For April. I needed every bit of your support. Thank you.

In Memory of David Farland
Beloved mentor of so many.

PENUMBRA

KEVIN A. DAVIS

Inkd
Publishing

Cover Design by Warren Designs

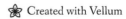 Created with Vellum

PENUMBRA

CONTENTS

INTRODUCTION

This is *Penumbra* Book One of the AngelSong Series. This is the story of Hadhira Dawson, Haddie, as she struggles to accept her powers and her place in an increasingly dangerous world.

A law student in Eugene, Oregon, she and her father have the power to spread matter back into time.

There are others like them, but with different powers, and different agendas.

PART 1

When we first came to this world, many of us saw it as a paradise.

CHAPTER 1

HADDIE STABBED another piece of egg, then glanced at Dad as she took a bite. He didn't look dangerous when people first saw him, usually stooped and withdrawn.

His buttered knife clattered as he placed it on the edge of his plate and crunched into the still dry rye toast.

He'd stopped shaving the left side of his head, so short auburn hair had grown out while the rest he kept braided into a long tail which reached his waist. He had that Viking biker look. The bent nose didn't help. She'd finally been able to dig out of him that it had been broken by a Frenchman in a barracks fight during WWI. He still didn't seem to like telling stories about his past.

As tall as she, just under six foot, he had a wide frame that took up a good portion of his side of the table. He wore an oversized Harley-Davidson T-shirt. Any piercings on his face had long since healed, though the summer sun tanned his pale skin and brought them out each year. To anyone, including her college friends, he looked as if he were in his mid-thirties.

People still gave him plenty of distance — and they didn't know the half of it.

How did he handle the thought of being immortal without getting lonely? Haddie had only dealt with it for a few months. She couldn't be sure it would happen to her as well, but just the possibility made her look at her friends differently. Her boyfriend, David, was twenty-nine. He was taller than she and had a solid build that he kept in shape at the gym. How would he look at forty, or fifty? His brown hair would turn gray.

Two of her closest friends, Liz and Terry, were in relationships; they had people they could grow old with. *Not something I need to deal with today.*

The restaurant had lights tucked into wagon wheels and an easy-going rural feel of a town's local breakfast joint. They'd managed to get a two-top table while most of the people sat at the counter or at one of the two long tables in the center of the room. The wood had been polished with age, and the most recent coat of sealer had started to wear at the edges.

Haddie faced the kitchen while Dad kept an eye on the pair they'd been following. Their trip had taken them north on 89 along the western edge of Wyoming, and they still didn't know where Dad's great-granddaughter and her uncle were headed.

Dad waved to their waitress. "He's going to pay with a credit card again. Idiot."

Haddie didn't turn. She shoved down the last of her eggs and swigged cold, bitter coffee that she should have added more sugar to. "I'm hitting the bathroom."

He gave her a twitch of a frown that told her to hurry. With a slow, deliberate motion he smoothed back his hair from his forehead to the tie of his braid. Haddie brushed crumbs off her blue T-shirt as she stood and turned.

Megan, the tween girl they followed, had Dad's auburn hair hanging loose about her shoulders. She twirled a strand with a morose, distracted expression while most of her pancakes sat untouched. It had to be expected; she'd just lost her parents two weeks prior. Haddie had been too young to remember losing her mother; still, it tightened her chest imagining what the girl went through. If Haddie wanted to brood and feel alone, it didn't compare.

The uncle, a plump man with a balding head, focused on the waitress and his bill. He refused the woman's attempts at small talk and jabbed the credit card at her without taking the check.

Haddie pulled her collar up and patted her scarf in case any of her white hair showed. Dad wanted her to color it black, but she'd gotten used to it. However, they didn't need her standing out, even if the uncle seemed oblivious. If Dad's concerns were correct, the man had done the right thing by getting them out of Utah. Whoever targeted her dad's previous family had wiped out all of them except Megan. Haddie hadn't realized the extent of Dad's loss until two weeks ago. Then, she couldn't tell if she thought he should have been more distraught.

Her friend Terry texted her as she locked the bathroom door. "Got a favor to ask," he typed.

"Of course. What?" Haddie raised her eyebrows; usually she asked for favors from him.

"Livia's looking at an apartment. They got a lease — contract thing. I told her you had helped me."

"Happy to. Send it to me." She could have Dad read it out loud while they drove; it would give them something to do. She'd seen the girl on campus once, and he'd described his girlfriend, but Haddie had never met her.

"Thanks." He dropped in a set of emojis. "I'll get it and email it. How's the trip?"

Terry had no idea what she and Dad were up to. He thought she'd taken a summer trip and probably assumed they'd ridden their bikes. "Beautiful. Mountains and all that. What are you up to?"

"Chatting on a post about Suicide Raves. There's been three now. Not all suicides either." As a tech major at her college, Terry loved his internet conspiracies.

Haddie sighed. "Sounds like fun. Gotta go." She exited the bathroom as the uncle and Megan were jingling the door closed behind them, heading to the parking lot.

Dad stood, dropping bills on top of the check, as Haddie headed for the door.

"Later, Buckaroo," Terry texted.

She slid the phone into her jeans and held the door as her dad worked his way toward her. He hid it well, but she could see how he favored aching joints. Haddie's had grown stiffer from using her power during the ski trip last winter, but her joints didn't seem as bad as his. The twinges had felt worst after she'd made a man vaporize; the guilt had been unbearable. Dad had said it got worse the first few times he used his abilities, then never went away. Never again. *I won't be using them.* The nightmare visions she got were the worst, and those didn't go away.

Her RAV4 had a layer of pale orange Utah dust. If this were one of their usual trips, they would have ridden, but Dad thought the bikes made them more obvious. When his mysterious friend had relayed that his great-granddaughter was moving, he'd asked Haddie to go along. He'd felt he needed to keep track of Megan. *Why involve me?* She'd jumped at the chance to help.

The uncle had packed a small moving van for the trip north. He'd been cautious, moving in the middle of the night without notice, except for Dad's man. Obviously Dad wasn't the only one who suspected the deaths in his previous family were anything but natural.

She took her time following the uncle's white moving van out of the parking lot. The roads along this section stretched out long and wide so she could follow at a decent distance. Mountains ridged the valley around them, and the wisps of white clouds couldn't cut the brilliant blue of the morning sky. Ahead, a blue sedan pulled between them from a gas station in town, and she settled in for the drive. She reached toward the radio.

"Can we have a little silence?" Dad leaned back in his seat, but he eyes watched the van.

"You just don't like K-pop." She dropped her hand back to the wheel.

"Give me a decade or two. I seem to catch up eventually. Led Zeppelin took me almost three decades to get into."

Haddie glanced over. "Really?" She'd grown up listening to Led Zeppelin and working on bikes in her dad's garage.

They'd just passed a church when a silver Mercedes E200 pulled past her on a curve and earned the blare of a horn from an oncoming pickup.

"Idiots," Dad murmured.

As the blue sedan ahead slowed to take a right turn, the Mercedes flew out to pass it. This stretch of the Wyoming valley had long roads; there was always time to pass. No need to rush.

The road straightened out again with large fields to each side and houses or storage buildings dotting the open areas on occasion. With an open stretch clear of oncoming cars, the silver sedan angled to pass the uncle's van.

Through the back window of the Mercedes, Haddie saw the driver's arm extend across the car. *Gun*. Haddie gasped, tapping the brakes. A flash lit from the muzzle and the uncle veered onto the roadside, kicking up dust.

"Haddie!" Dad yelled.

Haddie braked the RAV4 with only a short snag of tread and a squeal. No cars showed in her mirrors.

Dust churned in the breeze as the Mercedes slowed directly in front of her, pulling onto the edge of the grass. To the right, Megan and her uncle crashed through a pole and wire fence toward distant mountains, took out a smoothie sign as tall as their van, and coasted onto a field.

The driver's door to the Mercedes opened and a tall thin man ignored Haddie's RAV4, firing as he ran for the van. Dust swirled in the grass around him. Did he glow? A faint yellow light played around his head.

The van had come to a stop, tilted away from the road; the back windows faced Haddie.

Dad had the door open before she could brake to a stop. This time she felt the energy a fraction of a second before he started to growl.

The air rang like a bell around him and echoed inside the SUV. A hue of blueish light glowed on his face.

Amid the breezing dust, the shooter disappeared.

She sucked in a breath to calm herself as Dad stumbled over the torn fence. *Dad has to be in pain*. He limped and staggered from using his power. Her heart pounded.

Haddie swore before she slammed the RAV4 into park and jumped out to follow him. This was no accident, or even an attempt to make it look like one. Megan and her uncle had been attacked outright. What did this have to do with Dad and his previous life? He didn't say much other than he married a woman named Cynthia in 1962 and had three kids and bunch of grandchildren and great-grandchildren. *What am I missing?*

She caught up with Dad by the time he arrived at the van's passenger door. Another step and she could see the spray of blood across the windshield. The uncle's body slumped in its seatbelt against the wheel. Haddie froze and ice bled into her veins. The blue sky seemed a bright gray. Megan? If she'd been sitting in the front seat, Dad would have reacted differently. He would have paused for a second to look at her. Haddie turned to the van beside her. Holes puckered out in little steel kisses. Cracks trailed from the bullet holes in the side window and passenger window. She could smell gas and exhaust.

"Hell." Dad tried the side door without any success.

Steam rose from the front of the van. Dad's face already showed splotches of dark purpura. How bad would it get? After Harold Holmes, Dad's pale skin had looked worse than hers.

He broke the passenger window in a quick punch, with brass knuckles suddenly on his gloved fist, and reached in. The doors thunked around the car as they unlocked. Megan must be in the back.

As her dad opened the side door, a cardboard box jumped out spilling pens, folders, and blue ties onto the field. Haddie sucked in a breath.

Megan, dressed in a blue T-shirt and jeans, lay wedged between boxes so that only one side of her body and a tousled mop of hair showed. Dad extracted her like a limp doll. Inspecting her as he pulled the girl out, he seemed to relax when the last blue-sneakered foot yanked free.

"Devil take them." He raised Megan over his shoulder and moved around Haddie. "Let's go." The girl could have had a broken neck for all he checked.

"We should get her to a hospital," Haddie said.

He didn't wait for her, jogging through the field. "No authorities. She has to disappear. Don't touch anything."

Haddie reached in and grabbed a pink and white backpack before following. He might be right — unless Megan needed medical attention. Whoever had gone through this much effort would find the girl as soon as she came back up on radar. What did he plan on doing though? Kidnap her? He'd said none of the grandchildren or great-grandchildren knew him. Even his kids had thought him dead.

Dad made it to the RAV4 just before a black Silverado, decked in chrome and a lift kit, pulled up past the Mercedes. He was already in the back seat with the girl when a short man in a cowboy hat appeared, head high to the bumper. Haddie tossed the backpack onto the passenger seat.

"Wave him toward the van," Dad said.

"What?" Haddie stopped, half in her seat, and car door open in her hand.

Dad slammed his door shut. "Get rid of him. Wave him toward the van."

Haddie pursed her lips, but motioned toward the van. The man touched the brim of his hat and started to jog through the grass.

"Get back out on 89 north. First road left I think it is. 239? No decent signage. Use your map thing and head for Freedom, Wyoming."

"Dad —"

"Haddie. Argue later."

Another truck had slowed, passing her as they headed north, and pulled off to back up. The police would be there soon. Witnesses would see their plates. She swallowed, drove to the shoulder, then onto the empty highway. Clasping her belt, she rose to look in the mirror.

Dad sat with Megan's head on his lap, probing at her elbow. What if the girl had a concussion? Would he keep going? Did he plan on raising Megan? Her stomach clenched at the thought. *Am I jealous?* Her cheeks warmed. She glanced at the backpack; she'd had a red and black one for years. Dad probably had it in the storage above the garage.

Her phone had a missed call from her friend Liz. Haddie brushed past it and mapped through 239 to the town of Freedom. The turn lay just ahead.

Dad had to be in pain. She knew what it was like. What did he see in his nightmare visions? She was pretty sure that she saw his past uses of the power. Her mother's death and his removal of the killer had been clear. He'd grudgingly agreed when she'd asked.

Again, she rose up to look at them in the mirror, then turned it at a sharp angle so she could see both of them and the road. He just stared at Megan. Did he know what he was going to do? Was he working on a plan?

What if one of the trucks had gotten her plate? They'd find the uncle shot and no killer. That man was gone. What had been the glow she'd seen around the man? The dust, had that been the man, molecules disbursed back in time?

They really should figure out what their power actually did. No. Testing would mean using their power, and she hadn't dealt well with walking around bruised and aching.

First, they had to deal with Megan.

Her phone vibrated on the console. Liz had left a voice-mail. Taking a vacation from teaching at the college and the Eugene crime lab, she was leaving for a trip with her co-worker and new boyfriend, Professor Matt Arbor. Her relationship with Haddie had been a bit sketchy after the ski trip and the demons. Liz still couldn't admit to what she'd seen. She believed she'd panicked and hallucinated. Haddie hadn't clarified or filled in the gaps. Now, a certain distance lay between them. Liz's focus on Matt just made her and Haddie seem that much more distant.

A text popped up from her boss, Andrea. "New client 10 a.m. If you can make it."

Haddie groaned. Less than twenty-four hours, and they had at least a twelve-hour drive back to Eugene ahead of them. She'd planned on the day off from the internship at the law firm. Even half a year after all the trouble, Andrea kept Haddie from getting "too focused" on the higher profile cases, which meant rarely being allowed in on any interviews or depositions. It was understandable considering some of Haddie's obsessive behaviors when it came to their clients. *I don't dare give her another excuse.* She'd have to get Sam to take Rock for a walk.

"Got it. I'll be there," she texted.

CHAPTER 2

SAMEEDHA SAT ON A PADDED STOOL, her long golden hair carefully being brushed by one of her white-robed attendants. Two others prepared her outfit for the night's event, a floor-length dress of iridescent sequins with a high-collar and her monogrammed white gloves.

The hotel room stunk of Dylan's grotesque beast which sat beside the suite's door in the skin of a black German Shepherd. *I don't need protecting.* She was the Lord General's favorite, and He'd gifted her two of the foul creatures. She couldn't insult Him by refusing.

A fourth attendant brought out the makeup tray. Sameedha couldn't bear to see what her powers did to her face. She'd had beautiful skin, even in her teenage years. Her light brown hands, spotted with purple, were ravaged by these affairs.

It was a necessary price to pay for their cause. They needed wealthy patrons, and she brought them.

Her lips pulled up in an indulgent smile. *Come to the spider; welcome to my web.*

CHAPTER 3

HADDIE PULLED the RAV4 onto Route 239 with a wide tan field on the left and a green one on the right. Mountains in various grays rolled across the horizon around them. Sweat trickled down her sides and under her sports bra from their run across the fields — and her nerves. The car smelled funky after a couple days of travel. She'd pick up an air freshener at the next gas stop.

Megan let out a high scream with a delayed terror.

Haddie jumped and then adjusted the mirror to give her a clearer view to the back seat.

Megan had disappeared behind Haddie's seat.

Dad sat calmly, his hands in his lap. "It's okay. I'm family. Uncle Daw to you," he lied. "Aunt Haddie's driving. Uncle James had us following in case there was any trouble."

Megan stifled her sobs.

Haddie swallowed, trying to think of what to say. Dad had more experience with this than she did. How had he handled her after she'd seen her mother killed? The nightmare vision of it had been given to her after she used her power. She'd never remembered that her mother had been killed — that memory had been buried to her. *Until the visions.* He'd lied and let her believe that her mother had gotten sick. Megan, however, would remember all of this. Her parents had died in a car accident; she'd only survived because she'd slept at her friend's. What do you say to a girl who'd been through all that, had someone shot in front of her, and been attacked?

"We're going to drive for a while, get a hotel, and then you'll stay at my place for a bit. It's safe there." His voice had a calm, confident tone while purple bruises marked his cheek and around his lips. He looked somewhat horrific.

Megan sniffled and stifled more sobs.

Haddie cleared her throat, looking back at Dad. "Hey, I grabbed your backpack. Do you want it back there?"

Dad nodded and reached up a hand. "Do you have a phone? We have to make sure they don't follow us." He took the pink and white backpack as Haddie handed it back.

"Uncle Jimmy took it. He's —"

The crying took over, but Megan's hand reached out when Dad offered her the pack and they all sat in silence for a minute until Haddie's phone vibrated with a text from Terry.

Dad nodded toward her. "If you've got calls to make."

Did he think that would make things more normal for Megan? Nothing would likely help at this point.

Terry had texted, "In the morning."

She'd forgotten about his girlfriend's lease. Later would be better. Haddie hit the voicemail from Liz and it played through the speakers. "Hey. Just wanted to check in. We're on the road. Heading to Portland." A muffled man's voice, Professor Arbor, sounded in the background and Liz giggled. "Hope your trip is going well. Bye."

The giggle had stiffened Haddie. *Am I that petty and envious?*

"You should call her." Dad nodded in the mirror. Did he really think this was helping Megan?

She punched the call button with her finger. The last time Haddie had spoken with Liz was when she'd been packing for the trip. It had been short call, mainly to cancel a drink they kept postponing. Haddie could blame a lot on Liz's new relationship with Professor Arbor or on awkwardness between them since the ski trip.

Liz answered immediately. Heavy metal music cut off in the background. "Hey. How's the trip?"

Haddie held back a laugh. "Beautiful, a clear day." What did Dad expect her to say in front of Megan?

"You sound bored."

Haddie raised her eyebrows. *Hardly.* "Nah. But Dad won't let me play music."

"Am I on speaker? Hi, Mr. Dawson."

"He's in the back." *That would be weird.* "Resting."

"Oh, sorry." Liz dropped her voice. "So are you guys camping? Did you bring Rock?"

"Nope, motels. Sam's walking Rock and feeding Jisoo." Haddie tightened her lips. Liz might wonder why she wouldn't bring Rock. "What've you two got planned for tonight?"

"The concert. I told you that," Liz said. Professor Arbor mumbled in the background. "Want a shirt?"

"I'd just give it to Dad, I'd imagine." A metal T-shirt might fit his style better.

"True. Well, we're just listening to some of their playlists now. Have a fun trip." Liz sounded happy.

"Okay. Call me tomorrow, let me know how the concert

went." Haddie glanced at Dad; he seemed pleased, but it was hard to tell with him.

"Will do." The connection dropped.

Haddie took in a deep breath. She'd had to lie to everyone. Everything she complained that Dad had done to her, she did to her friends. The demons at the ski lift had been the worst. When Haddie had awakened at the hospital, she'd had no idea what Liz understood of what had happened. Her friend believed she'd hallucinated the creatures, and Haddie didn't correct her. Instead, she'd lied and let her friend wonder about her sanity.

She certainly couldn't explain what she did with her Dad on this trip.

"Who's Rock and Jisoo?" Megan's voice, small and wavering, came from the back.

Haddie let out a breath and smiled. "My pit bull and my calico cat."

"Will I get to see them?" Megan's tone sounded hopeful.

Dad nodded.

Haddie put a false cheer to her voice. "Of course. They'd love to meet you. That is, if you feed Jisoo."

"Okay." The tone came out serious and final.

Megan's response seemed larger than simply meeting Rock and Jisoo. Had she just accepted Dad's conditions? Is that all it took? The girl had lost her parents, and then her guardian. Maybe at this point she felt alone enough to accept anyone who didn't seem a threat. Did Dad really plan on raising this girl? She had no one. Did he have any other decent choices?

Haddie felt a sense of dread sink into her chest. She wasn't losing her dad, but it felt like it. She shook her head and tried to think of it as gaining a niece.

Terry texted, "Livia says midday. Will you be back? Or should I email?"

Haddie sighed. Megan. Terry. Andrea. The commitments piled up for tomorrow. At least David had been understanding when she'd canceled their hike. She winced. *I need to call him.*

CHAPTER 4

LIZ JACKED in her phone to charge and pushed her sunglasses back up to the ridge of her nose.

Haddie had seemed off. Something bothered her. Perhaps it was just her father. He had a way of getting her off-balance. Not that she didn't manage to get tilted over everything.

Matt turned the music back on and nodded his head in rhythm. Short brown hair bounced somewhat, and he conscientiously kept his eyes on the road and two hands on the wheel. He tended to overact around her, which was nice in its own way. This trip, their first overnight outside of his apartment, he seemed intent on making memorable. As proper as he usually held himself, she appreciated it.

What had Haddie gotten herself into? She hid some of her problems from Liz. That had been clear when that maniac Harold Holmes had been torching people. The FBI had gotten involved, and Haddie as well, somehow. She had gotten hurt and always hedged around the topic. *Not my business.*

A perfect example had been the ski trip. Liz had frozen when the man had been shot, but Haddie jumped in and disarmed the other man. She'd do better in law enforcement than as an attorney, but hadn't liked the suggestion. When they got attacked at the top of the ski lift, Haddie had ended up in the hospital. Then, she acted like nothing unusual happened. *Like I hadn't been there.* Liz couldn't explain what she thought she saw, but she knew when Haddie evaded talking about things. It had been worse this past year.

The song ended and Matt emphasized it with a grunt and gesture that seemed forced.

"Yeah," he said. "Let's hope they play that."

She smiled and nodded before the next song hit. They still had an hour before Portland. A few hours more before the concert. She took a sip of Diet Pepsi and glanced at the road ahead. The highway always felt unnaturally straight outside of the city. A road to nowhere.

She liked Portland. Tight and sprawling at the same time. Bridges over the river. Modern, tall buildings and established, older neighborhoods. Music everywhere. She could have lived there. Eugene came off a little — quaint. However, Liz had followed her first mistake from LA to get a job with the police while the jerk decided he liked blondes.

She rolled her head and watched Matt. he was the most conventional and sedate man she'd ever dated, maybe as a reaction to the two mistakes prior. She shrugged. He treated her nicely, even if she had to drag him out for some fun once in a while. He was a horrible but willing dancer.

Matt paused the music. "What are you thinking about?"

"Dancing," she replied. "Just having some fun tonight."

He beamed and nodded. "I'm glad we're doing this. A wild time."

She doubted it would be too crazy, but who knew?

PART 2

We were young then, the nine of us.

CHAPTER 5

THOMAS PULLED onto the exit for Coburg and headed toward the Ferry Street Bridge. The morning rush hour had already started with angry horns. He would have preferred getting into Eugene earlier, before everyone had reached that tense pulse they got themselves into on their way to work. Sedans and SUVs pressed onto the bridge, sure that they had somewhere to rush to, never stepping back and making a conscious choice about their pace or mood. Each era seemed to need more speed, more time, and more everything than the last. Money played a fiddle, and they danced a jig. People scheduled their lives into little pockets of time, then they cried and moaned that they didn't have enough morsels of moments to consume in a day. He'd experienced a swath of life when the day was cut only by the flicker of the sun from day to night. So much had changed in the last few centuries.

Haddie rarely noticed the mountains that surrounded her in Eugene. She could be forced — with her bike cooling on a roadside. She rested in the Willamette Valley which formed a paradise that she refused to slow down and appreciate. He'd watched her in the mirror as they descended down 126, ignoring the nature around, but still restful. Then, the cell towers and power poles grew up along the streets between the suburban houses and RVs, and her mood tightened. She checked her phone, suddenly focused on the minutes; she put the sun in daily boxes and counted them out.

Little Megan sat in the back seat seeming to absorb the signs that piled atop buildings and poles. She had just begun her journey through her loss. He'd seen so many crawl that cave. Some climbed and clawed for the light above, while others dug deeper, comforted by the darkness. He could only show her what life looked like outside that grief and let her find her path. She seemed interested in Haddie's pets; he couldn't ask for something better. Interactions with him, especially with the effects of using his abilities bruised across his skin, would take a while. He'd dealt with refugees from raids and wars who resisted help out of self-protection. Some, at least.

"I've got to get ready for work, but we'll make introductions and then you can feed Jisoo. Okay?" Haddie turned to the back, speaking to Megan who nodded carefully.

Thomas pulled into Haddie's space beside her bike. "We'll figure out how to get the car back to you, between you and Biff." He intended to get Megan settled in at the garage. She needed the time to get used to him and a new place. He had the summer to work out a plan for school and an identity for her.

Haddie barely acknowledged the comment as she jumped out and grabbed her duffel. The weather looked good for the next few days, so she would probably have ridden her bike anyway. She already chomped at those little bits of time waiting for her. To be fair, her boss had ignored her request for a few days off and enticed her with new client.

She popped the door open for Megan. "Ready?"

Thomas winced and slid out. They hadn't been followed. They would have been reported as being at the scene, but hopefully without a description the authorities could use.

Megan stepped silently from the other side. Haddie wore the blue scarf wrapped over her white hair. He could see strands most would assume to be blonde rather than white. She needed to dye it.

He turned as Rock dragged Haddie's dog-walker, Sam, stumbling toward them. Pitch black and small, the solid pit-bull had a white splash across his chest that Haddie called a giraffe. The dog had healed well from being shot, but Thomas could make out the scar on his chest.

Sam, wearing a trans pride T-shirt, stared awkwardly at Megan as Haddie introduced Rock to her niece. Noticing Thomas, Sam smiled, barely seeming to linger on the purpura dotting his face. The worst was on his hands, hidden by his gloves. She tucked her hands behind her back and swayed. "Hey, T." She'd picked up the nickname from Biff. It didn't matter, half the bikers in the state called him that.

"Hi, Sam." They'd have to explain Megan. He doubted a Wyoming "kidnapping" would make it to Eugene, but the internet did a funny thing to news. Maybe he could get Megan to color her hair.

Sam turned back to watching Megan, and eventually Haddie noticed.

"This is Dad's niece." Haddie blinked. "And mine. Meg." Her eyes flicked to him.

It would have to do.

The three of them headed up the stairs and he followed with cursed joints. Meg seemed engaged — that had turned out well. Hopefully she stayed focused on the animals and no other clues came out about her parents or the attack and murder of her uncle. It didn't seem likely the girl would bring it up.

Inside, Haddie disappeared to the back to get ready for work. She scattered debris about her living room like she had done growing up. He'd let her get away with it, hoping that she'd grow out of it. She hadn't. His better traits she seemed to rebel against. He'd lost the ability to discipline her after her mother had died; he just didn't have the heart.

Sam and Meg sat silently on each side of Rock, and the pit bull ate it up as they rubbed his sides and tousled his ears. Grinning at Thomas, he rolled on his back. Thomas picked up a familiar pair of pink jeans from a chair and folded them into a neat square before placing them atop some mail hiding a side table.

When Haddie's calico, Jisoo, started calling out, they went to the kitchen, and Rock came and leaned against his leg.

Thomas idly scratched behind floppy ears and smiled. "I wish I could borrow you for a few days. That girl's going to need someone."

When Haddie had finally left for work and he convinced a reluctant Meg back to the car, Thomas headed south for his garage. Traffic grew sparse, if not any kinder, and he pulled off 99 to his building. Biff's white wrecker sat at a diagonal in the front parking spaces by the highway. Biff started walking out of the garage bay, wiping his hands on a gray rag and managing a swagger.

His hair was brushed up in the air like some rock star, and he had a ridiculous beard that lined his jaw up to his sideburns. He thought himself some kind of ladies' man. Most, like Haddie, thought him a jerk. What people believed of Biff didn't seem to bother him, though. He'd come through a hard time in his youth and cleaned up well enough.

Biff jerked his head back in surprise when Meg climbed out clutching her pink and white backpack. They'd have to buy her some clothes. It would take more to get her set up with an identity, but Thomas had time. For now, he just needed to keep her safe — and get her settled in.

"Hey, T. What's up?" Biff nodded toward the girl.

His expression tightened as he saw the purpura on Thomas. The last time Biff had seen these bruises had been the previous autumn. There had been a lot of unusual activity and unanswered questions covering up Thomas and Haddie's use of their power.

Thomas could trust Biff to not ask questions or dig for answers.

"Biff, this is Meg. No questions. Got it?" Thomas grabbed his bag and slung it over his shoulder without expecting an answer. "I'm going to get her settled in. Might have some shopping for you." He gestured to Meg. "That's Uncle Biff. C'mon. We'll set you up in Haddie's old room."

CHAPTER 6

HADDIE WALKED to her cubicle in the back office of the Andrea Simmons Law Firm. She passed a tower of banker boxes that gave off a musty scent. The long, cluttered room echoed with the sound of Grace's typing.

Grace worked in the back cubicle near the copy room. She had a nearly perfect face, curly hair with rich black skin, and an unwavering focus on her pile of files and her computer monitor. She was the backbone of the agency and Andrea's paralegal.

Josh's cubicle across from Grace's lay empty.

Haddie tossed her legal pad and pen onto her desk and leaned on her cubicle wall adjoining Grace's. "An estate argument. That's what the case is about."

Grace didn't look up from her work. "Mm hmm. Putting notes on the will now. Josh scanned it this morning. The only will is from 1971." She wore a sun-yellow, button-down blouse and a black skirt; she hadn't stopped typing.

Haddie twisted her ponytail absently around her hand. "I just thought it was something important."

Grace's frown came from her eyes rather than wrinkling

her face. "It is — to the plaintiff. Andrea's not going to let you near her wrongful death suit."

Haddie feared she'd never be let near a real case again, or worse, that she'd never make a good attorney. "She's afraid I'll obsess on it."

"You would."

Haddie snorted and sat down. "I'm working on that."

She looked at the sparse notes from her pad. Andrea expected them typed up before lunch. That wouldn't be hard. Haddie almost regretted agreeing to come in early. After the trip east and all the excitement around Meg, her intern work at the firm hardly compared. She could be resting, hanging with Rock, and getting to know her niece. The drive to be an attorney had been everything, but now that she would be starting her final year of law school, it all paled compared to what she had learned about Dad and herself.

Andrea cleared her throat, standing at the doorway. She had her bright red hair tied back in a bun; the pale blue tips of two hair sticks poked up behind her head. "I've got a depo. I'll be back at 1:15. Haddie, notes done by then. Grace, everything for Taylor."

Grace grunted.

Haddie nodded. "Yes. Before lunch."

"Good." Andrea whisked back down the hall. Her voice carried as she detailed her schedule to Toby at the reception desk.

Haddie leaned into her seat and pulled up her phone. Lunch with David would help. She'd had to bail out on hiking Sunday to help her dad.

"Lunch?" she texted David.

She twisted her hair, looking through her notes while waiting for his reply. Usually she'd hit him up for dinner, but as tired as she was, she might not be up for it.

"Dinner?" he texted back. "I'm at a site in Roseburg until the afternoon."

Haddie pouted. "Okay. Your place?" He tended toward seafood, but he was an excellent cook. She'd end up crashing there, probably midway through the meal.

"I'll catch up on my Japanese lesson, then start cooking when you get here. I love you."

"I love you." She'd head straight from work and maybe nap on his couch while he cooked.

By the time Haddie finished her notes and peeked through some of the files on the other cases, Josh strolled into their back office wearing a leaf-patterned black, yellow, and green beach robe. He had hiking boots on, but his legs were bare. The way he carried the banker's box at his waist, Haddie hoped he hadn't opted for a Speedo again. Andrea had sent him home that day.

"Perish the tyrants who have dared break it!" Josh balanced three takeout containers from different restaurants, a small USPS mailing box, and a convenience store drink on top of the banker box, like a paper and plastic cairn. "They're building yet another anathematized building out on Green Hill Road. I've calculated one hundred and thirty-six more trees before we hit the nitrogen oxide threshold and Eugene smothers under a blanket of smog." His cup swayed as he came to a stop in front of their cubicles.

"You're late," said Grace with a sigh. "Get the expert's report scanned before you begin your feast."

"Damn, Josh. Let me help you, before you spill that all over the floor, again." Haddie jumped up to retrieve the tottering beverage.

He tilted his head, blond hair blending with his robe,

and smiled. "A true gentlewoman — see how it's done, Grace?"

Haddie raised her eyebrows and placed the drink on his desk. "Why are you dressed like that?"

"Don't," said Grace, never looking up from her screen.

"I'm surfing after work." Josh leaned on Grace's cubicle, the mail sliding atop the to-go box. "Want to come?"

Grace sighed and flicked an accusatory glance at Haddie. "I told you." She ignored him until he began whistling some movie theme, possibly a sci-fi, and juggled his load into the copy room.

Half an hour later, Toby walked to the back with Grace's lunch delivery. She smiled easily as she leaned on Haddie's cubicle. "What are you doing for lunch?"

Grace's delivery smelled rich and spicy, likely a vegan dish of some sort.

"Hadn't planned anything. What do you got in mind?" Haddie closed her searches.

"Craving mapo tofu." Toby raised her eyebrows in a question.

Haddie grabbed her wrist purse. "I'm in."

Haddie followed Toby back to her desk and waited in the hall behind her.

The door chimed and a familiar tall man entered. Blue-eyed with curly black hair, he wore a well-fitting, three-piece tan suit. A client?

"Toby," he said with a broad smile.

"Mr. Palmer." Toby dropped her purse into her chair.

Damn, I'm hungry. Haddie pasted a patient smile on her face.

"Please, call me Bruce." His eyes fixed on Haddie. "Ms. Haddie Dawson, if I remember correctly?"

Bruce Palmer. He'd come on as a new client during all

that trouble last fall. She hadn't thought about him again. "Correct, Mr. Palmer. Nice seeing you again." Those blue eyes pierced her.

"My pleasure." He looked past her into the hall. "Is Ms. Simmons in? I'm early for my appointment, I know."

Toby didn't need to check her calendar. "1:30 this afternoon. She'll just be back by then. I'm sorry."

Bruce checked his watch; a black utilitarian affair rather than the splashy gold that Haddie expected. "Not even noon. Are you two heading out to lunch? It seems I've got a bit of time to kill. On me."

Haddie hesitated, unsure how Andrea might feel about it. She wasn't dressed for lunch with a client; she had worn a simple outfit, partially based on what had been clean in her closet: an unflattering light blue shirt and a pair of black slacks that had pockets and plenty of Jisoo's fur.

Toby didn't seem to share her concerns and shrugged. "Sure. We were just going to the Chinese place on the next block."

"Excellent." He waited as they headed down the hall and came out into the waiting room. "Do they have duck?"

Toby nodded and laughed lightly. "I've never seen anyone eat it though."

He held the door open as they exited into a warm day. The clouds had come in gray to the north, but they didn't seem to threaten. City traffic mulled around them and a blossoming jasmine cut some of the urban air. Eugene stayed pretty clean for a city and left plenty of room for greenery, despite Dad's constant condemnation. Pedestrians bustled along the sidewalks, hurrying from heat or time clocks, except for a woman with rich brown skin and beaded braids over half her face. She leaned against a tree across the street with her nose tucked into a paperback. In all the hustle, she looked out of place.

Bruce did his best to spread his charm between both of them as they walked. He strolled leisurely on the sidewalks, and people moved around him accordingly. "The last time I saw you, Haddie, the firm had just cleared Mel Schaeffer of some horrible burning deaths. Right?"

"That's right." Haddie shivered slightly at bringing up what had been her single most horrifying and life-changing experience. He didn't know that, though. No one except Dad knew all of it. Biff had been there to clean up, but Dad kept him from asking any questions.

Bruce paused outside the door to the restaurant. "If I recall, it all had to do with a Harold Holmes. Have they ever found him? Any juicy clues?"

Toby shrugged and Haddie shook her head before saying, "He just disappeared."

"Curious, isn't it?" Bruce opened the door for them.

Rich scents filled the restaurant, and the distant clatter of the kitchen competed with the murmur and laughter of customers. Haddie's phone vibrated, and she pulled it from her slacks to see Liz calling. She'd been to her concert, likely slept in, and wanted to tell Haddie about all the fun she'd had with her new boyfriend. Haddie ignored the call. It wouldn't be anything important. *I'll check in later.*

CHAPTER 7

HADDIE OPENED the can and scooped a small portion of stinky fish onto the plate. Jisoo complained loudly from the floor, dismayed at the portion control.

"You're a pig," she said. "You'll end up weighing more than Rock."

Terry called from her living room, "Stop fat-shaming your cat."

Jisoo dove in, scarfing down the food as fast as she had an hour ago when Haddie fed her after coming home from work.

Terry sat on the couch dressed in cargo shorts and a "1984 is here" T-shirt. Lanky with short black hair, he slouched down with a fountain soda in his lap. He'd made space by moving her duffel bag onto some school binders.

Haddie moved back to her desk and started flicking through the lease, drafted from a template from the looks of it. There was nothing unusual and plenty she could warn against, but the landlords wouldn't change it. "She does realize that getting her deposit back relies on them being honest, right?" Haddie raised her eyebrows as she looked over to Terry.

"I guess. I've always gotten mine back. But, everyone likes me." Terry shrugged and took a sip.

"Debatable. You've only moved out once – from Carson Hall, a college dorm."

"Where they loved me." He raised both arms outstretched. "They still send me emails inviting me back."

"Everyone gets those. What they love is your money." Haddie closed up the lease. "It's a template. Nothing unusual and nothing they'd likely change if I did recommend it. However, if you plan on moving in, you have to get their permission."

His light brown skin darkened with a blush. "We're not there yet." As if in explanation, he added, "She doesn't like playing a cleric."

"Who does?" Haddie leaned back in her desk chair, lease on her lap. Rock came over to get scratched and pressed his muzzle on the thigh of her sweatpants. "What are you doing tonight?"

"Nothing. Livia's got a paper she's working on."

"She's got summer classes."

"Yeah. So, I'll just troll the suicide raves threads. Those Cali people get pretty bent." He took a sip. "What about you?"

"Sleep. I haven't caught up from the trip." Rock lay at her feet. Jisoo strolled from the kitchen heading for the bedroom, likely to use the litterbox. "We just got back this morning."

"Yeah. I didn't expect you back today. How was it? Fun? What did you do?"

A blast. Vaporized a murderer and rescued my Dad's great-granddaughter who we kidnapped and are holding at the garage. "Not much really. Just drove and looked at mountains. You know Dad."

"Your Dad scares the hell out of me sometimes. He just looks at me when I talk."

Scares me too, sometimes. "You've met him, like what, twice?"

"Still." Terry sipped on his drink, looking determined to finish it before he left.

Damn. She never listened to Liz's voicemail. Maybe she didn't want to hear how much fun Liz had with her boyfriend.

Terry waved his beverage. "You come off kind of dangerous, too."

Haddie held his lease in the air and raised her eyebrows. "Excuse me?"

"I just mean — you can handle yourself with your taekwondo. All that trouble last fall — you just plowed right through it. Wow, look at the time."

She scowled and handed him the lease.

Slurping at the bottom, Terry stood and took the lease. "Thanks, Haddie. We appreciate it. When Livia gets moved in, you'll have to come over. She makes a mean cauliflower rice dish with pine nuts and stuff. Not really sure what's in it. I think I'm afraid to ask."

"Sounds great." Haddie chuckled.

Terry jiggled the empty cup and then poked into the kitchen, tossing it deftly into the trash. "You have fun sleeping."

"I've got some stuff I gotta do. Dinner with David. Probably going to call Liz first, she left a message." Haddie absently twirled her hair.

"Oh, yeah. The concert. She having fun?" His hand was on the door, but he stopped and tilted his head.

"She and her professor, how could she not?"

Terry lifted his head. "Did you reschedule your hike with David?"

"Not yet. I'm heading over for dinner tonight. Now, if I can get rid of you."

"Got it, Buckaroo." Terry chuckled and headed for the door.

After Terry left, Haddie searched out her phone and found it on the kitchen counter from Jisoo's first feeding. She'd check the message, make a quick call to Liz, and then get to David's.

CHAPTER 8

HADDIE POURED hot black tea over the ice cubes and felt the mix of cold and warm swirl across her palm through the glass. Pungent and earthy, she took a deep breath through her nose before heading back to her desk. Rock waited by her chair, readjusting as she swiveled to her phone by the keyboard.

She played Liz's message on speaker. "Haddie, call me back. I don't know what to do. Matt is really acting weird. Last night was horrible. He was getting wasted and I feel like I got drugged. I don't remember coming back to the hotel. He's nasty this morning and drinking — damn it's after noon. I slept so long. This isn't him. Something is wrong. If it keeps up — I might need a ride. I don't know what to do. Call me, please."

Haddie sat up straight in the chair and her chest tightened. She'd ignored her friend's call when she actually needed her. "What is wrong with me?" she muttered.

Liz's phone rang once, and then moved to voicemail. Haddie twisted her hair, waiting for Liz's polite message to finish.

"Liz. I'm so sorry. I just got your message. I should have listened earlier. If you need me to come get you — I'll jump in the RAV4 and be up there in a couple hours. Please. Call me back. Let me know you're okay." Haddie stared at the phone. The back of her throat hurt, and she swallowed against it. *Damn.* "Please let me know you're okay. I'm sorry."

She hung up but continued to stare at her phone. She'd been so preoccupied with Dad and assumed that Liz was having fun. She should have paid attention to her friend.

Her phone didn't ring.

Rock nuzzled her leg and she absently rubbed around the back of his ears. Maybe she should just drive to Portland and be sure. *I don't even know what hotel she's at. Some friend.*

Tapping her spacebar, she woke her computer, typed "Matt Arbor," and opened the links into different tabs. Some were obviously the professor, and she dug through his twitter account, though it mainly highlighted his teaching focus, English major. She'd never taken his classes and barely recognized him from other social media. No posts in the past twenty-four hours. What had she expected? *Dammit, Liz, call me.*

Her phone vibrated and she jumped.

A text from Terry. "Livia says thanks! She wanted you to know she appreciated it. She's moving. Like next week."

Haddie tensed, ignoring Terry's text for the moment. Instead, she texted Liz. "Are you okay?"

Then she responded to Terry. "Can you track someone down in Portland? What hotel they're staying at? Liz is in trouble." Haddie started to type out a longer explanation, but backspaced and hit enter.

She waited a moment as he typed a response, then her phone rang. Terry had called her instead.

"Hey, I don't really do that. I started to type it, but they pick up on some key words quicker than others." Terry paused, likely overthinking his words; he really did believe a lot of the conspiracy theories he followed. "What makes you think Liz is in trouble?"

Haddie explained, as verbatim as she could, the message Liz had left her.

"Did you call her?" he asked.

Her teeth gritting, she answered, "Yes." Did he really think she hadn't?

"Sorry, of course you did." He took a long audible breath. "Okay, Portland. What's his name?"

"Matt Arbor. I can send you some of his social media."

"Nah, he's a professor. Easy to find that. I'll have to ask some friends to help. Can't promise." His tone shifted. "But, you know how awesome I am."

"I do, Terry. Thanks."

"Of course, Buckaroo. If she gets back to you, let me know to stand down, okay?"

"I will. Thanks." Haddie hung up and stared at the photo of Matt Arbor speaking at a seminar with an ill-fitting black suit and both hands clutching the podium. He didn't look like an axe murderer.

She flinched as the phone rang again. Dad. "Hey, Dad." She wasn't ready to get him involved. He had plenty on his plate with Meg.

His bike rumbled in the background. "Meg. She took off out your window."

Haddie closed her eyes. *What next?*

CHAPTER 9

THOMAS TROLLED DOWN 99 at a slow pace looking for signs of pink and white; Meg had taken her backpack with her, and he hoped it would stand out. A car, annoyed at his pace, passed too close and sped up with roar and a trail of exhaust. He tried not to let his own frustration grow with theirs. Haddie was on her way.

Biff checked inside any establishments where a child might go at this time of night. Meg had an hour lead. What had she been thinking? Quiet, and understandably morose, she had shown little interest in Haddie's old room or the new clothes that Biff had bought.

Thomas hadn't expected the transition to go smoothly, but the girl had given no indication of running off. *What exactly did I expect?*

At the edge of Creswell, he turned around and headed north, back toward Goshen. To his right and across the fields, I-5 traffic streamed with tall semis and a continuous flow. The girl couldn't have gone there. What had she been thinking? Haddie thought she might be headed back to Utah — home, even if she didn't have anyone there. The options grew the more time it took them to look. Ugly options. Some idea of her plan would help.

He'd ridden up 99 north toward Eugene originally, trying to gauge how far a young teenager could walk in an hour. Maybe he'd underestimated her pace. If Haddie was right, then the girl might have gotten directions to take 58, but she couldn't walk that highway. Thomas took a deep breath and settled his frustration. He would do what he could to make sure his great-granddaughter survived. He had control over those actions, nothing more.

Haddie called. "Got her, Dad." It didn't sound like she was on her bike; he couldn't hear any street noise at all.

His heartbeat started slowing, and he realized how tense he'd become. "Where?" The exhaustion from using his powers yesterday combined with the long day wore down on him.

"Behind the Academy. Meg and I are heading back to the garage now."

Meg hadn't even gotten out on 99; she'd headed down the dead-end street to the paramilitary high school at the end of the road. How had Haddie known?

Thomas opened his bike up and headed home, relieved and annoyed. "Thank you, Haddie." He couldn't hear her response over his engine.

Now that the crisis had been averted, he fought the temptation to grow angry. How could he get through to Meg the danger she was in without terrifying her? They'd had a brief talk about avoiding the people who hurt her uncle and keeping hidden. She hadn't responded much at all; he'd expected a teenager in this day and age to want their phone back and connect with their friends. That hadn't come up.

Haddie had withdrawn after her mother had been

killed. She'd been half Meg's age and spent a couple days brushing her hair and sitting in the tub, as if waiting for Nyra to come take care of her. That had led to days lying on her bed listening to music. She would eat her meals with Thomas, but conversation remained one-sided for almost a month. School started soon after, and that seemed to propel her into some routine. At home, she'd begun reading. The reclusive reaction to her grief had ended with a school friend, Annabelle, and afternoons at the girl's house where a mother still lived. Somehow, Haddie pushed it all aside and never talked about her mother.

It might not have been the healthiest reaction, but he'd embraced it — with a sense of guilt.

Haddie's bike sat out front when he pulled up to the garage. The smell of petroleum seeped from the building in a medley of gas, oil, and cleaning fluids. Country music played from an apartment behind. His building looked cold and dark with the bay doors down and no lights leaking out of the office. Biff had headed home. Thomas climbed off his bike and winced at aching joints and sore muscles. He needed sleep, but that would be hard while worrying about Meg running off in the middle of the night.

Haddie walked outside before he made it to the office door. She wore her brown leather jacket and a dark shirt, and her white hair trailed over her shoulders. She frowned as if pensive. "She's in bed. I don't think she'll be heading out again. She's tired."

Thomas resisted checking inside. "How'd you know?"

"I thought about it on the ride down here. Worth a shot, I imagined. I used to go sit out back of the Academy; sometimes they had an obstacle course set up, and I'd walk along it. It's just quiet back there." Haddie forced a smile. "She's got a lot to think about."

He took breath in and out. Maybe he could take Meg camping. Hiking and nature might take her mind off darker thoughts. Some people reacted well to being outside.

Haddie paced past him into the lot and looked north, smiling a false smile, but something nagged at her. She always had some cause or another. He didn't know that he had the time for one more concern.

Thomas focused his conversation on Meg. "What do you think I should do?"

"She probably just needs to think this through, Dad." Haddie turned, pausing to glance at him. "It's a lot to absorb. The shop is noisy, and so is route 99. You were probably hovering."

"I don't hover." Whatever that meant.

"You do. Drop by my place tomorrow and have her take Rock for a walk. She'd like that. I'll be at work." Her face twisted at the last comment. "You've got a key. Let her and Sam walk Rock, alone. Stay at the apartment and brood." She checked her phone and seemed frustrated.

"What's up with you?" He nodded toward her phone.

"Sorry. Missed a call from Liz — no, I ignored a call from Liz when she needed me, and now I can't reach her. I'm worried." Haddie punctuated her statements by shaking and gesturing with her cell.

"Liz. She went to Portland with some professor, right?"

"Yes. And now he's being a jerk. She sounded upset, scared. I should have answered."

So, Haddie did have a cause, possibly a good one, unless the friend liked drama. "What are you going to do?"

"Call her repeatedly and stalk her social media." Haddie grabbed her ponytail and twisted it around her fist, a habit she'd picked up as a child. She did it whenever she got frustrated.

"Don't judge the dog by its hairs. Either head up there or wait a day; you'll make yourself crazy." He regretted the tone afterward. Meg held his focus at the moment and his frustration laid there. "If you need my help, let me know."

Haddie bit off any comment she had started to make and then nodded slowly. "I'll get with Biff tomorrow and get the RAV4 out of here." She gave him a hug. "Love you, Dad. Bring Meg over tomorrow to visit Rock. That is the most boring bedroom ever."

"Love you." He watched as she climbed on her bike.

She stopped to answer her phone and groaned. "David. I'm sorry. I got caught up with Liz, then Dad. I'm at his garage. I had no idea it got this late."

Thomas waited as she listened to her boyfriend's response. The man seemed quiet and respectful, the two times he'd met him. Thomas could respect the man's healthy concern for the environment and his love of nature. Time would tell if he was a good fit for Haddie; she didn't tend to stay in relationships long. David seemed to accept her independence.

"No, I better cancel. I've got to sleep. I'm so sorry you wasted your night." Haddie slumped in the seat of her bike.

Thomas couldn't regret that he'd called her out here. She'd found Meg.

When she hung up, she turned to him. "I'm such a jerk."

"That's Biff's title," Thomas said.

Haddie laughed weakly. "Yeah." She fired up her bike.

As she pulled out of his lot, Thomas took a deep breath and headed for the door. *I'm going to have my hands full getting Meg adjusted to a new life.*

CHAPTER 10

HADDIE PAUSED on the stairs leading to her apartment. This late at night, barely any traffic rumbled in the streets around her.

Liz had posted a photo of a crowded dance floor, posing in a skimpy fringe bikini top that did not cover everything. *This isn't Liz.* Haddie wanted to deny, but despite too much hastily applied sparkling makeup, she couldn't mistake Liz's brown eyes, button nose, and unruly shoulder-length hair. In the photo, similarly clad dancers groped and jostled amid colorful lighting and a smoky haze. There seemed no walls in the murk except for a dark frame of small windows and an unreadable sign at the edge of a doorway. In the far-right corner of the image, a woman with a too-white face stood with her eyes closed and hands stretched overhead, palms touching as if in a yoga pose.

"Liz," Haddie whispered.

Scrolling back, she saw the picture before it had Liz and her professor boyfriend posed outside the concert venue. Strangely, no photos of the concert itself, but Liz had said she felt she'd been drugged. Still, Haddie had hoped for some hint of their hotel. She would have started driving already.

She texted Terry, "Any luck?"

Stepping slowly and watching her phone for his response, she made it inside before he answered. "Sort of a personal question." He followed with emojis and then, "Not yet."

Haddie sat down at her desk, letting Rock sniff across boots and her jeans. She set the phone beside her keyboard and typed with both hands. "Have you heard about people at raves wearing fringe?"

"Sure. Why?"

Haddie swallowed. "I think Liz is at a rave." Her skin chilled admitting the thought. She knew where Terry would go. These suicide raves had him full of conspiracies. However, she couldn't ignore the coincidence. Her hand shook as she reached down to Rock nuzzling her knee.

"Nooo. Did you try calling her?"

"Two minutes ago. When I got home. Then, I checked online. She just posted five minutes ago."

"Leave her a message. Tell her to get out. I swear, wrong time to be going to raves."

Haddie felt her chest turn hollow. Having someone confirm the same fear made it worse. "I'll do that now." She followed quickly with another text. "Find her hotel, please."

Haddie called, leaving a brief message pleading Liz to get out of the rave and call her. Jisoo cried in accompaniment.

Haddie swiveled toward her computer. Discarded mail piled by her mouse, orange folders with class notes stacked under the edge of the monitor, and a crumpled napkin lay at the top edge of her keyboard. She didn't dare start down the rabbit hole of looking up suicide raves. It would tear her apart. She put music on her computer and carried her phone with her to the kitchen to feed Jisoo. Work would have her up in five hours, and although her eyes burned and muscles dragged, she didn't feel like she could sleep. Liz risked some unknown danger at a rave with a demented boyfriend. Meg had lost everything, and Dad essentially held her captive at the garage. Emotionally exhausted between Liz and Meg, she would have to hope that a bath and a book would get her closer to sleep.

CHAPTER 11

HADDIE'S EYES glazed on the screen. Fingers perched at the edge of the keyboard jerked slightly when her cell vibrated.

She felt a flash of disappointment when she saw it was David. *Liz, where are you?* Terry would find something soon.

"Any word on Liz?" he texted. He'd spent an hour, maybe more, listening to Haddie on the phone last night. She'd kept him up too late.

"No," Haddie replied.

"Are you going to Portland?"

She'd threatened twice to do so, but she had nowhere to start looking. "No. At work."

"I want to help. Do you want me to come over tonight? I can pick up Thai," David texted.

Haddie sighed. She'd already agreed to a get together with Dad, Meg, and Sam. *I'm not ready to try and explain Meg yet.* "Can't. Dad's coming over."

"Good. Glad you have someone with you. I'm sure she'll respond soon. Probably lost her cell."

She wanted to see David and have his arms around her. *Tonight just didn't work.* Haddie sagged in her chair; she felt too worn out to even think straight.

"I'll be in Eugene tomorrow. Lunch?"

"Yes," she texted. Hopefully, she'd have heard from Liz by then.

David always managed to be sweet over these kinds of things. He didn't push her or pout when she missed something or had to cancel. How long would that last?

When they finished, she reached for the dregs of her coffee. *I should make some tea.* She'd need something to get through the morning.

Haddie, fogged after two hours of sleep, lifted her head over the top of the cubicle. She knew the voice coming from the waiting area. Detective Cooper.

The back office felt cool and dark with the musty smell of piles of paper and cardboard boxes. Stumbling over a pile of briefs she'd left at the corner of her cubicle, Haddie walked toward the open door leading to the hall, peering cautiously. The smell of morning coffee wafted in from the front office. The hall led past Andrea's office to the right and down to the conference room before it turned left. Along the left wall of the corridor, Toby's desk blocked the cutout into the waiting area.

Detective Cooper stood so that he could almost see into the back room. She came into his view as soon as she stepped into the hall. His face hardly scowled, but he wore the same carefully trimmed black hair and mustache that he had last fall during the Colman murders. Dark eyes darted to hers immediately. She felt her pulse rise.

"Ms. Dawson. Good to see you here." He forced a smile that made him look creepy.

Haddie came up behind Toby, unwilling to go around

into the waiting room nor run from the situation. What was he doing here? Old fears surfaced, as well as curiosity. He wore his black shirt and tie and his shiny seven-pointed star.

"Thanks. What brings you here?" He might think that rude. "Good to see you, too."

Toby spoke clearly into the phone as if to answer. "Andrea, Detective Cooper brought the records from downtown that you requested." She hung up the phone. "She'll be right out."

Haddie slowly drew in a deep breath, not wanting to draw any more attention to herself than she already had. *Not everything is about me.*

Detective Cooper kept his face awkwardly stiff, as if trying to keep a pleasant disguise plastered over his usual scowl. Why did they have a detective delivering documents?

Andrea walked out, tapping her hair and touching one of the hair sticks to make sure the buns remained in place. "Detective Cooper," she said, before turning the corner to the waiting area. "Were there no officers available? I did not expect you to be delivering these."

He shrugged and adjusted his tie. "I offered. I've got an interview down here in twenty minutes. I figured you could spare someone to drag them out of my trunk."

Andrea nodded, turned, and gestured toward the detective. "Haddie, he's got three boxes I need, can you help?" With a final glance to Detective Cooper, she said, "Thank you," and turned back into the hallway. Andrea gave her a quizzical expression as they passed and then continued into her office.

Haddie followed Detective Cooper to the door. It seemed even more unusual after Andrea had highlighted it. Toby shrugged and made a fake grimace as the detective turned his back to open the door. *Could this be about me?*

He held the door. "So how have you been doing, Ms. Dawson, after all that trouble last fall?"

"Fine." Haddie wore long sleeves, yet still consciously looked down at the burns on her wrists. She covered them daily with makeup, but she could always see them. They'd healed better than they should have. They were a constant reminder of her powers and the first day she'd used them. Detective Cooper only knew a small part of the trouble Harold Holmes had caused her. Was he digging again?

Gray clouds hid most of the sky. The smells of exhaust seemed packed into the city.

They walked toward a black Ford Interceptor and the alarm beeped off. "Did Special Agent Wilkins ever get with you? I know she had you on her list of people to interview."

Haddie kept her head down, focused on the license plate, not wanting to make any expression. "The FBI lady? Yeah, she didn't ask much, that I can remember."

With the back hatch open, Haddie grabbed two boxes of the three. If Detective Cooper wanted to dig about Harold Holmes, he would get nowhere. She had enough on her mind with Liz. Dad would have to deal with Meg while Liz needed help; she still hadn't answered any texts or voicemails. Her rave picture had been removed from social media, but Haddie had saved it earlier to zoom in on the sign. *I don't have time for Detective Cooper.*

He grabbed the last box, left the hatch open, and followed her. "We haven't found Harold Holmes or his brother." He spoke in a nonchalant and conversational tone, as if they discussed the clouds above.

Haddie managed the doorknob and nodded. "Mm hmm."

While she held the door open for him, he paused and studied her face. The extra inch she had on his height forced him to look up. Haddie raised her eyebrows and tilted her head at the door. Without a word, he stepped inside.

Infuriating man. Her apprehension boiled into anger in her chest. He'd chosen today to pick at an old wound, and she didn't have the time or inclination to figure out why.

Liz needed her, but until Haddie had someplace in Portland to look, she had to wait. Stomping with her load across the waiting room, she left him to trail behind.

A bit wide-eyed, Toby bit her lip and hurried to occupy herself on her computer. Her response helped calm Haddie, so by the time she dropped the boxes in the back room, she could offer Detective Cooper a fake smile. He couldn't have anything new on the case. They had scrubbed the house looking for clues, and nothing had come up that would implicate Haddie or her dad. Detective Cooper had ambushed her in the parking lot, but nothing more than digging for her reactions. What interest did he have in the FBI agent? She needed to get rid of him.

"Grace, are these for Josh?" Haddie asked.

Grace peered around the edge of her cubicle and nodded to Detective Cooper. "Yes. He's not in yet. I'll let him know."

Haddie moved quickly to her cubicle, leaving the detective to stack the last box. Exhaling with a shaky breath, she tried to focus on where she'd been before he'd come in. The sleepless fog still hung at the back of her mind, but he'd got her blood pumping.

"Goodbye, Ms. Dawson."

"Detective Cooper." Haddie made no effort to look in his direction.

The quicker he left, the sooner she could relax. She absently checked her phone, hoping for a message from Terry. Had she given up on hearing from Liz? The thought took her breath away. *I've got to do something.*

She didn't even hear Detective Cooper leave.

"Haddie?" Grace's voice came from the edge of their cubicle. She leaned atop the gray panel.

Haddie wiped tears and looked up. She hadn't even realized she'd been crying. "What's wrong?"

Grace's tone, usually crisp and efficient, took on a quieter and warmer aspect. "That's what I was going to ask you. I can tell you're tired, but there's something more. What's going on? Do you want to talk about it?"

"My friend Liz — she went to Portland with her boyfriend — they had some kind of trouble." Haddie closed her eyes. It didn't sound as desperate when she said it out loud. "She left me a message and I can't reach her."

Grace nodded. "You're worried about her."

"I am. I don't know what hotel she's at. I swear, I'd go there right now."

Grace smiled. "I believe it. You're a good friend. If you need to take off, I can cover your work. Or knuckle Josh into doing it if it's simple enough."

"Thanks, Grace. I —" Haddie jumped as her phone rang, an unknown number from an area code that she didn't recognize. Fumbling, she answered, "Hello?"

"Hadhira Dawson, this is Special Agent Wilkins. I wanted to schedule some time to discuss the Holmes case. I'm in Eugene for the next three days. When would it be convenient for you to come down to 7th Street?"

Haddie stumbled over her words. "Tomorrow?"

Detective Cooper's visit finally made sense. He'd found out the FBI agent had come into town; perhaps they'd already talked. The FBI had taken the Holmes case last fall. Did that bother him? What did Wilkins have now?

"Very good. What time?" Her voice sounded emotionless. Cold.

"Uh, noon?" Haddie sounded nervous, guilty.

"Thank you. We'll see you tomorrow." The connection dropped.

She sat with the phone against her ear while Grace rose up from her perch on the cubicle wall. Haddie swallowed. *I need to tell Dad. This can't be good.* What reason would they have to bring her back in for questioning?

"Everything okay?" Grace asked.

Startled, Haddie nodded. Should she tell Andrea? Dad first. He had a better way of thinking these things through. Haddie added as Grace lingered above, "Just an appointment."

"Okay. Well, if you need me to cover, let me know." Grace's tone cooled, as if she knew there were more to the call than Haddie alluded to.

Haddie cradled her phone as she stood. With the added stack of boxes, the back room felt confining. She had to let Dad know. He already had enough going on with Meg, but she needed him. It might affect him as well. However, only Biff knew that Dad had been at Harold Holmes' house that night. She drew in a deep breath, trying to push away the anxiety. The piles of briefs had spread out of her cubicle and were sliding across the floor.

Dad would likely be at her apartment by now, letting Meg walk Rock with Sam. This call she'd have to make outside.

PART 3

Our minds had been trained by our elders to further their purpose, their will.

CHAPTER 12

THOMAS WALKED down the road slowly, his joints easing at each step. Cautious birds called out from the trees as the sun set behind him. The mountains to the east had oranges and reds painted across the tips before they sank into dark purple bases. If it weren't for Haddie, he'd have moved closer to them. Her mother had been raised in Eugene and he'd never felt right taking Haddie from the city. Goshen had been as far as they'd gone. His garage had been at the junction of I-5 and 58, so he'd just built out one of the bays and called it Haddie's home.

The Academy stretched along the right in a dark line of plain brown wood and continuous windows that gave all the indication of being a school. He headed to the back where a taller building with a slanting roof gave off the sense of being a gym or auditorium. He'd rarely ever gone back there except to circle through the parking lot with one of the bikes he'd worked on.

Hopefully, Meg had slipped back here again, or else he'd have to recall the posse and troll 99.

Haddie had enough going on, but he'd call her if it came

to it. This business with the FBI bothered him. He'd hoped the whole Harold Holmes matter had been laid to rest. It had been Haddie's first use of her power. Would she stop aging as he had? She'd come to grips with killing the brother Dmitry, much as he had after he'd killed his first man — men. He'd known many people who were never the same after they killed. Some thirsted for it, but most never forgave themselves.

What she'd killed on the ski trip, that was a different matter. That description — wasn't human.

He rounded the back of the building where a large, groomed field stretched to a copse of trees backed by the grumbling I-5. Its traffic never ceased, no matter the time. It thinned out in the early morning until you could make out the individual engines and pick out a sports car or semi. This close, the sound echoed off the building.

Meg sat at the back of the school staring across the grass, perhaps up to the mountains. She wore one of the outfits Biff had picked up, a yellow shirt with flowers and jean shorts that reached her knee. She noticed Thomas but didn't turn directly toward him.

Grimacing, he settled down beside her. He didn't say anything, just watched the colors play off the range. He smoothed his hair. The rushing traffic across I-5 created a rhythmic sound, almost lulling.

They sat for a couple minutes before Meg took a deep breath. "I don't want to be here," she said.

Thomas nodded. "Where do you want to be?"

"Home, with Mom and Dad." She spoke with a firm tone, sure of herself.

He tilted his head. "You know that can't be anymore, don't you?"

She croaked and stifled a sob. "Yes." Wiping her face, she sniffled, unable to stop the tears.

He let her think about it for a moment before he spoke. "Then, we just have us right now. We'll have to make the best of that."

She didn't agree, but didn't argue the point, sobbing breaths softly between her fingers. He'd gone through plenty of loss, and he knew enough to let her work through it. No words could stitch a torn heart. Eventually, the tears slowed, and the sky turned gray.

She swallowed and stuttered. "Can we see Rock?"

Thomas grimaced lightly. Haddie had so much going on. "Probably fine. Let's get back to the garage and wash your face. We'll call Haddie." He winced as he stood.

Meg followed, wiping her hands on her shirt. Her cheeks shone in the dusk.

The Mini Cooper had enough gas to get them there and back. He pulled his phone out; 8:51 p.m. Hopefully Haddie hadn't planned on going to bed early. Her friend Liz had kept her in a near frenzy. She'd end up going to Portland. He wanted to help. Protect. But he had Meg now, and that complicated things.

CHAPTER 13

HADDIE PACED, yet again, into the living room where Sam played with Rock on the floor. Jisoo called out from the kitchen, but Haddie ignored her.

Sliding into the chair at her desk, she glanced at a silent, uncaring phone. Purposefully, she placed it face down beside her mouse atop a pair of unopened envelopes. It would vibrate if someone called or texted. Looking at the screen would not make anything magically appear. Her eyes felt dry and scratchy. The day felt like she'd worn it too long, and she needed a shower and a change out of clothes that smelled musty and overused.

Nothing new had come up on social media in either Liz or her boyfriend's accounts. It had been almost twenty-four hours since Liz had any activity. Liz's voicemail had filled, probably all from Haddie. Texting had become Haddie's only recourse; the messages stretched back to yesterday ranging from short demands to long pleading texts. No responses. Messaging on social media had never been something Liz used. Haddie messaged her anyway.

Sam had stayed, sensing Haddie's mood. She made no pretense about why and had helped make dinner, an actual cooked affair of spaghetti, chopped canned tomatoes, and garlic toast; aromas of basil and garlic filled Haddie's apartment, which would have been welcome had her mood been better. Most of it sat untouched.

The two crisp knocks on the door stirred Rock to a growl, but he stood attentively by Sam as Haddie got up. He gave her a quick look as if to gauge her reaction. It would be Dad and Meg. They'd come quickly.

Dad wore a black Harley-Davidson T-shirt and Meg stood at his hip in a cute little yellow top. She peeked around the corner to catch sight of Rock, and almost smiled.

"Hey," Dad said. He motioned Meg in, and she whipped past to Rock and Sam. His face still looked bad.

Haddie gestured to the kitchen. "Make yourself some coffee."

He frowned. "Nothing stronger?"

She knew he was joking in his own way. "Sorry, hit the last Two Hearts when I got home. There's leftover spaghetti if you and Meg want any." She leaned against the counter while Jisoo serenaded them.

Dad pulled the coffee and filters from the top shelf of the cabinet over her fridge. She kept them for him and on occasion Liz. Haddie drank coffee, just preferred tea. The coffee maker sat ignored on the counter tucked in the corner beside the fridge; she'd piled a stack of measuring cups on top of it. Jisoo wandered over as Dad began measuring out his coffee and Haddie absently petted her.

"How you doing?" he asked.

She fought the welling around her eyes. "Best as can be expected, I'd imagine."

"You take on a lot." He looked up before she could complain. "But I understand. You're a good friend to worry."

"And, if it were me?" she asked. What would he do?

Dad smirked. "I'd be showing hotel clerks pictures of a white-haired Amazon."

Suddenly, Haddie felt guilty. That is what he would do. Should she? It could take days, but it would be doing something. She'd thought of going down by the venue and doing exactly that, but they could be staying outside of Portland. Liz had mentioned other places they were going after the concert. Haddie hadn't paid enough attention.

"Should I?" she asked. "Should I go to Portland and try to find a hotel where they recognize her?"

"Liz, if I remember, is in her early thirties, shoulder-length brown hair, average height and build with only blue eyes to make her stand out. Right?" He started his coffee. "She's not exactly going to stand out. Half of the staff would think they saw her. You'd be sleeping in lobbies hoping to find her."

Haddie sighed. It would be futile. They wouldn't look up her name, and likely the room would be under Matt Arbor and he looked no less average than Liz. Unless Terry came through with something, she would end up calling the Portland police and filing a missing person report. The thought tightened her chest. Her schooling and internship taught her this would be the right way to deal with this; her Dad kept her skeptical of any authorities. Their recent activities, today's visit by Detective Cooper, and the call from Special Agent Wilkins reinforced it. Though, Liz didn't have the same kind of — problems — that Haddie did. She couldn't ignore the possibility that she'd need the police. Liz's voicemail waited on her phone just in case.

The smell of coffee fought basil and garlic. Haddie filled her teapot despite being tired. No one would care if she headed off to bed while Meg enjoyed Rock. With only a couple hours of sleep the night before, it wouldn't be surprising, but her mind couldn't turn off. Liz needed her help; she knew in her bones that something had gone terribly wrong. What she should do about it tormented her, along with guilt for ignoring the call — it could have ended right then.

Dad sipped black coffee as Haddie poured fresh brewed tea over ice. The comforting swirl of hot and cold rippled across her palm.

In the other room her phone vibrated on her desk. Haddie jumped, nearly upsetting her tea, and smacked the glass on her counter with a wince.

Terry called. Not a text. *This has to be important.* Haddie swallowed. "Hello?"

"Hey, Haddie." His voice did not have that usual chipper tone. "Got it."

"The hotel?" *Of course.* Her heart rose in her chest.

"And the room number, 311. I'll text you the address link."

Haddie smiled and glanced at her Dad, wanting someone to join in the excitement. "You are the best." She had to leave now. Portland only took a couple of hours. "Thank you."

"I'm awesome." Terry didn't sound enthusiastic. He hadn't been happy when she'd gotten his commitment to help.

"What did it take — to get this information?"

Terry remained silent for half a minute. He spoke with a quiet, emotionless tone. "Dealing with some people I don't exactly agree with. Let's keep it to that."

What cost had he paid for this information? "Thank you, Terry." She owed him, yet again.

He returned to a cheerful, if not hearty tone. "You got it, Buckaroo." The connection ended.

Dad leaned against the doorframe of the kitchen, sipping his coffee. His expression quizzical, he raised his eyebrows. "Good news, I take it?"

Haddie dropped her phone to her side. She really wanted Dad to go with her. They didn't need to pack. However, Meg sat on her knees rubbing Rock's white giraffe while Sam nuzzled his face with her forehead. Dad couldn't leave Meg, nor bring her.

"I'm going to drive up to Portland to check on Liz. Probably drag her back here."

Dad coughed. "Whoa, wait. Call the room."

I'm an idiot. "Of course. Yes. She could have just lost her phone and doesn't know I've been trying to get her." Haddie paused checking her phone. "It's pretty late."

Dad snorted. "You think she'd rather you pound on her door at 2 a.m.?"

I'm not thinking clearly. Dad thought so much better under stress, while she just flailed around. "No, you're right."

"Take a breath, Haddie. Two."

Haddie nodded, taking his advice. Her phone buzzed with Terry's text. Professor Arbor had booked the room. She sat down at the computer, partially to compose herself, and looked up the hotel's phone number. With a deep sigh, she dialed the operator.

"Hello, room 311 please. Arbor." She waited as a polite young woman transferred her. The phone rang endlessly before kicking to a hotel voicemail box. *I'm driving tonight.*

"Liz, check in with me. I'm worried." Haddie shook her head. "I'm coming."

She jumped from her chair in a burst of energy and moved to get a quick change of clothes in case it took longer than she expected. It would be 2 a.m. by the time she got there. She would be pounding on the door. "Sam, I've got to leave. Can you lock up and check on Rock tomorrow? I'll get with you at some point, let you know what my plan is."

Sam didn't respond immediately, and Haddie swiveled to find her turned toward Dad.

He pushed off the doorway and walked toward them. "You need to sleep a few hours first Haddie."

Haddie laughed. She couldn't imagine sleeping; it wouldn't happen. "I'll be fine, Dad."

"We haven't slept much in the past few days. Additionally, you told me you didn't sleep last night. Getting in an accident won't help Liz." He tilted his head. "Just four hours, you'd still get there by morning."

She couldn't sleep. Her bigger concern laid in what to do if Liz didn't answer. Where would she go from there? If Liz didn't answer the door at 2 a.m., 6 a.m. would not be any different. Could Terry get her the professor's license plate? Guilt pulled her upright. How much had she already pushed Terry into? She wasn't being obsessive — this involved her friend. No one argued that her fears were valid. Haddie needed to do something, now.

"T's right, Haddie. Get some sleep. Should you even go alone?" Sam swirled around from facing Rock and swept her legs to the side.

The question hung in the air, and Haddie dared not look at her dad. She watched Meg scratching Rock's chest as he wiggled, his head turning to look at her now that he'd lost Sam.

Dad cleared his throat. "I can't go right now."

Sam gestured dismissively. "Go, T. Meg can stay with me. Wait until she sees all my beasties. She'll love it." Smirking, Sam turned to Meg. "Wouldn't you?"

Meg's eyes had gone wide. "Yes." A hint of happiness lay at the corners of her mouth.

"See?" Sam spun her leg around so she sat cross-legged. "Haddie needs you. Liz obviously needs help. Sending Haddie out alone — who knows what she'll do?"

Dad frowned, staring at Meg. "I can't."

"Please?" Meg almost offered a smile she pleaded so hard with Dad.

Haddie nearly joined her. Sam could handle Meg, probably better than Dad. It did surprise Haddie though, to see Sam so engaged when usually she drew in at any chance of being exposed to other people. How did Dad feel about Meg? She hadn't asked him to leave, instead being able to stay with Sam and all her pets. Still.

She watched his face and imagined he worried most about what Meg might tell Sam. A valid concern. Haddie didn't have an answer for that, though she guessed that Sam would bring any questions to Dad or her rather than involve authorities.

He turned toward Haddie.

She shrugged and said, "I certainly wouldn't say no, but I understand if you can't."

He looked down at her feet and rubbed his head, holding the top of his braid for a moment. Her pulse rose. Would she always be like this — hoping Dad would come to the rescue?

He nodded decisively. "I'll ride my bike, in case I need to head back in a pinch." He looked at Meg. "And I'll bail if it takes too much time. I want to be back tomorrow night."

Haddie sighed in relief. Okay, so he didn't want to get trapped into one of her obsessions. That, she could understand, but this wasn't a simple obsessive windmill, as Terry called them. This concerned Liz, and he didn't deny that the situation warranted worry. They'd get there, find Liz, and probably bring her back.

"Thanks, Dad."

He held a finger up and she frowned. He did the same motion when she'd won an argument as a kid. Some concession or point that he would not negotiate. "But, we leave in five hours. I'll be here at 5 a.m. with some of Meg's clothes and stuff. The girls — ladies — go over to Sam's now to let you settle down. You," he said looking up to Haddie, "try to sleep until 4 a.m. or so."

Sam, and possibly Meg, giggled.

Haddie gave him a flat look. "I can't sleep."

"I can, and I need my bike and some gear." He shrugged. "Or go without me and have me worry."

Twenty minutes later, Haddie lay on her bed staring at the shadows her bathroom light made on her bedroom's textured ceiling. Dad had talked with Sam alone before taking them over to her apartment. Meg had been excited, if not yet smiling when she left for her sleepover. Rock curled up on the other side of Haddie's bed, seemingly pleased with the abundance of attention he'd received. Still, he'd sidled up to lay on her arm before sleeping.

"What are you doing, Liz?" Haddie held her phone against her chest, still hoping for a response. At least they had a plan, even if she just lay there thinking about it. She appreciated Dad going along, despite her random thoughts to just leave now. By morning they'd be at the hotel, and at least one step closer to finding Liz.

Damn. I need to leave a message for Andrea. They

expected her in the office first thing, not that they had anything important for her.

I'm not going to be able to sleep.

CHAPTER 14

THOMAS RODE through Eugene in the stillness of the dark morning hours. If he appreciated any time in a city, it came before its inhabitants began their morning routines. Most still slept at this hour, with only the occasional early morning driver or the waking flicker of a light in a house. The streets were his for the most part. Darkness hid a good part of the ugliness while lights masked the beauty of the night sky and stars. A place and time between — a couple hundred years ago the night sky still would have sparkled with stars, and nature would have dominated the few trails — in a couple of hours any sense of nature and sky would be erased in the hustle.

In the east, the gray of predawn shaped the mountains into a silhouette. There was a moist, comfortable smell to the breeze. A dog barked from its yard behind a fences as Thomas waited at a pointless red light.

Haddie's concern for her friend seemed founded, from what little he knew of Liz. A professor and a crime lab tech didn't speak of a frivolous or careless lifestyle, but sometimes secrets came to rise in people.

Secrets. His own. Haddie's. And now, Meg's. They swirled around him as if he were a whirlpool drawing them in. In the past, when they got too many and the current too strong, he just left to start fresh someplace new.

This time, he stayed. Haddie's friends, Liz and Sam, along with Biff, stood on the shore threatened with the rip of current. He'd been through this before and seen it all get sucked away quicker than anyone could expect. He'd been preparing since the moment Haddie had used her power on Dmitry, Harold Holmes' brother.

He'd selected parts from an innocuous collection in his garage, one stash of many. Then he'd rebuilt a 1909 Model 5-D Twin to the original condition it had when he'd bought it over a hundred years ago.

The sale had been quick and without any questions.

Haddie didn't know, but he'd purchased an identity for her in Abbotsford, Canada. He'd added one for himself there as well. The small property he picked up with the new identity lay on the north side of the Fraser River where he parked a registered and insured Jeep. Hopefully, they wouldn't need any of it, but he'd started the process of getting Meg one identity in Canada, and another in Eugene, just in case.

If Sam or Biff stumbled onto too many secrets, then Thomas had a plan. One contingency of many.

He pulled his Shovelhead beside Haddie's bike and killed the engine. Taking off his helmet and smoothing his hair back, he looked up to Sam's window on the opposite side of the road. A dim light, deeper in her apartment, silhouetted a feline who watched him. In Haddie's parking alcove, it smelled more like a city with gasoline and garbage.

She answered the door by his third round of knocking. Dressed in a long T-shirt with some cartoon or anime characters on it, she blinked furiously and wiped red eyes. "I slept. I'm sorry."

Thomas moved past her giving Rock a scratch. "Don't apologize. You needed it. I'll make coffee." He would have given her another hour before coming over, but feared she'd just have left on her own.

The calico begged until Thomas found some treats for her on top of the fridge. As his coffee brewed, it half-covered the scent of the pasta still on the stovetop from the night before. Moving one of Haddie's piles, he found a chair and grunted as he sat. Haddie swore from her bedroom, and he drank coffee while sitting with Rock, scratching the pit bull's ears.

The weather to Portland had looked good. There would be clouds, but no rain was expected. Leaving Meg with Sam risked stories coming out about the uncle being shot. It wasn't something he liked leaving to chance, but he could do a quick check on this hotel Haddie had found and then head back if it seemed as though it might drag on. Relationship issues had a way of never getting resolved quickly, in his experience.

Haddie appeared as he poured his second cup, so he made her one too. She dressed in a brown jacket that she likely wouldn't need, a black top, and jeans that covered her boots. Her face had been washed, though she didn't seem to have makeup on; the dark shadows under her eyes were from lack of sleep.

"Any word from Liz?" He leaned against the counter and watched her over the edge of his mug.

She tried to both blow on her coffee and shake her head. Now that she was awake, he could see her mind racing and worry tightening her lips. She needed to focus on the road, at least until they got to the hotel.

"No reason to worry at this point. We'll just head up there and find out what's going on. Often, it is far simpler than we make it out in our heads."

She remained standing in the living room and cocked her head in a way that implied she didn't believe his assessment. "I'm already worried. That's not going to go away."

"That might be. You can choose your focus though."

She snorted and worked on her coffee. This trip might prove useless, but until Haddie connected with Liz, she wouldn't let it go.

Her loyalty to her friends had always driven her. When she'd been nine, her friend Annabelle had been sick with anemia and hospitalized. Haddie had spent every hour outside of school visiting the hospital room. When they wouldn't allow her in, she'd sat in the lobby drawing pictures for her friend's wall. The ritual continued until the girl had been released a few days later.

"You ready?" Haddie asked.

Thomas sighed, winced as he stood, and took her mug, heading for the kitchen. He'd have to trust that Meg would be in good hands, but he had a good feeling about Haddie's friend Sam, always had. His only concern came from the possibility of Meg opening up to the woman. He'd be able to tell when he came back and interacted with Sam. Right now, he needed to focus on the ride. Then, Haddie's friend Liz.

He rinsed the mugs and left them in the sink with last night's plates.

Haddie held the door open, absently scratching Rock's ears. "Thanks, Dad."

"Let's go see about your friend." Thomas walked out of the apartment.

CHAPTER 15

IN HER EAGERNESS, Haddie strode ahead of Dad in the morning rush of pedestrians. Horns, engines, and people on their cells babbled around them.

The hotel stood thin and dark gray in the sun; it seemed gloomy despite, and perhaps because of, the windows and their reflections of the blanket of clouds that covered the sky. Yellow lights were still lit over the entrance as if night hadn't quite ended. The brick building rose eight stories.

"It looks depressing," said Haddie.

"Don't they all?" Dad looked at the city around them rising in tall blocks.

Inside the lobby, the yellow light shone warmly through globe lights hanging from chandeliers, bricks or blocks made up walls, and upholstered and wood furniture decorated the floor. It looked nicer than she had begun to fear.

Professor Arbor had not become a regular interest of Liz's until the past month. Throughout most of the spring semester there had been the occasional date, then everything had gotten serious. But with finals underway, Haddie hadn't given it much thought except that most of Liz's conversations had been about him. Now, between David and Matt, Liz and Haddie didn't seem to get any time. She should have been paying attention to her friend and perhaps looking into this man a little more. Instead, she stood here with no clear idea of who he really was.

Haddie started for the front desk and her dad discreetly scooped into her elbow and guided them for the elevator. "Don't we —?" she started to ask.

"Shh."

Evidently, he planned to go straight for the room and avoid discussion with the hotel employees — probably a better idea. They stood waiting for the elevator doors and he just smiled. There were few patrons sitting at tables and a pair of women checking out at the registration desk. More staff than anyone else seemed to trot about on one errand or another. *Nice hotel.* What if Liz's boyfriend Matt and his antics had gotten them kicked out? Would Terry's search have discovered that?

Dad spoke as the elevator doors closed. "Probably best we don't ask permission."

"I realized." She smiled nervously and breathed in and out. "I guess you have more experience in this."

"Not usually in hotels this nice, but there have been occasions."

The hall smelled of perfumed cleaner that masked the deeper scent of human musk and stuffy air. Light beige panels separated by dark brown partitions covered the walls, line art resembled graffiti along the floor, and ceiling lights shone brightly in the corridor. Stylish lettering on the brass plaque mounted to the door confirmed the room number. Food trays dotted the gray carpet beside many of the doors, but only a "Do Not Disturb" sign marked the outside of Liz's room.

Haddie knocked in a quick rhythm that matched her heartbeat.

She leaned in, but could hear nothing from inside the room. Three doors down, a man in a pale T-shirt leaned out of his door, carefully avoiding exposing his lower half while he slid a tray outside. He gave her a quick smile before disappearing.

She knocked again with a solid rap above the room number.

Still silence.

"What if they don't answer?" she asked.

Dad shrugged. "Have some coffee in the lobby? See if they show up? Maybe they went out for breakfast."

Haddie doubted they'd be up this early if they'd been going to concerts and raves. The call she'd ignored had come in midday and Liz had said they just got up. More likely this morning they'd just gotten to sleep, if they were even here.

Haddie pounded on the hotel room door again. A couple exited their room down the hall and maneuvered two wheeled suitcases out.

She needed Liz to be here. Otherwise, it could be worse than she'd imagined. What if Liz lay unconscious inside?

She waited until the couple turned into the elevator alcove. "We need to get in there."

"We can head downstairs and probably get them to check the room." Dad shifted and leaned up against the wall.

At least she'd make sure Liz hadn't passed out. What if Liz wasn't here? A rave would have ended by now, surely. Maybe something in the room would help them find Liz and her boyfriend. *They'll never let me in to look.*

"Can you —" She nodded toward the locked door handle. "Get us in?"

Dad rubbed his head. "Not without a key. I'm old school when it comes to locks. Unless you want me to try and break it in?" He studied the door and grimaced. "Looks pretty solid."

Haddie drooped. "Okay. Then we'll get them to check. I just thought we might find something, a hint, that could let me know what's going on if Liz isn't in there." They'd been knocking for a while; everyone awake would've heard by now.

This is what I was afraid of; that Liz wouldn't be here. Each time the thought came, she'd lied and reassured herself that her friend would be sleeping and come out grudgingly, hungover. In the back of her mind, she knew that she'd have to track Liz down and pull her out of some situation that had kept her friend from responding. At some point, Liz would have checked Haddie's frantic voicemails, texts, or messages and responded. *If she could.*

"You want to search her room." Dad didn't ask a question, he made a statement.

Haddie nodded.

Dad sighed. "Let's hope they start on the lower floors." He nodded for the elevator and led the way.

"What are you planning?"

"Just follow my lead." He pushed the button to take the elevator down and checked his phone for the time.

The second floor, identical to the third, had the food trays picked up and a maid's cart on each end. Dad headed down the hall.

When he reached the cart blocking an open door, he crouched over and laid his hand on the cart for support. "Hello?" he asked.

A young woman, dark brown hair tied into a ponytail, wore a gray uniform with wide, white collars. She wore pale plastic gloves and looked out at them. "Yes?"

Dad smiled and waved her toward them as he obviously swayed. "Can I have an extra towel?"

As she approached, he stepped back with an obvious limp, and swayed off balance. The maid smiled and grabbed a folded, white towel off her cart without question.

As Dad reached for the towel his leg buckled, sending him crashing to the floor. Haddie started, believing his act herself for a brief moment.

The maid dropped the towel with an exclamation and covered her mouth with her gloved hand.

Dad, rocking on the floor reached up toward the maid for help. The purpura still marred his face, and he would have looked ill if Haddie hadn't known better. She felt compelled to join them. "Dad."

Pushing her cart aside, the maid grasped his arm with both hands, ignoring his looks and that he outweighed her. Crouching she began helping him up. Twisting to get up on a knee, he dropped the same hand into her right pocket and a keycard flashed into his palm. Haddie joined to help, and they righted her Dad to a bent stance.

"I'm so sorry." Haddie apologized, salvaging the towel off the floor and leaving the woman open mouthed.

Dad smiled. "Thank you."

Haddie held the towel in one hand and supported her dad with the other, careful not to look back until they reached the elevator. The maid had disappeared into the hotel room.

"A pickpocket?"

He shrugged. "It's been useful at times."

Haddie carried the towel with her to Liz's room and followed Dad inside.

The empty bed had crumpled and twisted covers draped half off the edge. A variety of clothes, takeout food containers, and empty bottles covered the pair of chairs and table by the window. Brown curtains had been drawn almost closed, but a thin line of gray showed down the middle.

The bathroom light beside her was on, but Dad hit the switch on the wall and a light lit over the cluttered table. Haddie leaned into the bathroom without touching the doorway. Toiletries were scattered around and in a wide white sink. A pile of clothes lay in a sodden lump inside the shower stall. Towels of all sizes littered the bathroom floor.

"Dad." Haddie sucked in a breath pointing to a brown smudge across one white towel. "Is that dried blood?"

He grunted and passed her, kneeling down. As always, he wore riding gloves which he used to pick up the towel and smell it. He put it down and studied the floor. "You're right."

"Dad." Haddie shivered and the hair rose on her arms and neck. "What if something has happened to Liz? What if I'm too late?" *I could never forgive myself.*

"Don't go there yet." He stood up and studied her. "It'll muddle your thinking. The amount that is on that towel is less than some bloody noses I've had."

She looked at his bent nose that had obviously been broken. Not completely reassuring. Still, she took a deep calming breath and gave the bathroom another look before she led them out to the bedroom.

The mayhem looked all that more distressing. Some of it just looked like litter: the empty bottles of liquor and wine stacked on the bureau, the empty Styrofoam food trays on the chair seat, and the crumpled bags near the garbage can. The splat of food on the curtain looked as if it had been thrown, as did a pillow lying on the floor by her feet. The room smelled of alcohol with a tinge of vomit somewhere. Liz could never have been in her right mind in this room.

"Quite the party." Dad walked carefully across the floor, footsteps placed between mashed globs of food and discarded wrappers. "I don't see any signs of struggle or fighting though."

Haddie blinked. "How can you tell?"

"People get pretty violent when they're attacked and they don't avoid furniture, they push others into it. Chairs and tables are still standing." He pointed to Liz's suitcase behind Haddie on the folding stand in the corner.

Haddie's panic didn't lessen. *This isn't Liz.* Selfies in a revealing fringe bikini? Not on social media. They didn't talk much about each other's sexual forays, but Haddie had known Liz for years and she didn't do exhibition.

She took a few more steps between the bed and the TV. This didn't make any sense. "Where is she then?"

Dad gestured to the bottles "Partying somewhere, or sleeping it off there. Maybe they met some friends and went to their place. I'd guess from the state of this food, they weren't here yesterday."

Tucked under the table lay a somewhat neat pile of folded black T-shirts, some lanyards, a clear bag of pins, and a rolled poster, likely from the concert. She spied a small tray on the table, nearly covered by a cardboard sushi box. She approached and pushed aside the debris with her finger, but found nothing other than napkins and a pair of unused chopsticks.

A dark flyer with a rainbow of thin beams of light lay tossed on top of the clothes piled in one chair. Slanted to the side, it had nearly slipped out of sight. Haddie picked it up and glanced over an advertisement for a rave that had happened two nights before, the night Liz had posted the photo. Someplace in Portland — she didn't recognize the street.

"Dad." She held up the paper.

The flyer's tagline under the address and time read, "Wicked debauchery, dancing, food, and drinks. Fringe by Penumbra."

"That looks like a spot for these folks."

Maybe there had been another rave last night. Haddie checked her phone: 8:16 a.m. She sighed. "It was 10 p.m. to 6 a.m. a day ago. We've missed it by twenty-four hours." If there had been one last night, wouldn't they be back by now?

Dad lifted up the comforter, looked under, and tossed it to the bed. "That's the best lead I see here. Does she keep a purse?"

Haddie looked around. "Yes, it's not here." Where had they been all yesterday? Should she start checking hospitals? She glanced over at the bottles and rolling tray. Jails? *What have you gotten into Liz?* A welling of anger tightened her chest. Haddie should have dug into Professor Arbor's background long ago. Who thinks a professor would be trouble?

The only new information she had came from a two-day-old flyer that they likely picked up at the concert. Who's to say they even went to it? She could at least check it out, then call the police and start a missing person report. Probably best she didn't leave any fingerprints. She folded the flyer, tucked it into her pocket, and turned to the bed. Lifting a pillow, she found the source of the room's taint.

Someone had puked across the pillow and then flipped it over.

"Damn, Liz." *What have you gotten into?* She laid the pillow back down and turned with a grimace. "Take the RAV4 to the address? Leave your bike here?"

Dad nodded.

CHAPTER 16

HADDIE TURNED her RAV4 onto Thompson Street as she checked her phone again. "I think it's here, but I don't see a number." She rubbed her arm, apprehensive and not sure she could help Liz.

Dad squinted, looking at the two-story, white building. "We can walk around. Find the building number."

He pointed at a parking spot where cars were lined along the curb near a sidewalk where windows lined most of the walls. In her mirror, a clean white bridge had an arch that curved into gray clouds. A semi unloading into a warehouse across the way seemed the only indication of business in the neighborhood. The road ended at a dark underpass below I-5 where the tops of trucks were visible for a moment as they raced past.

Haddie stepped out and faced the graffiti tag on the building across the street. Someone had written "the neon gods fall" in red paint along the gray wall with "The Unceasing" sprayed farther down. Beside it, an odd symbol had been painted. Striding around the front of her car, she could see hastily swept glass on the sidewalk by the white building. The thick round pieces crunched under her boots and she caught the scent of alcohol over the exhaust in the air. She likely had found the building where the rave had been held.

Dad leaned against the tinted windows, cupping his hands around his face. "Empty. There's a light on in one of the halls."

Haddie headed toward an inset door under a fixed overhang. Through the small glass panes, she could make out an abandoned reception desk. The dark wooden door had a long bar from top to bottom as a handle. The building number stenciled on the wall confirmed she'd found the location of the rave. When they'd parked, they'd passed a smaller door, but this seemed the main entrance. She pulled against the locked door.

What was their plan?

Dad leaned against the windows surrounding the door, glancing at the semi unloading and the buildings across the street. "Let's check the other door and if that doesn't work, see what's in the back."

Haddie felt very obvious as they walked past her car toward the smaller door and overhang. No one stood and watched them, but there were plenty of windows. A Nissan Altima had a flat front tire, and someone had marked the car with a yellow sticker on the street side.

Liz had been here, two nights ago. *I know it*. Likely dragged here by her drug-crazed boyfriend. This area would be dead at 10 p.m. at night. Above the I-5 overpass, Haddie could see a couple houses or apartments that rose up an incline on the other side of the highway. They probably did not enjoy the warehouse view enough to look down here. Whatever had happened in those dark hours two nights ago had faded — disappeared like Liz.

Haddie felt a hollow forming in her chest as her hope bled out.

The plainer door had been locked as well. A nearly empty gin bottle nestled in the alcove. Everything here appeared abandoned.

Dad nodded and they walked to the corner and turned at the side street. Two more cars sat with yellow stickers on their windows marked with "Warning" and tiny words she couldn't read. She should have known what kind of car Matt Arbor drove.

"Lot of cars marked for towing." Dad nodded toward the sticker on a Ford Focus.

Haddie frowned. "Left from the rave? Is that common?"

Dad snorted, coming to the gate at the end of the building. "Do I look like I go to raves? I didn't even think they were a thing anymore."

There were two gates between the corner and a gray building farther down the side street. Dad stood at a short black gate that led to a fenced-in area with small dumpsters and stairs to a door. The other gate had a length of barbed wire and led to a gravel drive between the neighboring building where the only windows were on the second level. There, Haddie could see industrial lights hanging from an open ceiling.

Dad leaned over the black gate and opened it from the inside. With his height it barely came to his waist. Not very secure.

Haddie followed Dad toward the stairs. Above, windows on the upper floor opened out in random spaces. The music would have been heard all through this industrial area. Haddie had never gone to a rave. The closest she came was a farm outside of Salem where she'd gone with high school friends to dance and drink. She barely remembered the night, but woke up there the next morning.

How had people at this rave left their cars to be towed? At least they'd remember to come back the next day. What car did Professor Arbor drive?

Dad worked on the lock and Haddie pulled out her phone, glancing around to see if anybody noticed them.

She texted Terry. "Hey. Sorry. Another favor to ask."

Dad opened the door and checked the nearby alarm pad. Surprisingly, nothing went off. Haddie hadn't even considered it.

"Dad?"

He shook his head. "Don't worry. I could see the pad up front. Not armed. Just had to hope it was the same system."

She raised her eyebrows and turned back as Terry replied, "Ok."

Haddie typed, "Liz not at hotel room. Can you get me Matt Arbor's make, model, and maybe license number?"

"Sorry room a bust." He followed with two sad emoji.

After all he'd gone through. Haddie swallowed, following her dad. "No. It helped. She hadn't been there for a day. Found the rave she went to two nights ago."

"You're at a rave?" He added shocked emojis.

"No. It's over. We're trying to track her down." *The only lead I have.* "We found a flyer."

"Where was she last night? Another rave?" Before Haddie could reply, he texted, "Send me a picture of the flyer."

"Dad, wait." Haddie fumbled for the flyer in her jean pocket and stopped to unfold it.

He cocked his head, then went back to surveying the open room they crossed. "Is that your friend Terry?"

Haddie held out the flyer and sent a picture to Terry.

"Smart guy. Maybe he can find out where last night's rave — or better, tonight's will be."

Smarter than me, obviously. Haddie texted Terry. "Thanks."

"These raves worry me." He followed with emojis and typed, "Be careful, Buckaroo."

Haddie wrinkled her nose at the foul smell of rotted food, then folded the flyer and put it back into her pocket. Bottles, paper plates, and plastic cups littered the bottom of the stairs and trailed up. Two black garbage bags had been left by the front door they'd first tried to come in. Someone had started to clean up, or at least enough that a glance in the windows wouldn't alert them to the previous night's activities. The smell would have been enough alone. It reminded her of Liz's hotel room.

The stench and mess got worse on the second floor. Garbage had been crushed underfoot in some places until its identity disappeared and it became a collage on the wood floor. The thickest lumps were discarded clothing. Someone had painted a surrealistic mural with food and possibly wine on a cream colored wall. At the foot of the windows, disposable hotel pans had been left along with bottles, clothing, cups, and refuse shoved off the main floor.

Some smaller rooms divided a section of the second floor near the middle. A cream colored wall cut from the outer windows to form what could be offices. An open door into one of those had the only area that seemed free of debris, or had less at least.

This is the place. She opened her phone and brought up Liz's image that had been posted on her social media. "Dad."

He grunted as he compared the photo. "She was here. Now, where did she go?" He rubbed his head looking at the floor. "I'm sure they would have flyers for their next rave, wouldn't they?" He sighed, shuffling through the flattened debris. "What do I know?"

Haddie took pictures. She didn't particularly have a plan, but she had her phone out and wanted at least a picture of where Liz had been standing. The clear area appeared to be around where the woman had been doing yoga in Liz's posted photo.

"Keep me out of those." Dad grumbled and moved to a hall where the offices ended.

She'd never understood his avoidance of photos until she'd seen WWI pictures of him — looking not a day younger. He looked to be in his mid-thirties then and today.

Heavy wood beams split the ceiling of the open area. One of the supporting posts had gouges in it that looked like animal claws had dug into the wood. If it had been a human, she imagined they had no fingernails left. Haddie slumped under a weight which pressed down on her at the sight of the room. Liz had been here, in that outfit, with who knows who.

"Haddie," Dad called from the other side of the building.

She pocketed her phone and strode across the debris, careful not to step on the random beer bottles. Some were decent beer.

Dad faced her as she turned the corner. He blocked the doorway to a bathroom, and she could smell the sewage. Perhaps it came from the stains on the floor outside the door. She held her breath.

"It's just blood in there, but a lot." He stepped aside.

Haddie's veins froze. *Liz.* She shivered as she walked toward the open door. A white sink had brownish-pink streaks across it and the mirror above looked like someone had fingerpainted on the surface. The tile, which she had first thought wood, had been turned from a light color to brown with dried blood. Footprints blotted out each other in a bizarre design, and she could see dried brown tracks under her feet, as if the blood had been walked across the entire night.

"No one could have survived losing that much blood. I can't even be sure that it was only one body." Dad shook his head.

He caught her arm, and she realized she'd swayed. "Liz," she murmured as her vision cleared.

"Don't go there. You can't know that. How many people come to raves? A hundred? More?"

She had no idea how many people went to raves. Terry. He knew about raves. She only knew Liz had been at this one. And something horrible had happened in this room, and no one had cared. Part of her obsession had been searching the police blotters for accidents or deaths in Portland. No one had reported this. No crime tape hung at the doors. Terry called them suicide raves. Is that what happened here? Trembling, she took out her phone.

"What are you doing?" her dad asked.

Her lips didn't seem to want to form words. "Terry." She texted Terry three pictures, shivering between each.

Terry didn't respond immediately.

Dad had turned her away from the bathroom. There looked to be feces smeared on the window and wall. It stunk so foul she couldn't imagine how she hadn't smelled it in the other room.

Terry typed for a long while, but he only wrote, "No sign of Liz?"

"No. Help me find her." Haddie trembled as she typed.

"Whatever it takes, Buckaroo."

Haddie stumbled into the main room with Dad's help. She didn't believe Liz had been any part of that blood. Couldn't. The toilet seat had been smeared brown. She wanted to retch.

"I'll look around for a flyer. Why don't you go sit on the stairs?" Dad led her toward the steps.

"No, I'll look — in here." She wouldn't sit waiting while Liz could be out there. They needed to find last night's rave. Terry looked too. He could be amazing on the internet. She needed him to be amazing.

Every dark stain she saw became blood, and some of it might have been. The debris looked so much darker and twisted than at first glance. Her concern had turned to near panic. Liz could not have planned for this kind of trip — Haddie knew her better than that. Matt Arbor had to be the issue here. He'd brought her friend to all this. Maybe he hadn't known how bad it would get. Her anger focused on him, but it didn't matter. She needed to find Liz. Likely that meant finding last night's rave and she didn't see any flyers up here. Maybe that had been in the trash on the first floor.

"I'm going to look downstairs." Haddie headed for the steps.

CHAPTER 17

HADDIE TWISTED her hair nervously as she walked through the downstairs offices. Her dad searched above, and she could hear his footsteps thudding across the wood ceiling.

She'd grown sensitive to the scents, though downstairs smelled only of alcohol. Bottles and red cups comprised most of the litter in the vacant offices and abandoned storage rooms. In some, she found clothes — underwear. In a larger back room, some of the windows had been smashed, and the breeze coming in refreshed her. She paused to take in a breath. The blood and sense of mayhem built desperate images in her mind. They made her want to run from the building, hide in her RAV4, shut down inside, and wait for someone else to fix all this. She couldn't. *Liz is out there. I have to find her.*

Liz had always been the only friend Haddie had kept through her years in college. She'd met Terry later, once she moved to law school. She'd lost contact with her high school friends when she'd gone to college, and college friends when they'd graduated and she'd moved on to law school, except for Liz. They'd met four years ago when Haddie'd taken Liz's college course on forensics, a basic 101 class. Haddie had taken on a mission to meet a funding goal for one of the local homeless programs and gone to Liz with questions about police activity at Four Corners. Liz had ended up helping, and they'd been friends since.

Haddie picked her way through the light debris, still not finding any flyers. However, she found a locked storage room. A gray, painted, metal door had been locked with a zip tie in the loop with a hasp bent to fit the door jamb. Unlatched, the door lay open a finger's width. Not enough to see inside. Someone had worried the door enough to bend the hasp straighter, but it would have been easier to cut the tie. Unless, someone inside had tried to get out.

Haddie hurried back to the stairs. "Dad, come check this out."

Wincing, he came down the steps with slow deliberate footfalls. "What is it?"

Haddie couldn't be sure of her assumption, better to just find out. "A locked door."

He grunted as she led him toward the storage room. "That's a bit odd for an abandoned building." He stepped up beside her. "You okay?"

"A little freaked out." She shrugged. "I'd imagine, I should be."

The door had no markings or indication of a previous plaque or sign. Some of the offices had been marked with comptroller or such. This seemed a regular storage room, except at some point someone had added a lock above the keyed knob.

Dad frowned at the zip tie and pulled out his knife. "You think there might be someone in here?"

"A zip tie won't keep you out," Haddie tilted her head, "but it might have kept you in."

"Agreed." He flicked the zip tie loose with the tip of his knife. "Back up." He kept the knife out as he unlatched and opened the door.

A dark pile of angular rubble was scattered across the floor of the room. Dad reached around the edge of the doorway and clicked a light switch, but no light turned on. A tray for a fluorescent light hung from the ceiling, but there were no bulbs. Without it, the debris gave up nothing except indistinct shapes.

Leaning over, Haddie almost placed her hand against the door, stopped, and noticed the path of gray paint that had been scratched off. A chill tickled across her neck. Someone *had* been trying to get out.

Dad took a step in and Haddie followed. Gray shelving had been mangled into a heap that barely rose knee-height off the ground.

"There." Dad leaned in with his left hand and touched a pale shape.

His gloved fingers rested on the neck of a man, perhaps in his thirties. Clean shaven with hair well trimmed, he looked peaceful. Too peaceful. She swallowed down a rising fear that he'd died in here. She scanned the other dark recesses wondering if there were others under the rubble. If he lived — well, he had witnessed part of the rave. If they could get him awake, then he might have some answers. Maybe he'd seen Liz. A small hope flowered in Haddie's chest.

"He's alive. Let's get him out of here."

At Dad's voice, the man's eyes opened. Haddie had stepped forward, her boots close to the man's shoes. Or shoe. He only wore one expensive looking leather loafer.

"It's okay," Dad said, his voice firm but calm.

"There's nothing," the man whispered in a dry croak.

He wore a tan, long-sleeved shirt with a darker decorative piece along his left shoulder. If it weren't for the stains and a tear near his stomach, it would have been a nice shirt.

Haddie sighed. "Let's get you out of here. Is anyone in here with you?"

He started scrambling up. Bent shelving groaned and clanged as he jerked to his feet. His bloodied hands slipped off unstable grips. His eyes widened and his face grimaced in a rage.

Dad stepped back, and a metal brace rose as he stepped on the opposite end.

"There's nothing left. Nothing left." The man's graveled words came out like the ravings of a madman who spoke to himself. As the man gained his feet, Haddie expected him to move toward her, toward the open door, but he launched onto Dad with surprising speed.

Dad pushed back with gloved fists, trying to throw the man away, but the madman laughed and grabbed at shoulder and hair. Shelving rattled around them, almost deafening in the confines of the storage room.

"Nothing." His voice had dropped to an angry whisper grinding out of clenched teeth.

Haddie sucked in a breath and stepped forward. The two men squirmed as Dad punched, trying to pry the man off. She'd thought the man trapped, near death, and now he fought crazed, with no apparent reason or purpose. They'd come to help him.

She grabbed his wrist, but the pressure point had no effect on him. She switched to his thumb, and it nearly broke before she was able to pry his hand off Dad's braid. The man reeked of alcohol, urine, and feces. She grabbed his wrist with her left hand and began twisting it back, trying to put pressure on his joints.

The man grunted from a kick or punch in his stomach. Then his head rocked back as Dad caught his chin. Slumping, the man dropped to the ground with his face nestled into the mangled shelving.

Dad sheathed his knife. He'd been wrestling and punching with it in his hand. The madman didn't seem to be bleeding.

In the silence, Haddie could hear herself panting, not from exertion, but from frenzied panic. Despite all her years practicing taekwondo, she still couldn't master her emotions when she actually needed to fight.

Dad remained calm. "Help me drag him out of here, before he comes to."

"He might —"

"I'd rather deal with him in some open space, than in this hell of a closet." He nodded toward the man's feet.

Haddie swallowed and reached for the man's ankles. He reeked and she imagined his socks wet. They had to untwist him from where he'd fallen, and the metal squealed around him before Dad had his arms and they shuffled him out to the open floor. The gray haze through tinted windows suddenly seemed bright.

The man's pants were soaked from his crotch down; they were black slacks torn along the side and snagged nearly everywhere. Someone had locked this madman away to die. How many hours had he been left without food or water? Is that what he meant by 'nothing' or had he run out of booze and drugs?

Dad gestured for her to follow as he moved back toward the storeroom. He searched through clattering metal as she watched the limp figure on the floor.

Liz is in trouble. Had she even survived this? Haddie had hoped to find something at the old rave site — something helpful, not more worries. The blood in the bathroom disturbed her the most. People had walked through it without a care, it seemed. Or maybe it had been too dark to see it. Perhaps the light had been taken from there as well. She had no intention of going up and finding out. They hadn't found a flyer for last night's rave. She had no way of finding Liz. Did they dare go back to the hotel? Certainly the maid had discovered she'd lost her keycard and may even suspect Dad.

Haddie could book a room there. Request the third floor and hang out in the hall. At least until Terry came up with something.

Dad stepped out. "Nobody else. Let's find a bathroom down here to rinse off."

Haddie pointed toward the front of the building. "There's one up there. I'm scared, Dad."

"I don't blame you. We need to find your friend — quick."

She sucked in a deep breath as she followed. If Dad had concerns, then it made it worse. Haddie could obsess unreasonably about situations and blow them out of proportion. Dad didn't.

She let him wash first. Then, he watched as she washed her hands. They trembled as she soaped them a third time. "Dad?"

"We'll find her." He shifted behind her. "Any thoughts about where we should look next?"

Maybe the police were her best option. If Haddie brought them here, they'd find plenty of reason to investigate. She had the photo of Liz as proof that she'd been here.

Could she just say the door and gate were open, and they went in despite the no trespassing signs?

Her phone vibrated in her jeans, and she lunged at the paper towels, drying off as she pulled them free. Still shaking, she pulled her phone out.

Terry had sent a text.

CHAPTER 18

HADDIE SWIPED OPEN HER PHONE.

"Terry?" Dad asked.

Haddie nodded, taking in a cautious breath. She needed Terry to come up with something. Standing there, she felt Liz drifting further away. She tapped opened the message.

Terry texted, "Chevy Cruze Silver 968-KXR Matthew Barlow Arbor."

Matt's car Haddie waited a moment, perhaps sagged; she wanted to know the location of last night's rave. That, above all. If nothing else, to make sure that Liz wasn't locked in some closet, or her blood didn't cover some room. The license plate helped, though how much she couldn't know. She could still smell a lingering stench over the dispenser soap and freshly washed hands. Their boots. She waited as Terry typed.

"Nothing recent in police records on his name or tag number. You have a number of people looking. We've got someone who can look up cell phones - crazy good. Send me her number." He added a grimacing emoji. "You may owe some people legal advice when this is all over."

Haddie scrambled through her phone and shared Liz's contact with Terry. "Thank you."

"Looking for information on the people who are running this. Hoping they did a legal rental on the property. Owned by a Cali corp under Anthony Prizer. Checking his company as a lead as well. They may have more properties in Portland."

Thank you, Terry. Haddie imagined the work it took to track down everything Terry suggested. She'd be happy to do anything for the help. However, considering how badly she'd botched things at Andrea's law firm, she didn't know if her legal advice was worth much. If it meant getting Liz back, she'd hire Andrea herself. As many hours as she could afford.

"Can't thank you enough." She paused, considering taking a picture of the man they'd found. "We found a man locked in a closet here."

Terry took a long moment before typing, "Call the police?"

Haddie paused, not wanting to put in writing that they'd broken in. "Not yet." She did need to find a way to get the madman help. "Thank you."

On the way in, she hadn't seen a Cruze outside, but they should check, maybe on another side street.

"Team Haddie, Buckaroo." He continued typing, then texted, "Be careful."

Dad raised an eyebrow as Haddie closed her phone and tucked it into her pocket. "Anything?"

"Matt Arbor's car information." She sighed. "Something."

Dad nodded thoughtfully. "Wipe down the sink. We need to get this guy some help. I don't think your prints would matter, but better to be safe." Then he gestured for her to follow, heading toward the door where they'd come in.

Haddie hurriedly wiped handles and the basin where she might have touched. "Wait, are you going to call the police?"

He stood by the alarm panel. "In a form." He studied her for a moment. "We head for your SUV, and we can drive around looking for this Matt's ride."

Stabbing the away button with his gloved finger, he opened the door and gestured her out. He followed, leaving the door ajar as the beeps counted off inside.

She found herself taking a deep breath of the city air, tinged with exhaust, but seemingly fresh compared to the warehouse. He strolled down the sidewalk to the corner with her, glass crunching under their feet. His even pace kept her from wanting to run.

She heard the whine of the tow truck before they turned the corner. The man, squat with short, red-brown hair, never saw them approach as he winched a yellow-tagged LaCrosse onto his flatbed.

Dad spoke as they neared the tow truck driver. "Excuse us." He paused as the man flinched. "Have you seen a . . ." He trailed off suggestively, looking to Haddie.

"Chevy Cruze. Silver." Haddie stumbled through her words. Her mouth felt dry. It was barely after 10 a.m., and her body felt drained. She hunched slightly, waiting for the alarm to blare from the building behind her.

The man frowned. "None from here, if that's what you're asking. I've towed thirteen and we've got another dozen to go. Some party. I saw their bus yesterday morning."

"Bus?"

"Yep," He turned back to his truck and winch. "One

of them big black party buses. Must've been fifty people out here getting in it." He motioned out at the intersection. "I came in for work and had to wait on them to get out of the street. Our yard's right down the road, got the call yesterday afternoon to clear the cars they left. Idiots." With the LaCrosse pulled all the way onto the flatbed, the man turned and wiped his face, looking up at the clouds.

"And no Chevy Cruze?" Dad asked.

The man showed a gap in his front teeth as he smiled. "Not yet. Still getting calls though. From three streets out." He motioned to the building and noted Haddie's white hair. "So, you forget where you left —"

The alarm in the rave building whined lightly from the back. Dad looked behind himself and then back at the tow truck. "Can that set off a window sensor?"

"Damn." The man looked toward the windows of the building. "It shouldn't." He ran for his passenger door. "I've got to call this in to my boss."

Dad gestured her past the truck and toward the RAV4. Haddie walked and remembered to take a breath. The alarm sounded louder toward the back end. It had taken longer to go off than she'd expected. Long enough that she'd gotten caught up in the party bus story. Were they bringing them from rave to rave? That made no sense.

She stepped around the front of her car; the driver of the tow truck stood at the windows of the building waving his hand as he spoke on his cell. Opening the door, she looked down at her boots and loathed bringing them into the car with her. Once the doors closed, she'd surely smell them. Kicking her soles on the asphalt, she sighed and got in.

"A bus?" her dad asked. "Is that normal?"

Haddie shrugged and started the RAV4. "I wouldn't know. I'll check with Terry."

They weren't much better off than when they'd gone into the building less than an hour ago. No closer to Liz for sure. If anything, Haddie had formed a horrendous fear of the danger that her friend faced.

She turned around and pulled quickly past the tow truck. She rolled down her window and then slowed taking a left down the side street to look for Matt Arbor's car. The alarm whined pitifully.

They had nothing to continue with. If anything, she had more reason to go to the police than she had before. She didn't know where last night's rave had been, nor where tonight's might be. She could wait and see what Terry came up with, but what if they had Liz locked up in some closet going mad? Or had she been on the bus, dragged off for what — to continue the party? *Or worse?*

She turned down a street to her left and drove toward a dead end where a line of trees and brush hid I-5 and a steel warehouse lined most of the left side. Cars parked in parking spaces facing it. On the right, near the end of the street, a single-story white building formed around a gated central yard. The structure returned to the road and ran down to the edge of the vegetation. A roofing company, according to the signs on one of the trucks and the abundance of ladders.

A silver Chevy Cruze was parked at the end of the street.

"Dad." Haddie pointed it out and then pulled in directly behind Matt Arbor's car.

Finally, a spot of good luck. The windows on the building were above head height. Perhaps no one came down to the end of the street often, or not within the past twenty four hours. Only a Mitsubishi Lancer was parked at this end of the road, leaving plenty of space for a couple cars.

Dad grunted and slid out his side, and Haddie followed, closing her door quietly. The metal warehouse across the street had an office at the end with stairs up to a door and a long window. She couldn't see any motion inside the glass. Up the street, an open bay door gave a glimpse of high shelving and stock, but no one worked at the entrance.

The traffic of I-5 droned by. Haddie stepped along the sidewalk beside Matt's car to join Dad. The tall white wall of the building beside them and the plants ahead almost gave a false sense of seclusion. As he leaned down to look inside, his phone rang.

"Hell." He pulled his phone from his pants and frowned. His eyes locked Haddie's before he answered, "Hi, Sam."

PART 4

As youth, we sought our passions, our purposes, our will.

CHAPTER 19

THOMAS WATCHED HADDIE. Did she catch the nuance that Sam called him instead of her?

"Hey, Mr. Dawson." Sam's voice muffled as she walked away from the sound of a cat, likely Jisoo, crying out.

She'd switched from calling him T suddenly. It could be the use of phone versus speaking with him in person, or their relationship had distanced. He didn't like the latter option and itched to be on his bike. The air hung heavy with exhaust. Portland had more smog than Eugene or Goshen.

He kept his voice calm and even, still facing Haddie. "What's up, Sam?"

"I know what you said, about not bringing up Meg's parents — that she still couldn't handle that discussion." Sam had moved into a quiet space, possibly Haddie's bedroom. "But she started crying this morning, like out of nowhere. So, I asked her what was wrong."

"Okay, sounds reasonable." And exactly what he feared would happen.

He couldn't regret being here for Haddie, especially if she'd confronted the deranged man in the storage closet alone. He'd considered sending Biff in his place. Now, it seemed that would have been the wiser choice.

"Well – so —" She stumbled through her words. Awkward, not panicked or accusing.

He waited through a long pause as he pictured her preparing her words. Meg had either gone into the shooting death of her uncle or being estranged to him and Haddie and compelled to stay with them anyway.

"She said that you are the last of her family, but she doesn't know you. That most of her uncles and aunts and cousins have all died this year. At least the ones she knows. It sounds horrible. She seems really upset about their deaths. She said she's afraid that someone will kill her next."

A concern we share. "She is right about most of that, though she may be exaggerating some aspects. Out of an abundance of caution, our family has decided to keep her with me." He hoped that placated Sam, with enough concern that she wouldn't make any rash attempts at finding Meg's family. With the internet, people could find more than he expected. He'd grown up with it, but spent so many centuries without it that it hadn't seemed potent until these last few decades.

"So, what should I do?" Sam's voice rose, indicating concern. That could lead to irrational results.

"Is she still crying?"

"No, we took Rock for a walk." Her tone dropped.

"That's good. I'll be home soon, and I'll talk with her some more."

Haddie raised her eyebrows at the comment. He shrugged. She knew the situation. He could still ask Biff to come out and help her. She had the option of going to the police, and it may come to that.

Sam's tone lightened. "Did Haddie find Liz then?"

Haddie looked away from him. Her lips had tightened, and she'd started tugging at her hair. He almost hoped that nothing panned out with the car. This way, maybe she'd go stake out the hotel instead of digging around warehouses.

"No, unfortunately we haven't found Liz." He looked at the boyfriend's car. "Haddie's still looking."

"You don't have to leave her just because . . ." Sam trailed off. "I like spending time with Meg."

"I can't leave Meg there for too long. She needs to acclimate to her new life." *At my garage.* Maybe he needed to consider a better situation for her. "When I get back, we can all hang at Haddie's. Hopefully Haddie will be following me soon."

Sam seemed to brighten at that. "Okay, good. I was going to make Meg some dirty rice for lunch; she's never had it. I'll make extra for when you get here."

"That would be nice, Sam." He stared at Haddie. "See you soon."

"Bye, T."

She'd switched back to T — a good sign. He moved the phone to his pocket with a sigh. "You got that?" he asked Haddie.

"Yeah. Meg's starting to talk about her family. You don't want Sam getting skittish, bringing the authorities in." She shrugged. "I knew your time might be limited. I appreciate that you came out, though."

"I can send Biff, if you'd like a little muscle." He grimaced at her expression. "Or not. I'm going to worry about you. Maybe I could circle back here with Biff and Meg, just to see where you'll be?"

"I got this. It's looking like I should go to the police anyway." She nodded toward the car. "Want to help me get in?"

Thomas leaned over and opened the unlocked door. "Least I can do."

CHAPTER 20

HADDIE SNORTED. "How'd you know it was open?"

Dad motioned to the driver's door. Leaning down, she noticed it was unlocked. She'd been focused on the bottle of rum on the passenger floor. He slid into the passenger seat and popped open the glove compartment. Haddie leaned her forearms where the door met the top of Matt's car. It smelled like fried food and rum. The clutter on the floor included fast food wrappers and bags, gas station chips, and some empty water bottles. Copies of the same rave flyers were stuffed in the console. Dad pulled them out and rifled through them quickly, but they all had the same date.

I don't want to lose Dad. She couldn't expect him to ignore Meg. It had been a surprise when he'd agreed to go, though he likely did that more to force her to sleep than anything else. If they didn't find something, she'd have to go to the police. Liz was in too much danger.

Haddie pulled her long sleeve down to act as a glove and opened the back door. Just one wadded up burger bag and an empty liter of soda that reminded her of Terry. *If they took the bus, there might not be a new flyer.*

Haddie backed out of the car. The trash in the front looked like little more than a car trip that no one bothered to clean up. It wasn't as bad as the hotel room.

She pulled out her phone and sent Terry a text. "Found Matt's car near rave. Have you heard of party buses at raves?"

"Sure. Why? Did they have one?"

"Supposedly yesterday morning they picked up 50 people," she typed.

"That sounds like a lot."

"They're out here towing a lot of cars." Haddie glanced around; no one had noticed them digging in the car, unless someone sat in that office across the street.

"Odd." Terry continued to type. "Still digging on the properties. I'll send you a list to check out soon." Before she could respond, he typed, "Nothing on the flyer or any planned raves. We're still looking."

Dad stood up out of the car. "There's blood on the dashboard. Looks like the driver punched it."

Haddie drew in a breath and walked around to the driver's door. She could make out the brown smudge and what might be a crack in the molding of the dash. If Matt Arbor raised a hand to Liz . . . Haddie found her teeth grating.

Terry texted, "?"

"Sorry. Nothing here at the car. Thanks, Terry."

"We'll find her."

He hadn't ended with "Buckaroo," and for some reason that disturbed her. Terry worried about this situation, as did she. Somehow, no matter how impossible it seemed, she had to find Liz. Police or not. In reality, beyond her reluctance to involve the police, she didn't trust their abilities. Andrea's cases had convinced her that sometimes they gave up before they put in any real effort. She might be jaded between Dad and interning at the firm. He had, in a way, involved the police. She couldn't hear the weak alarm from only a few streets over, but the tow truck driver had called someone.

"Pop the trunk while you're up there." Dad moved to the back.

Haddie pulled her sleeve and opened the driver's door. She clicked the latch open to the trunk. He had it open by the time she headed back.

Dad rifled through an orderly and nearly empty trunk. *I found Matt's car, but there's nothing here.* She'd lose Dad soon; he'd have to be dropped off at the parking lot by the hotel. By that time, she'd have to make a decision. Her options didn't look good.

He closed the trunk quietly and rubbed his hair back. "Well. Not much here to work with. I looked through every flyer up there. I doubt they ever came back here from the rave. Maybe took that bus."

"So, back to your bike?" Haddie looked up at the ceiling of gray clouds. Not that rain would stop him. "I imagine I've got two choices. Wait at the hotel for some information from Terry, hoping that Liz waltzes in." She offered a wry smile. "Or file a missing person's report, show them the picture and the flyer."

Dad frowned. "Not any good options. I agree. I'd suggest the latter, more for my peace of mind than yours. I don't like the looks of this, and I can't be here. Not right now." He raised his hand as she started to speak. "And Liz can't wait. I know that."

Haddie walked toward her RAV4, checking the street and the office window to see if anyone showed any interest in their search. A Ford truck groaned in the driveway behind them, ambling into the construction yard with clanking ladders. She imagined that the night of the rave all these blocks were like a graveyard. Liz and Matt had walked down this street in the dark, heading for the rave. Leaving felt like abandoning them.

She finished the last of her water as she started the car. Wedging the water bottle into the cup holder, she began driving back to Dad's bike. As they crossed the dark Willamette River, she leaned forward to look at the clouds that rolled, bubbling, over the city. The sky seemed an endless gray blanket. A dreary day all around. *Where are you, Liz?*

Still a short time from lunch, the streets weren't too crowded with cars or pedestrians, so she made good time. *I feel like I'm giving up.* Her chest tightened in the silence, so she turned on some music. Dad didn't complain. EXO played an eerie song that started to push out some of Haddie's more desperate thoughts. She would have to go to the police.

They pulled into an empty parking space across from Dad's '32 Shovelhead and Haddie turned off the car. She'd be alone now. The silence welled around them for a moment before Dad opened his door and the city noise seeped in.

Haddie climbed out, twisting her hair into a knot. She couldn't let him feel bad for leaving. He had to take care of Meg. "Ok, Dad. Be safe." She pointed up at the clouds. "Rain?"

He shook his head with a frown. His demeanor told her that he didn't want to leave her. A small consolation. The madman in the building and the blood had disturbed him, probably as much as they did her, but she had to see it through. Liz would be in danger from the looks of the mess.

"I'll be okay, Dad. I'm going to call Liz's room one last

time, then go up and see if the keycard still works. If nothing, I'll drive over to the station and make a report. Probably get a room and see where this goes. On your card, if that's okay."

Dad's expression softened, perhaps relieved. "Yes. I hate to say it, but the authorities might be your best choice. If you take off though, call me."

"Sure. Let me know how Meg is." Haddie wished they could have dealt with his issue before running off on hers. She still hadn't come to terms with how she felt about Meg being in their lives. It changed things. That couldn't be helped.

"Okay. Love you, Haddie. Be careful." Dad turned, walking toward his bike and rubbing his hair back.

"Love you." She took in a deep breath. The parking lot took up an entire block and seemed nearly full. Down the street, the hotel stood between stacked buildings. Red ornamental streetlamps marked the corners of the sidewalks. Beyond the hotel and to the right, a tall glass and concrete skyscraper reflected the gray sky and poked at the blanket of clouds. Dad complained about Eugene, but Portland felt tight and foreboding. She shivered as his bike rumbled out of the parking lot, and she started walking.

The phone in Liz's room went to voicemail, and Haddie hung up without leaving a message. Her pulse rose as she checked for the keycard in her back pocket. The air had warmed since morning, and exhaust tinted the air. She imagined the polluted Willamette just a few blocks away with I-5 hugging it. Dad would be out of the city as fast as he could. From the few stories she'd pried out of him, he'd spent some of his life in the largest cities in Europe — during amazing times — yet he seemed to hate cities. Why had he raised her in Eugene? Why not up in the Rockies? She probably shouldn't ask, or Meg could end up a hermit.

She got a few glances walking through the lobby, but no one stopped her. Her height, and now her white hair, always brought her more attention than she usually wanted.

The maids had removed the trays from beside the rooms, and a cart of laundry waited at one end of the hall. Otherwise, the third floor seemed quiet. Haddie walked over and swiped the card. The light flickered red. She tried a second time before knocking. "Liz?"

Alone in the hall, she pressed her head against the door and listened to silence and the blood rushing in her ears. Noon, and still Liz had not returned to her room. Haddie knocked a second time. She'd reached the end of her procrastination and knew it was time to involve the police.

Her phone vibrated in her pocket and she jumped eagerly. She still hoped she'd get a call from Liz, but more likely a text from Terry. She stared at the unusual number calling her for a moment. The area code looked slightly familiar, but she couldn't place it.

"Hello?" she asked.

"Hadhira Dawson?" The connection buzzed and crackled. Special Agent Wilkins.

Damn. She'd forgotten to cancel their meeting. She'd meant to. Meg, Liz, Dad, and Terry had piled into her brain and pushed him out.

"I'm sorry. I had a family issue that came up. Could we reschedule?" When? If she planned on waiting in Portland for either the police or Terry to come up with something, then how long would that take?

"I only —" the connection dropped.

Haddie grimaced, fumbling as she tried to dial back. No reception. Wilkins would think she was avoiding her.

Damn. She jogged toward the elevators with a quick look back at room 311. Punching the button down, she saw a bar show on her phone. She needed to explain to Special Agent Wilkins that she wouldn't be available today, and might not be tomorrow. Hopefully, the woman didn't take that as Haddie avoiding her.

She stared at the extra bar. The call might go through, but it would be better to get downstairs, even outside, where she could hear the agent clearly. What did the woman have to talk to her about? It couldn't be that they found Harold Holmes; Dad had used his power on the man. She imagined that the man's atoms or molecules had been spread back through time and had settled around Harold Holmes' torture room. She based her theory on her own experience killing the twin brother, Dmitry. Before she'd used her power on him, she'd seen fragments, more a mist, of him. The images still plagued her.

The phone showed one tempting bar.

The thing she'd killed during the ski trip hadn't helped her understand her abilities any better. She and Liz had been moving in a gondola when Haddie vaporized the demon.

The elevator bell rang at the same time her phone vibrated. Special Agent Wilkins called again, and Haddie stepped back to answer it. A middle-aged couple ambled out; the woman wore a nice pink and gray long-sleeve top and a quick smile. The man carried a garlicky take-out bag that made Haddie immediately hungry.

"Hello?" She cupped the phone to her ear and listened to the crackle.

"— thought we —" Wilkins' voice came through for a moment, then disappeared into static.

Haddie waited a moment. She should have gone downstairs to get a clear connection. Instead, she spoke slowly and loudly. "I can't hear you. Let me call you back."

The elevator door had closed and the down button ignored three pointed stabs before it lit.

"Damn." The connection had dropped. Haddie grimaced and pulled the phone off her ear. "Damn."

She would call the agent on the way to the police station. She wanted to know what information or questions Wilkins had, but it would have to wait. Concern for Liz beat the anxiety over whatever the FBI had to ask Haddie. The madman's ramblings and rage still haunted her. The memory of the blood in the bathroom made her shiver. Even after she got the police involved, she wouldn't be able to resist looking on her own, but she didn't know where to search next.

The elevator rang and opened, empty. Haddie jumped in and stabbed the lobby button. Annoying Wilkins did not seem like a good plan when she wouldn't be able to meet with her — not today. A breakfast burrito at seven in the morning hadn't been enough, and now she felt thirsty. Everything seemed to be piling in at once.

Her phone vibrated despite being in the elevator. Usually she had less coverage.

Terry texted, "We've got a lead."

She stared at the message long enough that her phone turned off the screen. Her fingers scrambled to open her phone and read the message again. The doors opened into the lobby, and a mother held back a young boy who had been about to jump in.

"Sorry," Haddie mumbled as she slid past. Glancing up enough to keep from stumbling into furniture, she started typing back to Terry.

"What is it?" she texted. If they found last night's location, she could go check it out. Tonight's rave would mean waiting.

Wilkins called.

Haddie groaned in the middle of the lobby. She flushed as a couple sitting at a table turned. Hurrying past, she cupped both hands around the phone. "Hello?" she asked. Wilkins might think she'd been playing her, trying to avoid the call. "I'm nearly outside, my reception should be better. Sorry about that."

"Ms. Dawson. I thought we had agreed to meet today." The woman sounded irritated.

Haddie stepped onto the sidewalk and moved to lean on the brick wall. It had gotten warm and humid outside, and someone cooked Chinese food. "I'm sorry about that. Unavoidable. I've got a family emergency." Her phone vibrated and she resisted the urge to check Terry's response. "I meant to call." She'd have to remember to save the agent's phone number in her contacts.

"Your father?" Wilkins asked.

"What?" Her pulse rose. Did the FBI have some evidence that her dad had been at Harold Holmes' house?

"Is your father the one with the emergency?" Wilkin's tone had turned calm and assured.

She didn't want to lie to the woman. Drawing in a deep breath she imagined Andrea and ignored yet another message vibrating her phone. A refusal to answer, a polite one, could not be construed as a lie.

"I'm sorry, Special Agent Wilkins. I truly am. I should have called. However, this is a personal matter. I'm hoping to be back tomorrow." She did want to know what the FBI's questions were. Did they have new information? "Can I call you at this number when I'm back in Eugene?"

Wilkins took too long to respond. Long enough that a

third vibration announced another message. Haddie rolled her hair into a ball at the back of her head. Sweat trickled under her sports bra.

The agent sighed before responding. "We need to speak, Ms. Dawson. I have questions."

Haddie pulled in a tight breath. The woman hadn't agreed, but she hadn't threatened or demanded either. Haddie acted as if the woman had accepted her statement. "Thank you, Special Agent Wilkins. I'll do my best to be available."

They disconnected and Haddie let out a breath. Wilkins hadn't pushed her. Haddie did want to know what the FBI's questions were — if they had any new questions. But right now, Terry's messages waited.

She needed something to drink and time to sit for a moment and look at her phone. The street had started to thicken with pedestrians; most looked to be office workers off for lunch. Heading back into the air conditioning, she pulled up Terry's messages.

CHAPTER 21

BREATHING in the cool air of the hotel, Haddie navigated toward one of the seats at the counter. A few people sat about eating, and the smell of grilled sandwiches and fries focused her hunger. She tapped the counter as she read.

Terry texted, "Yaass. We've localized Liz's cell to an area that has warehouses. One belongs to Anthony Prizer's company, same owner of the first property."

He followed with another text. "I'll send a map link."

Her eyebrows raised, both surprised and excited. She had given up somehow. The last message had only a map link. *If only Dad could have waited.* She shook her head and opened the link as her stomach churned with hunger. Another location just this side of the Willamette River. Right down I-405.

"You think this is where Liz is?" she texted.

Terry took a moment to finish typing. "Her phone at least. Or it could be in any of those warehouses. Or along the river there. Best guess from the towers."

A young man with long lashes and a smile came up to

take her order. He wore a black tie pinned to a white button-down shirt and offered a thin menu.

Haddie tilted her phone toward herself. "Hi, I just need some water, a black coffee, and something to go." She swallowed. The location was only a short bit up the road; Haddie could be there in a few minutes. She didn't take the menu.

He leaned on the counter. "We've got a full lunch menu available, if you want to look at the menu, or some pastries if you're looking for something continental."

Haddie tapped the edge of her phone. She imagined the crazed man locked in the storage room and thought of Liz in her skimpy fringe bikini top. "I'm sorry." A shiver ran down her arms as she pictured the bloody bathroom.

The server stood, looking surprised as she jumped off her seat. "I'm sorry," she repeated before she dashed for the door.

Outside in the midday heat, she nearly jogged down the street, darting between people milling along the sidewalks. The street had grown heavy with the lunch crowd. The humidity added an oppressive air to the gray clouds above. She felt the press of people until she crossed the street at the corner and ran through the parking lot.

The cars, at least, didn't have that same urgency, but they packed the lot to nearly overfilling, and drivers prowled for a spot. Heading for the RAV4, she realized Terry had texted while she'd been running.

"So, what's the plan?" he'd asked.

He followed with another text, "?"

She texted quickly. "Thanks. On my way now." Jumping in her car, she blew out a deep breath trying to calm herself.

"Okay," he replied. "Be careful, Buckaroo."

She set the map for directions, and it showed a couple turns and ten minutes. She'd need gas at some point, but not for this short of a trip.

Her stomach complained as she pulled the RAV4 onto the street and took a right at the corner. The buildings grew up around her, and then for a brief moment she drove through a park with trees. It made her homesick to be back in Eugene — with Liz. Her hopes didn't rise too far after a morning of expectation and let-downs. They'd found Liz's hotel, the rave where she'd taken the picture, and her boyfriend's car — but still no Liz.

Once Haddie got past the more congested downtown area, she moved quickly onto I-405. *What does Wilkins want?* She shouldn't let the woman fluster her. Dad should know about the call even if he had his hands full. Worrying about all the other things, besides Liz, wouldn't help Haddie. She needed to focus.

Her phone buzzed and she gritted her teeth. The console showed a text from Terry, so she had it read. "The boards just lit up on tonight's rave. Sending you the flyer."

Haddie sighed, juggled her phone into her hand, and opened the image.

The flyer showed a neon diamond along with the location and date — hosted by Penumbra. *Hours from now.* Hopefully, she wouldn't need that information. Maybe Liz and her boyfriend just slept off their excursion at the last rave scene. She couldn't imagine that scenario, and she found herself passing cars on the highway. If she headed toward the location of last night's rave, who knew if Liz actually had her phone? It might have been left behind. Then Haddie would need tonight's location. She could give it to the police, as part of their investigation. No. Haddie had to believe that she was heading toward Liz at that moment.

The industrial neighborhood looked much the same as the last, if not larger. Shipping companies had semis backed into warehouses. She drove down Thompson Street toward the address. Semis, trucks, and cars lined the sides, and none seemed to have any towing stickers on them.

The warehouse itself stood a couple stories tall, though it didn't have windows except for a low brick section facing the small front parking lot where an empty, forgotten flagpole jutted from the roof. That section looked like an office, and a few cars were parked in the lot, with more along the street. Haddie pulled into the lot. *I wish you were here, Dad.*

She stepped into the humidity. *Maybe it'll just rain and get it over with.* Should she just walk up to the front door and ask about Liz?

Her phone vibrated and she pulled it out, fully expecting to see Terry texting her.

David texted, "Are we still on for lunch?"

Haddie groaned. *How could I have forgotten?* She felt guilty using Liz as an excuse, but it was the truth. No excuse for not telling him. "I'm sorry, I ran to Portland. Lost track of time. Going to check a building for Liz."

"Is your dad with you?" David didn't even chastise over her being a jerk and not calling.

"It's abandoned." She looked at the cars parked in the lot. *Mostly.*

"You're alone? Call the police. Don't risk yourself."

She swallowed. "I have to. I'll text you as soon as I get back to the car. Promise."

It took a while for him to respond. "I love you. Be careful."

Haddie put her phone back in her pocket and twisted her hair into a knot. *I'm a lousy girlfriend.*

The first door she approached had a set of windows, and she could see an empty room. A concrete floor stretched to the back where a dark blue wall opened into a hallway. The outer door was locked. Haddie went from door to door and could even see in the higher windows of the bricked offices. All empty. All locked. She worked her way down the right side. Even under an overhang, where a picnic bench marked an employee area, the building had been locked tight. Around the table it smelled slightly rancid.

The higher part of the building continued down the street, and Haddie tried the one door there, ignoring the large bays with closed rolling doors. A set of disused railroad tracks ran down the back, and she followed it to another locked side door. *If Dad were here, we'd have been in by now.*

At the corner, a barbed-wire fence blocked in a long back parking lot with a few cars. She'd have to circle the entire building to check the doors. Sweat already trickled down her stomach and sides.

A black movement caught her eye. The rear of a black bus backed up momentarily. The party bus. It moved forward at the front of the parking lot and disappeared.

Haddie ran.

The ground around the tracks was uneven and spotted with trash. She took long strides, nearly jumping at points. They could be taking Liz away now. *Why would they bus people from rave to rave?*

Rounding the corner, she hit the sidewalk and raced toward the employee table and the brick walls of the offices.

The black bus took off down the road ahead of her. It

moved at a good clip, so she knew by the time she made it to the RAV4 she might not catch up to them. If they headed for I-405, then she knew that route. If they turned on any side street, she'd lose them. They probably headed to tonight's rave, so she'd catch up to them when they arrived. She hadn't looked at Terry's location. *I should have.*

Haddie leaned on the door of her RAV4 to catch a breath. She'd search here first, then catch up to the bus.

Making her way around the other corner of the building, she came to a single locked door on that side. In less than a minute she came to the gated parking area where some cars sat and the bus had pulled out. The bay doors were all closed and she only saw one gray door, though the building extended past a couple of low trees planted beside the beige walls. If Dad hadn't left for Meg, she might've already found Liz. Haddie frowned at herself. She couldn't resent him going back for Meg. Haddie'd been lucky enough that he'd been with her when they found the madman.

Litter here reminded her of the previous rave site. Red cups, some broken bottles, and general trash speckled the parking lot. A bright green, furry hat with the eyes and lips of a frog hung over a concrete post.

When she tried it, the gray door opened.

Haddie paused with the door cracked barely a finger's width. She hadn't expected it to be unlocked. Taking a deep breath, she moved to the edge and peered inside. Dim lights lit the ceiling high above, bleeding away as they reached a cement floor covered with crushed litter. Debris flattened in the open area and piled at the edges.

She leaned her head inside and gasped.

In the middle of a huge room, bodies littered the floor as if they'd dropped where they'd stood. A man in a white business suit stretched his hands above his head and clasped them palm to palm, much in the way that the woman had in Liz's social media post. Motionless, his stance looked fixed and awkward, and the bodies lay in a ring about him. He emanated a tone. No. An echo.

A tone, like that which her Dad, herself, and Harold Holmes had emitted, rang in the air, wavering. She felt it stirring her hunger, which had abated in the excitement and running. Famished, it returned with a vengeance.

The man in the white looked like any businessman, with short trimmed dark hair and a clean-shaven face. The white suit had been stained, spattered with dark brown droplets along the side and left leg. She could feel his power urging her to eat - to have more. Thirst burned in her throat until she glanced to the side, searching the litter for the bottles she'd seen.

One of the bodies shifted with a light groan. Haddie blinked and fought the man's power. Whatever the exact nature of his ability — his song — it came from somewhere else. He just echoed it. She seemed able to resist that, but it made her angry to do so.

Slowly, she opened the door and stepped inside. The door creaked as it closed.

"Hey!" called a burly man leaning against the wall to her left. Pallid, almost sickly, he had a light brown beard across most of his face.

In her hunger and focus, she hadn't noticed him.

Some of the bodies on the floor stirred at his yell. Was Liz among them?

He moved with a steady gait toward her. He could have been a body builder. Short and wide, his muscles bulged at the arms and neck.

Haddie set her jaw against the cravings. Anger boiled against burning need — lust.

He didn't pause or threaten with his step; he didn't seem intent on scaring her out the door. His eyes wide and keen, he seemed intent on attacking her.

Haddie's rage escalated. Furnaced by her manipulated hunger and wanting, she growled as she rushed toward him.

He stepped quicker. Most people slowed when charged. His head glowed with a yellow haze, like the man who had been shooting at Meg's uncle.

She dropped and kicked low. Her heel aimed for the inside of a still moving knee. Haddie connected too high and rebounded to his side.

He barely reacted to her kick. A slight stumble.

Haddie sneered, jumping back. *I can take him.*

The tone from the man in the white suit haunted her. She wanted to satisfy her hunger — to feast.

The no-necked man came at her with a telegraphed right punch. Muscled, but not trained in fighting.

She lunged with a punch to his ribs and dodged a slow swing.

Thick muscles bulged as he swung repeatedly at her. All strength. No speed. No skill.

Her urges raced from one sensation to the next. The song ebbed against her, persistent. She backed up, step by step, toward the corner. They moved away from the motion-less crowd and the man in the white suit.

One of the people jerked in their sleep. Haddie glanced. *I can't be distracted right now.* Shaking her head, she tried to dislodge the song, and focused back on the guard. She had to stop this man. *Find Liz.* She came for Liz.

Haddie dropped and swept the man at his knees. A grunt escaped as his head and shoulders slammed to the floor. It should have been enough to knock the sense out of most people.

She rolled to a crouch with a raging satisfaction. *Stop this man. Find Liz.* That tone.

Shaking his head, he rose up on his elbows. The yellow haze shimmered around his face in the dim light. Only slightly dazed, he shifted to sit up.

Haddie kicked him in the forehead. He almost grabbed her ankle, even as she connected and slammed his head back. Scrambling, she got to her feet and danced to his side. The tone rang in her head, threatening to strip away any control. The fight and the Adrenalin made it more difficult. The rage fed the hunger. The need. *Liz.* She needed to find Liz.

Almost sneering, the bulky man rose.

Haddie waited until he got to his feet. Before he had a chance to adjust his stance, she spun, snapping her heel inside his closest leg. His knee separated and he howled. Momentum carried his backhand to her temple before she could dodge it.

His blow slapped Haddie toward the door, and she threw her hands out to catch her balance. Debris kicked under her feet. Alcohol permeated the room and she craved it. Fighting the song, she got her footing.

The guard lay on the floor, trying to get up despite a distorted knee. The man in white had dropped his hands, and several people moaned on the floor; some were trying to get up.

Liz, a mop of brown hair sliding off her face, rolled to her back, still wearing her fringe bikini top and underwear. She'd found Liz.

CHAPTER 22

HADDIE'S JAW TIGHTENED, fighting against the urges that swelled inside. Her head throbbed from the punch.

The man in white turned away and yelled, as if to someone else, not Haddie. The song echoing from him remained a constant melodic hum. Churning her. Pounding into her pulse.

The crowd at the man's feet, possibly twenty or thirty people, ranged from naked bodies to a woman dressed in a red and black gown. Many murmured as they woke.

Lying motionless to the right of the man in white, Liz breathed slowly.

Haddie needed to get past three people to reach Liz. One of them, a man dressed in a red neck scarf and boxer shorts, started to rise. His eyes blinked, and he mouthed silent words.

Haddie found herself angered and aroused at the sight of him.

The guard still floundered to her left. He would not be able to get up, but that didn't mean there weren't more around. Pushing down the cravings, she searched the darkness for any other threats.

Haddie took a deep breath. The smell of alcohol excited her, overcoming the sharper urine, sweat, and vomit. Absently she glanced at the glint of a bottle in the litter, then forced herself to stagger toward Liz. She had to fight the song. It was a power like her own, but different. Harold Holmes' ability had been different as well. *Liz. Get Liz out of here.*

The man in white had begun backing up, heading for the far side of the huge bay. The upper corners of the room, lit by the dim ceiling lights, hinted at its size. The lower edges were black depths.

She stepped around a topless woman wearing a black skort; one of her nipples had a gold pastie. Aroused, Haddie leered. The woman rolled, pressing the palms of her hands at her eyes.

The man in the scarf started yelling something unintelligible, stirring more people among the crowd. Liz rolled her head.

Haddie stepped over the legs of an older woman, possibly in her fifties, who had a red cut on her forehead. Blood had trickled down and dried into dirty blond hair. She didn't seem to be breathing.

Liz had bruises on her arms and chest. A larger red scrape started under her armpit and went past the thin tie of the fringe bikini top. Smeared makeup distorted her face, but she looked unharmed. She smelled of urine and alcohol.

Haddie shook her friend. "Liz."

The song faded; the man in white had disappeared into the darkness. It still hung in Haddie's mind, a persistent tune.

"Liz!" Haddie spoke louder, earning a glance from one

of the rising crowd. She grabbed Liz by the shoulders and shook her. Nothing.

She'd have to carry Liz out, about a hundred and twenty pounds. The rising moans and muttering around her reminded her of the madman. *Ignore them.* Three had risen and seemed to search the floor. She heard a bottle clink, but the urges had faded in her.

Dad had walked her through a dead weight carry. In all the possible scenarios, none had been through a crowd of moaning zombies.

The guard dragged his way toward her. The odd yellow haze ebbed around his face.

Lying with her back on Liz's stomach, Haddie reached back and got a grip under the knee. She did a test roll, hearing Liz grunt. Taking a deep breath, Haddie rolled opposite the knee and leaned Liz up and onto her shoulders. Scrambling for the arm, she pinned Liz and got her own legs ready for the lift. Dad would be proud. Liz moved slightly, not resisting, but reacting to the movement.

Someone's hand touched Haddie's ankle before she got to a standing position. She jerked it away. Panic lit her chest. The blinding rage had faded. The guard still crawled toward them.

A rectangle of light opened on the opposite side of the bay from where she'd come in. A shape moved there. The man in white? He might be going for help. She had to get Liz out.

A man with dark brown skin and a vest pushed past her, running for the door.

Haddie staggered and turned for the exit she'd come in. Liz moaned and resisted the grip on her wrist. "Hang on, Liz. It's Haddie."

The downed guard, his face fuzzy with the yellow haze,

crawled closer. More of the ravers had started for the door behind Haddie. The song had drifted away, just a haunting memory. Some of them growled, others moaned, almost pleading.

Just a few more steps. Haddie fought a rising panic in her chest. She only had to worry about the guard; the others ignored her, but their scrambling sounded ominous. She remembered the frenzy the tone had brought her to. Still it tugged, and she'd only been under its influence for a couple minutes. Taking short, quick strides, she plotted a wide arc around the guard and made for the door.

A gunshot echoed in the bay just as she reached the door. A dot of light appeared in the wall to her right. She imagined the sound of the bullet scraping through metal.

Liz jerked, fighting against the hold on her wrist.

"Stop it, Liz." Haddie hissed through clenched teeth.

A second shot rang out, and someone behind Haddie shrieked.

She didn't look back. Using the hand under Liz's leg, she opened the door and let in fresh air. Even with the gray blanket of clouds, the light forced her to blink. Kicking the door wide, she stumbled through, fighting Liz.

She'd parked her RAV4 out front, where the man in white had been running. At least on this side, there might be workers on the street to witness and hopefully help them.

Gas pumps sat across the street. She hadn't noticed them on her way to get Liz. Of course, they were empty. It looked private. A quiet parking lot with tankers and cars stretched behind the equipment. There was no one to help.

Haddie turned the corner and strode toward her car. "Hang on, Liz. Don't fight me."

"There's —" Liz rasped in her ear and still pulled weakly at Haddie's grasp.

Did Liz even understand her? Haddie tried to imagine the number of steps she could take before whoever had the gun could get out of the bay and turn the corner. If they even followed. With Liz dangling across her shoulders, it would take precious moments to turn and look. Who were these people? What were they doing with the raves?

Harold Holmes she had understood. He'd organized his own illegitimate business and kept it under control using his power, if a bit sadistically.

This — a power to make Haddie want to satisfy every urge — what did that get them, other than violent raves and madmen?

I just need to get Liz safe. Haddie took her steps carefully, feeling Liz's weight stagger her. Her back prickled, waiting for a gunshot.

A couple cars lined the side of the road next to some thin oaks. She could dodge behind them if necessary. Then what?

Did they follow? She didn't dare turn to look. Ahead, cars parked against the building. If she made it that far, they'd offer some cover to the front parking lot. She moved so slowly, it didn't seem likely she'd make it that far.

Each step tensed her taxed shoulders — waiting for that bullet. Liz tugged persistently and shifted her free leg. It made Haddie's pace difficult and unsure. Her face swelled from the backhand. Her cheekbone hurt.

"Let me go." Liz jerked hard, nearly sending them both to the ground.

"It's me, Haddie."

"I . . ." Liz trailed off into a mumble, relaxed, and then

struggled with a fury. Moving all her limbs, she used her free hand to hit Haddie on the side.

Haddie stumbled, caught herself, and avoided looking back to see how close they might be. Perhaps they didn't want to risk firing their weapons outside. Haddie tightened her grip, trying to pin her wriggling friend across her shoulders. What would Liz be to them? None of it made any sense.

Constant hunger and craving? *Is this what Liz had been trapped in for the past few days?* Haddie shivered.

"I can't —" Liz slumped and whispered, "Where is it?"

"Where is what?" Haddie asked.

Liz exploded with movement. Together, they tumbled to the pavement. Liz rolled off Haddie's shoulders. Haddie held onto her friend's wrist and ended up on her own back. Only a few steps from the cars parked against the building, they sprawled onto the black tar.

Haddie scrambled onto her elbows. Her black sleeves snagged and the stones bit into her arms. She held Liz's limp wrist.

A guard, a fuzzy yellow glow to his face, skidded to a stop only two dozen paces away. Like the first, he wore a couple days' worth of beard. Thin and wiry, this one could probably run. She saw the flash. Haddie winced at the gunshot.

It didn't hit her. A sound registered behind her, possibly the ricochet off tar. He would fire again, and hit her or Liz. He stood too close to miss. She'd never make it to her car. Witnesses obviously didn't matter. No one came to their rescue. Dad rode on his way home to Meg. If the guard didn't have a gun, she might be able to fight and win. *But, he does have a gun.* She sucked in a breath.

Haddie yelled.

CHAPTER 23

THE AIR AROUND HADDIE SANG.

The guard faded. She saw it clearly this time. Like snow blown off a porch, parts of him wisped away. Clumps lasted longer around his face. His eyes stared in surprise. But in an instant, everything about him had disappeared. His gun and clothes faded with him.

Pain wracked Haddie's hands, face, and neck. Her blood shattered in pinpricks across her skin, causing the purpura that would speckle her. Her joints burned as if on fire.

The world around her turned black, and the image of thick, leathery leaves appeared before her face. A man dissolved in the dark green, and she caught a glimpse of a short blade before its glint winked out. The nightmare lingered a moment before morphing into a similar scene where someone she knew as a friend exploded in gunshots that ripped through flesh and uniform. Her song — Dad's song — rang, and the gunfire stopped. The body dropped at their boots.

Liz tugged her wrist away, and Haddie focused on the

green leaves of the oak above and the gray clouds that boiled in the sky.

She shivered at the pain and couldn't bring herself to push up her elbows. Groaning, she rolled to her knees. Pebbles bit into her palm. She could smell Liz: sweat, urine, and alcohol.

Liz mouthed words but said nothing. Her eyes wide, she stared where the man had been. Bare heels scraped on the tar, but she didn't stand.

"Liz." Haddie's mouth tasted like metal, and her tongue felt thick — dry. "We need to get out of here." *She saw it. She has to know now. All the lies.*

The man in white could have more guards. They weren't safe yet. They should go to the hotel and get Liz dressed. She looked bizarre, nearly naked in the daylight on the side of the road. Even after the gunshot, no one stirred in the parking lot across the street.

They couldn't just sit there. Haddie got to her knees, grimacing.

Liz pulled away.

She's afraid of me. "I won't —" Haddie rose to her feet and grabbed Liz under the armpit. Leaning back, she lifted her friend to a bent position.

Liz licked her lips slowly. Frowning she studied Haddie's face. "What?"

What am I? I don't know. How much had Liz understood of what happened? They didn't have time to discuss it. Haddie felt a chill. Could Liz accept her, as she was?

Haddie pulled Liz toward the front parking lot. Right now, they needed to get safe.

A silver sedan pulled up to the corner of the side street and Thompson. The car barely stopped before squealing and heading down the road away from them.

Liz resisted, slightly, but Haddie barged forward. Her knees screamed at the pressure. Every joint hurt in her arm that pulled Liz.

No one moved in the parking lot ahead, nor followed from behind. Perhaps there had only been two guards. Why did they need guards? In case someone like the madman came awake? Or someone like Haddie came looking for their friend? Did they protect the man in the white suit? Somehow, she knew it wasn't his power that sang to her. He'd just been an echo.

"Are you okay?" Haddie asked.

Liz didn't make eye contact, but she resisted less. Her eyes searched the ground ahead of them. The fall had scraped her right arm and she walked slowly, tenderly, either from pain or her bare feet on the parking lot. She seemed disconnected — in a fog.

"Liz, do you know where we are?"

Her friend didn't react to the question. Her lips twitched as though she might speak, but her focus remained on the ground.

"What do you remember?"

Liz sniffled, then gagged. Her expression turned to a pained confusion, but she still wouldn't speak.

They cleared the corner of the building and no one waited for them in the lot. She didn't know if she could handle one more fight, and she wasn't sure she could bring herself to use her power again. She could still feel the memory of pain bursting across her skin. Too much more and she doubted her joints would move. Hunger, thirst, and fatigue smothered her like the clouds above. They just had to get to the hotel, get Liz washed up, and rest. Then they could go home. Fortunately, Liz had stopped resisting.

Haddie opened the passenger door and retrieved her

brown jacket. Liz stared at Haddie trying to hand it to her. Could there be permanent damage?

"Do you want to wear this?" Haddie kept an eye on the building. She assumed Liz would want to cover up. It might be an awkward scene, going through the hotel lobby.

After not getting a response, Haddie sighed and slipped the jacket loose over Liz's shoulders before ushering her into the seat. Each move seemed awkward, like Liz dug deep to just remember how to get into the car. After she sat, though, Liz sprang on Haddie's empty water bottle, only to shake it with disappointment.

"We'll get room service at the hotel," Haddie promised. "Let's just get out of here."

She closed the passenger door and watched Liz carefully as she rounded the front of the car. Part of her expected Liz to leap out and run like a feral cat. Instead, Liz sat looking desolate and disconnected, staring at her feet.

Haddie started up the RAV4 and checked the parking lot as she made for the side street. No one else had come out of the building. Her heart rate slowing, she took in a deep breath. Her wrists, elbows, and shoulders complained at every turn of the wheel. But, Liz was safe.

The car connected to her phone and prompted a text from her Dad. She let the car read it out loud. "Anything?"

She stopped at the intersection and texted, "Yes. Got Liz. Going to hotel." Two mechanics had come out of the automotive bay across the street and stood wiping their hands. Had they heard the gunshot?

Terry had texted as well. "Anthony Prizer rented properties connected to the suicide raves in the US. The raves started in India, then Brazil, before Cali."

Haddie dropped the phone back onto the seat with a sigh; she'd have to message him later. *I can't obsess on this and risk everyone.* Someone else could figure out what these raves were all about. They needed to get clear of here. If the police had been called over the gunshot, she didn't need them finding Liz like this. She took a left onto Thompson.

What about Matt? Anger flared up. Partly because she blamed him, and worse, because she felt guilty abandoning him. Liz could go to the police. The police could find Matt.

"Seatbelt." Haddie glanced over, but Liz didn't seem to hear her or understand. Haddie didn't want Liz to look at her face; she would look hideous bruised and with the purpura.

The raves did bother Haddie. What was the point? And why did she see yellow on the faces of some of the men? She'd seen it briefly on the man who shot Meg's Uncle. They couldn't be connected.

Dad hadn't mentioned seeing it, and Haddie hadn't wanted to ask when they were with Meg. Did she see it because of her powers? This whole rave situation had something to do with another one of them, someone like Haddie or her dad. Someone with powers. The police would have to clear this up. *Not me.*

Haddie drove down Thompson. Liz didn't buckle up, and she hadn't put on the jacket. She looked in no shape to go to the police. They would need proof. Liz could say they shot at them when they left. Haddie would have to be involved, which meant explaining the bruises and purpura. Liz obviously didn't have her phone; it would be back at the rave. That might help their story. Haddie might have to explain the fight with the first guard. Her chest tightened at the thought. Maybe they could anonymously report Matt's disappearance.

In the rearview mirror, she caught a motion.

A man ran behind them, faster than should be possible. She glanced back. His eyes seemed to be orange dots.

"Liz, seatbelt." Haddie started to accelerate, focusing on the road ahead. Flatbeds were parked on both sides of the road, and a black Dodge Ram pulled onto Thompson toward her.

"Damn." She drove tight against a load of rebar, and the truck stopped, letting her pass.

The figure behind had reddish-pink skin and a thin gangly neck and chest. He didn't have any clothes on. Haddie chilled. It wasn't a raver, but a demon. Its skull formed a too thin, oblong shape with an open mouth and wide eyes. There didn't seem to be a nose. The eyes glinted a fluorescent orange. The ones she'd seen during the ski trip had been very different. *Except for the eyes.* Only a couple car lengths behind her, it jumped, leaping out of her view.

To Haddie's right, two women stood smoking at the opening of a warehouse. They stared at them — frozen with cigarettes in hand.

The demon landed on Haddie's roof with a thud. Nails scratched on metal.

Haddie slammed on the brakes.

Liz crumpled against the dash and onto the floor.

The demon flipped over onto the hood of Haddie's RAV4. The flesh on its face looked taut and too raw to be skin. It hung with its left hand from the top of Haddie's windshield. Its legs flopped off the car. It held her hood with its other hand. One long nail protruded from its thumb. Its eyes glowed orange.

The women screamed, a sound distant and disconnected.

Haddie punched the gas.

The demon swung onto the hood. Liz flopped back

against the seat. Haddie drove with the creature leering open-mouthed at the two of them. It slapped against the windshield, its large nail clicking. This thing had been at the warehouse.

Ahead, the road crossed the tracks and would merge with the highway that led to I-405. Speed might not be enough to fling it off. Large nails on its hind legs dug into crevices where the hood attached.

It shifted toward the passenger side and slapped the window there.

The nail dotted the windshield with a small crack.

Liz rolled her head back and stared at it. Blood smeared her nose. She barely seemed aware of it.

Haddie slammed the brakes again. She didn't have the same speed as before.

The demon held, barely shifting. Nails ground on metal. It glanced at Haddie, and then slammed the glass in front of Liz again.

A spider web of cracks spread out. The glass wouldn't hold. The creature would break through into the car. It would kill Liz.

The mouth seemed stretched open, fixed in a silent scream. Sharp pointed teeth menaced. It pulled its arm back for another blow.

Haddie screamed. The song rang in the enclosed car, threatening to deafen. Pain exploded across her skin like a raging fire.

The demon vanished like a pile of leaves blown before a gale. A lingering yellow glow remained where its neck had been.

Liz jerked, glancing at Haddie and wincing before her expression turned to surprise. Had she heard the song? Some recognition glinted in her eyes. Did she remember?

The world turned dark. Hot and humid air cloyed against Haddie's skin. A monkey cried out far away. A knife struck Haddie's shoulder. She yelled with surprise and the burn of it. A South Asian face, young and angry, vaporized as it came into view. The teeth lasted just long enough to create a leering grimace. The darkness swirled, exposing a gray that lit the pool around her. Water sloshed from the side, and a line of dirty soldiers crouched in a paddy. Shoots of green grass wavered in the air. An explosion tore through three of them and slammed a fourth into her. Water, grass, and mud sprayed above. A woman rose from the water, screaming and firing a torrent of bullets over Haddie. Voices cried out from behind. Haddie bellowed. The water rippled where the woman had once stood.

The nightmares flickered away. The RAV4 crawled forward, and again Haddie slammed the brake down. The movement burned her hips and knee. Her hands shook; even the light tremor flared pain in her elbow.

Liz stared. She'd remained on the floor, but leaned away from Haddie. Her lips moved, then delayed she said, "What?"

What am I? Haddie blinked. "I don't know."

PART 5

Finding fault with our freedoms, the Gatekeepers, the Seroveilm, named us when they locked us here.

CHAPTER 24

THOMAS WALKED up the steps to Haddie's apartment. Birds called from the trees planted about the courtyard. It was a simulation of nature, a contained and cultured swath of green for the designer and architects surrounded by ugly squat structures, clones of each other placed on some vision of aesthetic value. There had been a time he'd found beauty in architecture, especially in Norway, but also Europe. Decades of living in or near cities had burned away that naïveté.

Haddie had found Liz. They'd be back soon, no doubt. No mention of the boyfriend, but with Haddie, that wasn't surprising. She didn't have the same need to bond with a mate for validation as her girlfriends did. Hopefully this David didn't expect that. All through high school, her friends had been about their boys; Haddie picked up causes, which at times had been worse. He didn't really have cause to judge Haddie about crusades.

Thomas tapped at the door. Rock grumbled in the living room, and Sam's voice moved closer.

A familiar warmth of smells came from Haddie's apartment, like a locker room with faint perfume. Today, spice from something Sam had likely been cooking, added a sharper note.

"Hey, T." Sam was dressed in a pink, white, and blue sweatshirt and jean shorts.

Meg glanced up as he walked in, but turned back to Rock before he could see her eyes. She sat on the floor, wearing an oversized T-shirt that he'd seen on Sam before. The too long yoga pants crumpled at the ankles might have been Haddie's. The apartment had been straightened up. School books were piled neatly at the wall by Haddie's desk, and there were no loose clothes on the floor. The room looked bigger.

Sam tucked her hands behind her back. "How's Haddie? She find Liz?"

"She did." He closed the door.

She bounced. "Good! Should I check with her? No, I'll wait until she calls. I hope Liz is okay."

Thomas waited until Sam finished. "How did the overnight go?" He spoke in Meg's direction, not necessarily expecting her to be the one who answered.

Rock rolled to his back, lolling his tongue and seeming to smile at Thomas. Meg scratched his chest.

Sam dropped down by Meg and spoke. "We had fun. Watched some anime." She smiled and gestured toward the kitchen. "We had some Spanish rice for lunch. There's a bowl left if you want it."

Thomas shook his head, but strode toward the kitchen to make coffee. "Been eating dried garbanzos most of the ride. But thanks."

He filled the coffee pot in an empty sink. Sam, and perhaps Meg, had cleaned the kitchen as well. Jisoo yelled at him from the counter.

He couldn't let Meg completely acclimate to Haddie's or with Sam. It would be the easiest for the girl, but he couldn't put that burden on the women long term. He'd taken the responsibility. Meg would have to work through uncomfortable new surroundings and find some peace at the garage. He'd have to find something to engage her in her new home. He knew so little of her life before her parents had died. She'd open up in time. In the fall, he'd get her into school.

It would always be a risk — her sharing a past he needed to keep secret. Once she settled in better, he'd explain his concerns. Other than moving out to the hills and secluding there, nothing would guarantee her silence or discretion.

He brought out a mug of coffee and passed Haddie's computer on the way to the couch. A brown mongrel with a white chest sat on a webpage. Thomas caught the name "Louis" and the offer to adopt. He sat on the couch and closed his eyes. A puppy would be the easiest way. He didn't know Meg well enough. She might not be responsible. He sipped his coffee and caught Sam looking at him. She raised her eyebrows questioningly.

It had helped Haddie. She'd had Annabelle at first, through school. A year after her mother had died, Haddie started wanting a dog. Despite the highway right outside the front door, he'd acquiesced after a week. When he'd first expressed his concern that she needed to be consistently responsible and walk the dog daily, she'd rolled a tire up and down the street for four days, three times a day. They'd gotten a three-year-old mutt. She'd named it Mula, despite his explanation that it meant 'mule' in Spanish. She never expected him to care for Mula, except when she spent the night at friends' houses. She'd claimed the rights and responsibilities.

"So," Thomas drawled. "Louis?"

Meg turned up, brown eyes growing wide. Still, no smile. She didn't say anything, but she blinked and seemed to be waiting.

Sam stood. "Isn't he cute? Eight months old. All trained. Sit, stay, lie down, and no. Very cuddly. Sounds a bit needy, but —" She chewed her lip moving to the computer. "Got all his shots. Neutered."

Thomas snorted. "You get a commission?" He grimaced at his stiff knees, getting up off the couch. "We haven't had a pup at the garage since Rock. Couldn't keep him inside. Lucky he had a good sense of 99."

Meg just watched, forgetting to scratch Rock until he smacked her hand with his paw.

Louis's owners, east in Vida, had put the dog up for adoption as it became clear he didn't handle their older dogs well. Thomas had a property near there, north of Nimrod. Less than an hour ride.

Sam swayed side-to-side, arms still behind her back. "And that means . . . ?"

"That I'll need to go back to the garage." Thomas turned to Meg. "Louis can't ride on the back of my bike. We'll need a car so we can all go pick him up."

Meg blinked and the corner of her mouth twitched. Not a smile, but it would do.

Sam hopped. "Can I come?"

Thomas nodded. "It'll be a while before you're back here though. We'll have to hit up a pet store to get Louis settled in."

He headed for the kitchen, ignoring Jisoo's complaints. Sam followed him, and he held up the half pot of coffee as an offer. She made a face and he poured it down the sink.

Sam nodded knowingly. "This will help. They gave away her dog when her parents — died."

Thomas frowned as he rinsed his cup. He remembered the article now; Meg had been at a friend's house, walking a dog when the fire trapped the parents upstairs. The friend he had watching them never mentioned a dog with the Uncle and Meg.

He nodded. "Thanks. I appreciate it."

They walked out together and found Meg's pink and white backpack had been brought out to the living room. Meg sat with Rock. The pit bull lay with his head in her lap as she rubbed up his nose and over his brow. It seemed she'd be willing to put up with the garage, and Thomas, if she had someone to share it with. Maybe she'd come up with a different name than Louis. It reminded him too much of the French, Napoleon, and all the mess that Thomas had got himself caught up with before he'd come to America. Back to America.

He took a deep breath in and out. Haddie had her Liz. Meg looked like she could deal with the change — with this small bribe. Things were looking better after a rough couple of days.

CHAPTER 25

HADDIE SHOOK AS SHE DROVE. Her joints cried out with each move of the wheel or press of the pedals. She only had a few minutes before they would be back at the hotel.

Liz murmured to herself in the passenger seat. She'd moved up from the floor and wrapped the coat around herself. Her hair was clumped, and something glued a thick strand to the back of her neck. Her face had scratches, and her arms, sides, and thighs were scraped. Occasionally she snuck a glance at Haddie, but wouldn't put on her seatbelt or respond to any questions. Staring at her bare feet, Liz could still be reacting to the song at the rave, the demon's attack, or from seeing Haddie's power. Hopefully, she'd come out of whatever this was.

After their incident with the demon on the ski lift, Haddie had ended up in the hospital. The next time they had talked, Liz had believed she'd hallucinated the demon. Haddie let her believe it. *Does Liz realize that I lied? Worse, does she wonder what I am?*

Like Haddie had learned with her Dad, no explanation

would be enough. How could she even begin to explain things she didn't understand?

As a jerk in a white caddy veered across her lane, Haddie braked, wincing. They were almost to the exit that would bring them to Liz's hotel. They both needed food and a bath. Liz first. Haddie had almost become accustomed to the smell, but sweat and urine reeked off her friend. Haddie's own hunger had eased to an ache, but she kept wanting to grab her empty water bottle.

In her murmuring, Liz mumbled, "Haddie." It repeated before the words became obscure again.

"Liz," Haddie said. "I'm here. Right here."

Liz glanced then shook her head. "Haddie, Haddie." She went back to unintelligible words and didn't react to any of Haddie's attempts to coax more out of her.

Haddie swallowed. *She's going to think she's crazy.*

In a few minutes, they pulled up to the parking lot and found a spot near the sidewalk. The sky still looked gray and gloomy, without rain, but the clouds pressed on the city. Haddie turned off the RAV4 and forced herself not to cry. She'd found Liz.

Now, she had to walk to the hotel despite joints that burned with each movement. Haddie slid out of her seat, groaning and wincing like her dad. Liz sat quietly, staring at her feet. The front hood had deep gouges from the demon's claws. The windshield would need to be replaced. Parts of the front grill had separated.

Haddie opened Liz's door. "Let's get inside. Get a shower. Some food in you." She offered her hand.

Liz turned to look at the hand. "Nothing," she said.

A chill crawled up Haddie. The madman had said the same words.

"We'll get food brought up to the room."

They couldn't avoid a stop at the front desk. They'd need a new keycard; Liz obviously wasn't hiding hers anywhere. Haddie, having used her powers twice, would be covered in purpura. She could see the swelling in her cheek. Together, they would make a spectacle.

"Hungry," Liz said. She turned to study Haddie's face, frowning. Still, she didn't get out.

"Food. We'll get food." Haddie smiled, trying not to imagine what she looked like. She reached in and shifted Liz's legs to point her friend out of the car.

Liz flinched, but didn't resist. She allowed Haddie to pull her from the car, and she stood on her own. She allowed the jacket to be put on her, but showed no reaction or emotion. She flinched again when Haddie closed the passenger door.

Haddie took Liz's hand. "We're going to walk to the hotel now. Get some food."

"Food," Liz repeated.

"Yes, food." Haddie's throat swelled and she fought tears.

She took a step, pulling lightly on Liz's hand, and her friend walked with her. Slow and shaky, she stepped as though her feet hurt. They made it to the smoother sidewalk, and Haddie ignored the odd looks from a couple who passed them. It was past lunchtime, and the crowd had thinned. The air had become a humid summer's day.

I found Liz. They'd survived whatever the raves actually were. Finding another demon made Haddie shiver. *Orange.* This time, she'd seen orange eyes. The tall scientist they'd met on the ski gondola, Dr. Aaron Knox, said he could tell they were demons even disguised as human, and that was why they hunted him. Is that what he saw — orange eyes?

Hand in hand, she walked Liz into the lobby. Gratefully, no one waited at the registration counter. Two attendants, a woman Haddie's age with tan skin and a paler older woman, stood in white button-down shirts and black ties. Both widened their eyes at the sight of Haddie and Liz, and the younger woman stepped back.

Haddie ignored them. "We need a new keycard for 311, Matt Arbor. This is his fiancé, Elizabeth Backhus."

Liz looked up, her tone pitiful. "Matt." She looked drugged — stoned.

The younger woman stuttered. "We can't give out a key card to anyone other than —"

The older woman cleared her throat and pointed to her screen. "I'm sorry. It seems the gentleman's card has been declined." Her tone and expression indicated actual regret. "Ms. Backhus is listed on the room, but —"

Haddie smiled, imagining the horrifying sight she made. "Ms. Backhus and I need to clean up and rest after the accident. I can place the room on my card." Hopefully, an accident would seem plausible.

"I can give you a new room, but the belongings will be held until the room balance is paid." The older woman offered a pained, apologetic smile. "I'm sorry."

Liz needed her clothes. Haddie handed over her card, Dad's card, to the woman, followed by her license. "She'll need something to change into. Please place the room balance, and tonight, on my card."

The older woman started to speak, glanced at the younger woman, and turned to work on her terminal.

Haddie's phone vibrated. She groaned at David's text. *I forgot to text him.* He had to be worried.

"Everything okay?"

Demons and guns — everything is normal. "Yes. Getting Liz into her hotel. I'll text you once I get her settled in." She'd have to take some time and make up a story, something that wouldn't sound too bad but would make up for her being an ass.

Haddie nervously glimpsed into the lobby. The few people there turned away as she looked. *David can't see me like this.*

"3 1 1?" The older woman spoke into a two-way radio.

Haddie didn't understand the response, but the woman seemed to. She smiled and nodded. "Bring up linens. They'll be returning to the room," she said into her radio.

"Food." Liz started to move and Haddie reached out for her shoulder.

A server crossed the room with a tray. Haddie stood in front of her friend, blocking the view.

"We'll be upstairs soon," she said. Her nose caught the hints of fresh food over Liz's rank smell. Her own stomach ached for anything, and her throat begged for simple water.

The older woman's eyes watched from over the terminal, but she kept working. The younger attendant worked beside her, keeping her eyes down. Silently, the older woman placed Haddie's ID and credit card on the counter. It took another half-minute of awkward silence before she slid two key cards across.

"Sorry it took so long. It may be a few minutes before they come up with sheets and towels." the older woman forced a smile.

"Thank you. Room service still open?"

"Twenty-four hours." The woman's smile warmed.

Haddie took the cards in one hand and Liz in the other,

navigating across the lobby and avoiding the table with fresh plates. Even she wanted to grab a sandwich. *Liz just might.*

Still, Liz tugged as they passed the bar lined with bottles. *No.* Haddie slipped her hand around her friend's shoulders and guided them to the elevators.

Inside the elevator, Haddie sighed in relief. "We're almost there. I just need to wash up and rest a bit. Then we'll head home."

Liz looked up, blinked, but said nothing.

I could eat three meals and sleep a week. The idea of driving two hours didn't sound possible. She still had to decide what to do about Matt Arbor. She'd talk with Terry about an anonymous reporting. Going to the police in this state wouldn't be wise. And Liz — she'd be in no shape for the police. What would she tell them? Haddie's jaw hurt, and she realized she'd been gritting her teeth. She blamed Matt.

"Haddie?" Liz looked up from where Haddie still had her crooked under her arm.

Haddie's eyes watered. "Yes. We're safe."

"Haddie?" Liz repeated, she started to lift a hand as though reaching up, then stopped. "Where . . . ?" She trailed off, and her hand dropped.

"Here, at the hotel. We're going to get you washed up, and we'll eat."

Liz looked to the floor. "Hungry. Nothing."

Again, that word chilled Haddie. She hugged Liz tight as the elevator doors opened.

The room had been cleared, if not cleaned. Leaving Liz at the bathroom, she peeked into the room. They'd stacked two suitcases in the corner and the comforter lay off the end of the stripped king bed. Haddie returned to the bath and started the shower. Liz stood, at least cognizant enough to watch.

Haddie laughed. Someone had replaced the glasses with fresh wrapped ones. Of all the things she could have wanted right now, this felt like a present.

Her smile faded when she looked in the mirror. Two blackening eyes took her initial focus. Then, she noticed the tiny bruises that dotted her between her nose and lips, along her cheek, down the neck. Her usually rich, light-brown skin looked mottled. Her cheek puffed out around one eye.

Haddie drew in a breath and filled a glass. Handing it to Liz, she waited until her friend had a firm grip. Haddie left the water running as she finished a glass. The water seemed to bring some life to Liz, who quickly downed hers as well. They were on their third round when the door opened.

A surprised maid stopped halfway in the door, arms full of white towels and sheets. "Sorry." She swallowed and stared before she could say anything else.

Haddie knew what she looked like. She put out her hands, "I'll take the towels."

It still took seconds for the maid to recover and comply. She stuttered as she pointed toward the bed in the other room. "I'll make the —"

Haddie nodded and closed the door. She checked the water and adjusted it to a hot but not scalding temperature.

"Let's get you washed up." She got Liz out of the fringe bikini and tossed it into the trash. The panties were more difficult, but she finally got Liz under the spray of water.

Her friend stood motionless, her back to the stream with her eyes closed. Awkwardly, Haddie got shampoo into her friend's hair as she heard the door to the room close. She worked up a good lather and left it. When she pulled up Liz's hand and squirted body soap into it trying to coax her to wash herself, Liz left the soap in her palm and promptly sat on the shower floor.

Haddie sighed and stepped back. *It won't hurt to sit there and rinse.* The lather from Liz's haired trailed off. They needed some food anyway. She put the bottle of body soap beside her friend.

She left the door open as she ordered room service, plenty of it. The man on the other end sounded a little more curious with each entree. He stopped asking if that would be all.

By the time two carts of food arrived, she had Liz out of the shower and wrapped in a towel, and had washed her own face and hands. Haddie had spread the contents of Liz's luggage across the bed and was trying to coax her friend into dressing.

Haddie pushed the carts into a line and left the man standing outside. Everything smelled delicious.

"Alright," she said, stopping a cart in front of Liz and lifting lids off.

Liz already had a piece of cake in her hand, frosting on the palm, and began shoving large bites in her mouth before Haddie had exposed the entrees.

"Good choice — dessert first." Haddie raised her eyebrows. A second bath might be in order. "I probably should have ordered more finger food."

Haddie sat in the other chair and went for the Alfredo. Of everything she'd ordered, it needed utensils the most. It was rich and creamy and tasted like the best she'd ever had. She still ached and desperately wanted to throw the clothes off the bed and sleep, but for now, she ate.

Liz wiped her hands and face with napkins, when prompted. She even used a spoon, when Haddie placed it in her hand, on the nearly melted ice cream. Still, her towel wore much of the food until Liz started to slow down.

"Are you feeling better?" Haddie asked.

Liz actually nodded. Food seemed to be helping. Had they drugged Liz? *How long before it wears off and I have my friend back?*

Haddie could make no sense of the raves or the power behind them. However, she'd heard the song, or the echo of it. Someone with abilities like her own wanted these raves to happen. But why?

"I saw — that thing." Liz had stopped eating. She had a finger resting on the edge of a plate, but she didn't move.

The demon on the hood of the RAV4. "Yes." Haddie swallowed.

"Like on the ski lift."

Haddie started to cry. "Yes." This was Liz. The friend she'd lied to and let believe she'd hallucinated monsters — all to keep Haddie's secret. "Yes. I'm sorry."

"You're real. You are the real Haddie?" Liz looked up, crying.

"Yes, of course." What had Liz thought — that she just dreamed or hallucinated escaping? What drugs had they given her?

Liz puked onto the serving cart.

In half an hour, Haddie had Liz rinsed off again, dressed, and sleeping on the bed. Liz didn't rise to the same lucidity, but she responded to prompts. Haddie took what reaction she could get as a good sign and hoped sleep would cure the rest. The carts and some of the towels she'd used to clean up with she moved into the hall.

Haddie took her own shower, though she hadn't brought a change of clothes. They would get a bit of rest, then deal with Matt. She probably should check in with Terry, but she was too exhausted and sore. A couple hours of sleep. Then she could deal with the world. She crawled onto the bed and Liz stirred.

Asleep, Liz's eyes fluttered. "Matt?"

"Shh. Sleep."

CHAPTER 26

SAMEEDHA STARED through the tinted glass to the glowing diamond light and the churning mass of revelers that she stirred with her song.

The raves had been going well, and the Lord General had been pleased when He visited. Then, after He left, there had been trouble at last night's rave location. He'd turned hard and angry at her news of missing people and enraged when she couldn't find one of Dylan's despicable creatures.

Her people had identified at least three rich patrons to further the cause. Shouldn't that count for something?

She had her men investigating. They would find out what happened. The reports so far had been surprising. If she could believe it, there might be a new Noveilm.

Without taking her eyes off the rave, Sameedha put her hand out for a champagne glass. A vision was coming. They were particularly ugly at this point.

Another Noveilm, with a power that she had never witnessed. Surely, He would be impressed with her if she found the woman first.

CHAPTER 27

HADDIE JERKED awake to find Liz sobbing against her shoulder.

The gray haze that lingered outside seemed too bright, and the hotel room clock said 5 p.m. The room smelled like a mélange of pungent food. Haddie rolled to her side, blinking away a thick crust of sleep. She could barely focus on Liz's features or words.

"Liz. Liz. What's wrong?"

"Matt." Liz sobbed after the word.

Haddie hadn't really looked for the man once she'd found Liz. Average and nondescript, she remembered him more from her recent social media searches than the little she ever saw of him on campus. Surely, even in her haze from fighting that indulgent-urging tone, she would have recognized him if he'd been among those around the man in white. Maybe not.

Liz ebbed out of the sobbing and seemed to drift back to sleep. She wouldn't want to leave him at the never-ending rave, stuck in that craving. If she were fully aware, she'd insist they find him. They'd be traipsing down to the upcoming rave or the police station even now. Maybe after a couple more hours of sleep.

"Matt's gone." Liz sounded frantic. Haddie blinked her eyes open again. With a surprising alertness, Liz was staring at her, not a hands-width away.

"We can call the police. Explain . . ." Haddie faltered. There were certain events she certainly did not want Liz explaining. "Matt is missing and possibly at a rave." That statement likely wouldn't alert the police too much in the way of action without more detail. "Maybe say that you think they kidnapped him, on the party bus. They took you on that bus, right?"

Liz didn't reply. She quietly repeated, "Matt's gone."

The finality of the statement sent a chill through Haddie. Had something happened to Matt? Something that Liz just now remembered? Haddie vaguely remembered a woman who seemed unmoving. Could she have been dead? The man in white had guards, there'd been a demon, they'd locked a madman in a closet — the blood in the bathroom. Anything was possible.

"Where did he go?" Liz mumbled. Her eyes had closed.

Haddie started to say she didn't know, but Terry had sent her the location for tonight's rave. Unless something had happened to Matt, he likely would be there. "We can call the police."

Liz whispered. "No. There are drugs. Pills on the floor. The hunt." She sucked in a wavering breath, and her lips moved silently for a few words before she spoke again. "It would ruin his career."

The school wouldn't likely hear about the police report, unless Matt did get charged with something. Certainly the people putting on the rave would be the focus, not their victims, though the police might not see it that way.

Haddie couldn't ignore Matt — leave him behind — no matter if she blamed him or not. They had time before the rave. Hours. Watching Liz drift into gentle rhythmic breathing drained Haddie of any initiative. Her friend still looked rough, with scratches on her face and along the side of her hand. Haddie's own joints ached and her face throbbed. The bed felt too good. She was thirsty, but didn't have the energy to get up and fill a glass. She had to let Terry know Liz was safe . . . after some sleep.

Liz snorted, jerking awake. "That creature — it just disappeared. Tried to break the glass. Didn't get in."

Haddie swallowed, fighting back a sense of guilt or shame at having her power.

Liz's eyes seemed to be searching hers for an answer. How much did she remember? Could Liz hear the tone that rang out? Liz blinked, and her lids lowered as she drifted back to sleep.

Haddie sucked in a deep breath. Liz remembered the demon, and she might remember Haddie's powers. Would they have that conversation, later, when Liz woke up fully? *Will I lie again?* She didn't really know how to explain her ability, even to herself. She certainly couldn't explain demons.

She had truly never expected to see them again. How were demons connected to the raves — by someone with powers? If only she'd had time to talk with that scientist, Aaron. He reminded her of Terry, a conspiracy nerd.

Exhausted, she rolled onto her back and stared at the ceiling. She didn't understand any of it, and this time she wouldn't try to. She didn't have to get in the middle of whatever these raves were. Haddie groaned, sliding out of bed to get some water. She'd let Liz sleep, and then they'd go to the police. Maybe she could shut off her mind and catch another hour of rest before then.

CHAPTER 28

LIZ BLINKED AT A GRAY CEILING. She smelled like soap, and her mouth tasted like bile. Snoring rumbled beside her.

The room looked familiar. *Not my bedroom.* Gray light filtered through a window to her right. A familiar table and two stiff chairs. Thick curtains draped to the carpet. Ugly art on the wall. The hotel room.

She felt sore everywhere and had a pounding headache. Hungry. A hangover for sure. Her feet felt as though she'd been on them for a full day. Bruises and scrapes covered her sides and arms. Even her forehead hurt.

Something vibrated. A phone.

White hair flowed across the pillow next to Liz; Haddie snored beside her. When did Haddie get here? A ride in her SUV, and something broke the windshield. The memory seemed so distant, like a dream, or nightmare, if Haddie didn't lie right there on the bed. Why was it so difficult to think?

Where had Matt gone? They'd been dancing. All night. Forever. No wonder her feet hurt.

Liz pulled the cover off and winced at the movement. A pink scrape covered the back of her arm. She wore a new black T-shirt from the concert, stiff and smelling slightly chemical. She started to take her feet off the bed and stopped. Her ankles were swollen. The bottom of her right foot had light bruises and a blister. *What were we doing?* She sat on the edge of the bed, staring at the table. Dim gray light lit the buildings across the street. *Morning or evening?*

Matt had been angry. They'd gone somewhere, after the concert. Or had she dreamed that? *Where the hell are you, Matt?* Did they have a fight? Perhaps Haddie had come to pick Liz up.

Liz had to work up the courage to stand on her feet. The bruises hurt. *I need to call him.*

She didn't find her phone on her side of the bed. Someone had straightened up; it wouldn't have been Haddie. Wincing, she hobbled around the bed to Haddie's side. A black shirt and jeans lay on the floor, and Haddie's phone vibrated on the night stand. Liz's bag had been packed, but sat open on top of Matt's. *He's not gone then.* No sign of her purse or phone.

Wobbling, she made it into the bathroom. No purse, but towels littered the floor. Did she leave her purse in his car? She didn't do that. Maybe in the trunk. But why leave the phone there? *I must have gotten drunk.*

She looked like crap. She had scratches on her face, arms, and legs. A bruise down her side. Her hair, its usual mess. She used the toilet, drank some water, and stared into bloodshot eyes.

Tottering, she returned to the room. Haddie wouldn't care if Liz used her phone.

Haddie looked worse than Liz. A huge bruise covered

her face, her cheekbone swelled out on one side, and little bruises dotted everywhere. Liz grimaced. Had they been in an accident? She vaguely remembered a shattered windshield. A nightmare face. *Did they hit someone?*

Nothing explained Matt not being there. *I need to call him.* She picked up Haddie's phone.

Liz stared at the date and time. It took a moment for her to realize she'd lost days. *What is the last thing I remember?* Checking into the hotel, certainly. Matt being angry — what day? Dancing — from her feet, that would be recent.

She dialed Matt's number and it dumped her directly to voicemail. "Where are you?" she asked.

She hung up, closed the screen, and an image of a flyer for a rave lay behind it. Liz frowned at the picture on the cell phone. Yes. They'd gone to a rave. She'd never been, and hadn't really wanted to, especially not with him in such a foul mood. However, this flyer had today's date on it.

The neon and black image brought memories. She'd been eating pills. "Shit." *What have I been doing?* Music. People scrambling across the floor, howling, sex, and even fighting. Images of bottles, red cups — so they'd been drinking. Matt dancing wildly with no shirt on. She'd had sex with him, and people had been dancing around them. She shook the memories away. What kind of insane drugs had they been doing?

Even now, hearing the music in her head, she wanted to be there. Where, though? She remembered a man in a white three-piece suit with strange, dead eyes.

Haddie had driven her back here. Where was Matt? Still at the rave? Hard to imagine mild-mannered Matt in that party, or herself. Did Haddie just leave him there?

Liz looked at the flyer on Haddie's phone. Is that where

Matt is? How had they been partying for three days? They were supposed to leave today, to head back to Eugene.

"Where is my damn phone?" Liz shook her head, stumbling for her suitcase.

She hadn't packed it. The pants she wore during the car trip were rolled up and shoved next to clean, folded jeans. Someone had shoved clothing where it didn't belong. Her toiletries were tossed in a corner of the luggage, not even in their bag. Annoyed, she grabbed her toothbrush and paste.

The pills must have had something to do with the lost days. She'd gotten too old to party for twenty-four hours, let alone three days. She did remember sleeping and taking a bus ride. Why hadn't they driven Matt's car?

Anger toward Matt shifted toward dread as she brushed her teeth. She stopped, staring at the mess she'd made of her face. What if Matt was hurt? Or was he still at the rave, getting high and dancing? If so, he needed to end it and get her back to Eugene. The more glimpses she remembered of the rave, the scarier it seemed. She'd been out of control. Drinking, kissing, on her knees searching for pills, trash everywhere, and always the music.

Liz left the toothbrush and paste on a hand towel and stumbled back to the main room. She considered waking Haddie, but there might be an argument about Matt. Haddie seemed to resent the time Liz spent with Matt. Some of the comments had been obvious. *She has David.*

Snatching Haddie's phone, Liz grabbed a pen and pad from the nightstand and wrote the address from the flyer. She left them all on the table and hobbled back to her clothes.

Her sneakers from the car ride were tucked in Matt's bag. She'd almost committed to going barefoot until she thought to check there. Had the hotel packed their bags?

Haddie would have at least put the shoes in the right bag. She unzipped the side pocket inside her bag and pulled out two twenties, an emergency stash that had sat for five years. *Well, this constitutes an emergency.*

Dressed, Liz picked up the hotel phone and called the front desk.

CHAPTER 29

HADDIE STARED at the flattened pillow beside her for a moment. The wrinkled sheet stretched to the edge of the bed. A light behind her lit the walls and curtains of her hotel room, while an artificial red light glowed on the buildings outside the window.

"Liz?" Haddie sat up in the bed.

Stumbling against stiff joints, she hobbled to the lit bathroom and blinked at the light. Liz had left. Downstairs? Maybe she'd gotten hungry. She hadn't held down much of the food. Hopefully, she hadn't gone to the bar.

Haddie splashed water on her face and caught sight of herself in the mirror. Purpura not only flecked her face but her neck and hands. Her face had swollen around one eye, but mainly along the cheek.

She shook her head and searched for her glass. She couldn't call Liz. Her cell likely lay on the warehouse floor somewhere. She flicked the switch, and the light lit over the table by the window. 8:13 p.m. Haddie grabbed her pants and shirt off the floor and ignored her thirst. She'd check the lobby first. Why would Liz just leave? *I shouldn't have fallen asleep.*

She still felt exhausted and needed something to bring down the swelling in her face. Hopefully, Liz sat quietly at a meal downstairs.

Hopping over as she pulled on her pants, Haddie went to her phone on the table. She stopped, fingers pinching the pants at her hips. *I didn't leave my phone there.*

A hotel notepad and pen sat beside it. Sliding her pants up, she sat at the chair and opened her phone. She didn't recognize the most recent phone number dialed, but it had a Eugene area code. Matt? That would make sense. Liz would wake up, perhaps more lucid, and try to find Matt.

Her text messages with Terry had been opened, or she'd left them open. He'd sent an image of the flyer for tonight's rave. *Liz saw this.* She'd been in such a fog. Did she even remember the escape? If not, she might not realize how dangerous it was.

Panic tightened Haddie's chest. She couldn't lose Liz after all they'd been through. Scrambling, she jumped up, grabbed her shirt, and yanked it over her head. How would Liz even get there? Haddie touched the lump her keys made in her pocket. Picking up the room's phone, she dialed the desk in the lobby.

"Front desk, Nicholas, how can I help?"

"Did Liz order a taxi?" She took a breath. "Did my roommate order a taxi from room 311?"

"Uh, yeah. Probably an hour ago." He grunted. "I think they're gone already."

"Damn." Haddie hung up the phone. As she shoved the key card in her pocket, she heard her phone vibrate on the table.

Sam sent a picture of a puppy. Haddie almost closed it

without a thought before she recognized her room at Dad's garage. He'd gotten Meg a puppy. Smart. Haddie closed the thread and realized she'd missed texts from Sam and Dad; she opened Dad's.

"Check in with me. Been a while." He'd texted over an hour ago.

Haddie sighed and typed, "We slept. Liz left, looking for her boyfriend. I'm headed out to look for her now. Again." She sent it and then realized he'd worry. "I'll text you when I get to the rave."

Sliding the phone into her pocket, she ran for the door. The corridor seemed busier than earlier in the afternoon, and she had to wait for the elevator. A rising dread scrambled her thoughts. She cursed Liz for not knowing better than to go alone, and herself for not being awake to dissuade her.

She rode down with a large man in a red and pink striped shirt. He had a salesman's smile even when he cringed at the sight of her. He stood as tall as she and made a show of letting her off the elevator first. He didn't have to offer; Haddie planned on running to her car. Liz had a short lead on her. If she could get there before the rave started, it might be as simple as slipping in and out. She might even worry about Liz's boyfriend this time, just so they could get on the road and get back to Eugene.

In the middle of the lobby, Haddie came to a stop midstride.

At the front desk, two men talked to a young male attendant. The first had a scraggly black beard, dark skin, and a yellow glow about his face. The second wore a tired thin face but had glowing orange eyes.

Her blood chilled. They argued with the employee, seeming to grow annoyed and frustrated. They hadn't seen her, but it couldn't be coincidence. A demon and a man with whatever the yellow glow indicated had attacked her at the rave, and now, there were two more at her hotel.

The large man from the elevator passed, and as he blocked her view of the two men, he gave her an odd look. Still, he smiled.

Haddie blinked and then jumped to keep up with the man's bulk. She crouched a little. He gave her some cover, but if they looked over, they still might spot her. Her heart raced as she approached the front doors of the hotel.

They'll turn and see me. She expected the demon to slough off his human skin and begin killing, or for them to spot her and begin a chase. Her body ached despite the sleep. She couldn't imagine handling the pain that using her power would cause. She would, though, if it came to it.

The large man opened the front door with a practiced smile and paused, giving her a nod. "Ma'am." He had a Texas accent.

The demon and the man had never noticed her. As she slipped outside, Haddie whispered, "Thanks."

Cars rambled down the street, but she dodged carefully through them to get to the opposite sidewalk. The humidity had dropped, but the heat remained.

The two men still worked on the young attendant who had a tight expression, possibly nervousness. The man with the yellow haze motioned to his hair, as though describing. *White hair.* Then he gestured up, perhaps commenting on her height. She needed to take Dad's advice. Color her hair or at least consider a wig. How had they tracked her?

The attendant's eyes turned up from the counter and he found her quickly, as though he'd followed her departure.

Haddie stood stupidly on the opposite sidewalk, gawking. The few other pedestrians had been streaming about her as if she were a lamppost.

The man with the scraggly beard and yellow haze turned to look out the window, searching her out.

Damn. Haddie jumped and started running toward the lot and her car. She couldn't help but turn her head to watch them.

The yellow-hazed man yelled, causing the attendant to pull back wide-eyed.

Her pursuers were out the hotel doors in a second. Pedestrians parted as they pushed through. A car sounded its horn and brake lights flared.

Haddie heard a man's exclamation just before she barreled him over. She spun to the side and caught a glimpse of a black shirt and jeans floundering on the pavement and a black cap rolling across the pavement. "Sorry!"

"Ms. Dawson?" Special Agent Wilkins approached down the sidewalk. She had a concerned expression. She had rich brown skin, dark eyes, tight black curls, and round, gentle features. Dressed in a black suit, she wore a blue and gray striped tie.

Haddie froze. What is she doing here? *How did she find me?*

She whipped around, ignoring the man sitting on the ground, and searched the traffic for her pursuers.

The demon jumped past a car, his glowing eyes sharp in the night. She needed to keep running, past Wilkins.

"Ms. Dawson, are you looking for Harold Holmes?" Wilkins blocked her path.

The man she'd knocked over had pushed himself to his knees. Glaring and swearing, he reached for his hat.

Haddie moved to slide past. "This isn't a good time."

Wilkins reached out to stop her. "What is going on

here? What happened to your face?" The woman held her hand in front of Haddie, not wanting her to pass.

The pursuers were only a few paces from her. "I'm being chased." Haddie gestured wildly at the two men. The demon had a clear path up the sidewalk, and the yellow-hazed man dodged between antagonized cars. She wasn't sure what she expected Wilkins to do, but didn't the FBI carry weapons? She remembered the scientist's advice — he'd been right. "You have to shoot it in the head. Other wounds won't stop it."

"What?"

Haddie pushed the woman's hand away and started squeezing between her and the building. Panic overrode Haddie's surprise at the FBI's presence.

A gunshot rang in the street, and the bullet ricocheted off the bricks beside her head. She jerked down into a crouch. Sucking in a ragged breath, she shifted behind Wilkins. The agent pulled back her jacket on the right, as if to reach for a gun.

A woman far behind had begun a long piercing scream. Some pedestrians ran; a woman in green had fallen near the curb, frozen.

Between the wall and the side of Wilkin's left arm, Haddie locked eyes with the demon. *Orange eyes*. Its skin and clothing had begun to slough off like sludge, leaving an impossible form. It was just like last winter in the ski gondola with Liz.

The demon had two flabby ridges of thick, ruddy flesh left over the eyes and a mouth that distorted to the side in a voiceless scream. Three or four strides away, it leapt for Haddie as she tried to hide between the wall and Wilkins. It only had two black-nailed fingers at the end of a seemingly boneless arm.

Wilkins stepped back brusquely, sending Haddie to her butt and palms. Skidding on the pavement, she saw the agent's arm raised in the air with a gun as the woman grappled with the monstrosity. "Run!" Wilkins yelled — likely to her. However, the man with the black cap took the advice first.

Other pedestrians stood frozen. Some, screaming, ran from them. Cars honked and continued down the road, oblivious to the struggle. The woman in a green T-shirt sat on the sidewalk nearby, staring at the demon. She should run.

A second shot shattered a brick beside Haddie's face. Surprised, she felt a hot shard splinter into her jaw, just under her left ear. She could smell heat.

The man with the yellow haze skittered to a stance in the gutter and aimed a small gray gun at her head. He wouldn't miss from barely three steps away.

She would die if she didn't move. Haddie lurched into a roll before he fired. The gunshot shook the air. Her hair tugged. She could smell the gunpowder.

Her jump rolled her toward the man. Dirt from the sidewalk pressed into the sweat on her face. A disorienting view spun around her.

The woman in the green shirt had begun crawling. Wilkins had crumpled to the ground. She struggled with the flailing demon. Losing, it seemed. Her black suit had been slashed at the shoulder. It looked wet.

Haddie slammed into the legs of the man with the yellow haze. She hoped he'd fall. Feral and frantic, she grappled with his legs. His pants smelled sour with old sweat. She waited for his next shot. Pressing her weight against him, she got a fist behind his knee.

His body finally crumpled. She'd gotten him off balance.

Haddie flinched as a deafening shot went off. *So close.* She waited for pain. The screams all around them stifled to a distant buzz outside of the ringing. She held onto his legs as he fell.

Tires screeched.

His body jerked, nearly out of her arms.

For a foot, Haddie dragged with the body. She could make out the dark blue door panel of a car beside her. Fumes, heat, and oil wafted around her.

The shooter didn't struggle anymore.

With her face pressed against his pants, she took a quick breath. She needed to run. *Move.* She shook when she scrambled up to a knee.

The man lay along the gutter, his yellow haze gone. Flowing blood painted the right side of his face. Somehow, he'd fallen headfirst into the passing car. No, she'd pushed him into it. *I killed him.* His face was mangled, cheek flattened, and the eye looked askew. She'd done this. An empty candy wrapper fluttered against the side of his face that hadn't been crushed.

Even without rain, the asphalt felt wet and slimy. Something, not his blood, smeared under her palm. She could smell his blood. *Leave.* She wanted to puke.

The woman in green crawled away.

Haddie wanted to hide. *No, get up — run away.*

A weight slammed her into the car door. Haddie brought her right arm around and felt the clammy, flabby skin of the demon. Her left shoulder was pinned against the door, and her neck bent at an awkward angle against the weight; she tried to get leverage against the creature. She tasted a foul slime on her tongue.

The demon stuck two piercing nails into the top of her left shoulder. Not deep, but painful.

Hot, rotting breath panted against her face. The lopsided mouth didn't attempt to bite, but it hung just over her eye.

It's going to kill me. She pushed, and her hand sunk deeper into straining muscles. No bones.

The creature's nails raked out painfully. The face moved back as the creature lifted its boneless arm back for another strike.

Her neck felt exposed. With her left arm pinned under her back and hips, her right arm could do nothing but press frantically against the demon's flaccid, yielding side. *I'm not going to die here.* Enraged, she squirmed.

The claw whipped toward her.

Haddie screamed. The tone seemed to come from somewhere far away, rising, bursting through her.

The creature faded away; its flesh blew into the past like soft mud under a hard rain. The last bit, a glowing yellow medallion at its neck, winked out.

She imagined that the slime she'd felt had been its residue. A gasp stuck in her throat. Nausea couldn't compete with the pain that raced through her. Her skin seemed to explode. Her fingers felt as though her skin had burst open. Her lips tightened as if prickling needles laced over her face. her shoulder and spine, twisted against the car, flared in searing heat. Her body yielded, and she slid down to land atop the man's legs.

The world faded from darkness to a glaring hot, sunlit day. Fat-leafed trees rose around her, and pain flared from behind. A knife tip protruded from her soldier's jacket, and she saw a drop of blood fall from its the tip. She bellowed. The knife disappeared.

Darkness. A gun flash through the jungle. There were bodies dropping beside her. Hot metal in her leg. She bellowed. Silence. Darkness.

The nightmares faded, and her eyes adjusted to the Portland street outside Liz's hotel.

Wilkins lay on the street, her arm outstretched, pointing her gun above Haddie. Perhaps it had been aimed at the demon's head a moment before. Blood oozed from the woman's torn ear. Her free hand covered the tear on her shoulder. She mouthed a word. Or possibly, she spoke, but the ringing in Haddie's ears was too loud. Had she said "run" — or something else?

Haddie scrambled up, moaning — whimpering — at the pain in her elbows and knees. Were there more? She had only seen the man and the demon. Her hands shook.

Wilkins folded her arm, brought the gun to her chest, and seemed to be trying to rise. Again, she spoke what seemed a single word.

Haddie stumbled away, in the direction of her car. The woman in green had finally gotten to her feet and run. Haddie hunched; she glanced around, waiting for another attack.

One man had stopped in the street, blocking traffic. Standing at the edge of his car door, he fumbled with his phone.

She had only seen two pursuing her, but imagined Wilkins had been telling her to run. What if that wasn't what the agent had said? *Then, I'm running from a crime scene.* One where she'd thrown a man into traffic and exposed her powers against a demon.

Passing the woman in green who stopped to gape back toward Wilkins, Haddie dodged into a thicker group of people. Some focused their cell phones on the fallen agent.

Behind her, the woman in green plowed through the unwary. Like Haddie, she ran for her life.

Haddie felt sick. Her skin, throbbing, felt moist when she rubbed her lips. Red slime smeared across her hand. She couldn't stop. Her legs wobbled from pain and terror.

People at the crosswalk stared at her, and then turned to hurry toward the disturbance farther down the street. Gawking, they headed toward Wilkins.

The agent had to be okay, with a small gash in her shoulder maybe, unless her injury was more severe or there were others pursuing Haddie.

I killed a man. The police would be looking for her. She would have to face them and eventually Wilkins. There would be no hiding this. First, she'd get to Liz, get her free again. Then, she'd deal with whatever the police and the FBI came up with. *How?*

Stumbling, she spotted the RAV4 and veered toward it. How had the yellow-hazed man and the demon known where she was? The FBI she expected it from. Dad had always made comments. They could have tracked her phone for all she knew.

None of that mattered. If the people who ran the raves sent a demon and the yellow-hazed man after her, then Liz could be in more trouble than Haddie imagined. Anger welled up, at them and at Liz for running off.

As she started the car, Haddie caught a glimpse of her pink hair in the mirror.

Pink.

She rubbed the red slime off her face. She raised her eyebrows, realizing she'd always imagined that her power pushed people, and creatures, back in time. Ever since Dmitry, Harold Holmes' brother. She'd seen his misty ghost for a couple minutes before she used her power on him.

Tonight, during the struggle, she'd been lying for a moment in the same spot, before her song had pushed the demon, molecules perhaps, back in time. He'd been misting down onto her during her fight.

Haddie opened the car door and puked onto the asphalt.

CHAPTER 30

Liz passed the twenties to the cabbie and waited for her change. The front seat smelled strongly of garlic and she felt her hunger rising.

An older black man made the change while looking around the desolate parking lot and three-story warehouse. "Are you sure about the address? Looks pretty empty. One car in the entire lot."

Liz tried to smile, though it probably came out more of a grimace. "I'll be fine, thank you."

It did look empty, but maybe she was too early. The air hadn't cooled by the time she arrived; humid summer air made her appreciate the thin T-shirt. Her nerves had her sweating in the cool air of the taxi. More and more of the past few days had been trickling into her memory, and she was confused by the constant, sometimes vicious party that she never would have been a part of, but couldn't have left at the time. What drove them to stay?

She'd smoked on occasion, and experimented in high school, but had never just eaten random pills off the floor. Who knew what was in her system? She barely remembered Haddie bringing her to the hotel. She'd been hallucinating from the drugs. Monsters and a broken windshield. She should have left a note for Haddie.

The white warehouse had two or three floors, and the windows at the side were confusing. Red awnings covered the windows and the front doors. It didn't look like a rave, but she had never been to one, until this trip, and couldn't remember the other buildings. Hopefully, Matt was here and safe. Then, she could get him out of here and kill him for all this.

Taking a deep breath, she hobbled toward the main entrance. The building looked closed with dark hallways. Her tension rose as she tried the door and found it open.

"Hello?"

It smelled musty, unused. She could hear a distant throb in the back somewhere. Music. Well, she had come to the right place after all.

Her eyes adjusted and she shuffled straight, hoping there would be an entrance in the darkness. Matt better not give her any trouble about leaving. They had to leave. This ranked high as her worst outing ever with a new boyfriend. Some of the memories scared her. They might have to cool down a while after this, talk some things out. Violence she couldn't handle.

"Follow me."

Liz's arms jerked out to the sides in surprise as she stopped. Even looking in the direction of the voice, she couldn't make out any features. A reflection off his eyes, a darker shape against shadowy, brown walls.

"You scared me. I —"

He'd already started walking, leading her in the same direction she'd been heading. If he hadn't said anything, she would have passed right by him. She looked back at the light of the door, partly considering running in fright, and partially to see if she'd passed anyone else.

She followed. When he opened the door, light bathed him in silhouette. He was tall and had a solid build.

Inside a large bay, a neon diamond hung from the ceiling, and she remembered it. A ragged group danced underneath. Some jolted around, while most lumbered as if half asleep. It felt familiar and inviting.

A sickly, sour miasma hung in the room. Dance music beat low from all sides. Liz moved toward the dancers.

The man grabbed her arm with a firmness that inflamed her bruises. "This way."

"That hurts." She tried to pull away, but he had a firm grip and the muscle hurt.

He ignored her, dragging her down the side and past a pair of doors. *Where's Matt?* Four or five dozen bodies writhed in a tight mass, despite the size of the floor. Some looked familiar. A man in a white suit stood in the center, unmoving.

Emotionless men stood along the sides. Metal stairs climbed the back wall to the right; under it, a door led out the back. Liz could see windows at the top looking down onto the open bay. The glass was reflective, so she could only see a couple dim shapes.

He pushed her ahead on the steps and reached around to open the door when they came to the top.

Inside, a tall woman stood at the window staring down. She had long blonde hair, nearly white, and wore a high-collared, black and purple dress with long sleeves. White gloves on her hands held an almost empty champagne glass. The neon diamond hung directly ahead, flashing its myriad colors.

Beside her waited a black German shepherd, large

enough to be a wolf. It had turned its head to glare at Liz. A gold medallion hung at its collar.

Three women in white gowns sat against the far wall working on laptops, adding much of the light to the room. They ignored Liz. A fourth stood at a podium with a writing board and pen. She wore the same white gown, standing just behind the tall woman, and watched Liz intently.

Everything about the room screamed strange to Liz, and she had difficulty breathing.

The man pushed her inside. He closed the door behind them and stood waiting beside her.

The tall woman turned and studied Liz. She wore white face paint as a base with rainbows spraying across her forehead. Sparkling colors shot from under her eyes. Her cheeks had been darkened to give a gaunt look to her face. Red lipstick glittered.

"Elizabeth Backhus. It is a pleasure to meet you. You've brought us quite a surprising and delightful treasure. I hope she'll be joining us soon." The accent sounded Indian.

"Who —?" Liz stopped as the man beside her stiffened.

The woman shook her head slightly. "She doesn't understand the protocol here." She tilted her head with a shrug. "Doesn't really matter, or it won't soon. I call myself Sameedha, but you might think of me as Penumbra."

She flowed over to a table, her gown dragging across the floor. The woman with the writing board rolled the pedestal behind her. Bizarre.

Sameedha raised her phone. "Do you know why I can't reach my men? Did your friend dispose of them? Is she that good?"

"Who? Haddie?" Why had she assumed Haddie, not Matt?

A smile creased the woman's face paint. "Haddie. A name. How delightful. What a helpful girl you are." She sipped down the last of her champagne. "I imagine she'll be here soon."

Liz blushed. *What is going on? Haddie?* She couldn't be sure what just happened, or what issue this woman had with Haddie, but she felt she'd made a mistake.

The woman with the writing board scratched on it with a pen. Another woman, dressed similarly, had been kneeling unnoticed to Liz's left. She stood, uncorked a champagne bottle, and poured a glass for Sameedha. The heavy bottle clanked as the woman dropped it into a garbage can along with the tall woman's empty glass.

Liz stared at waste, yearning somewhere deep inside. Whatever insanity went on at these raves, Liz wanted no part of it. They couldn't make her. She stiffened and took in a deep breath. "I'm just here to get Matt."

The man beside her grabbed her arm painfully. Liz sucked in a breath.

"You'll be joining him shortly. He's downstairs. We made sure." The edges of Sameedha's lips curled slightly.

Liz pulled at the man's hold. "I just want to leave, with Matt. No trouble."

"No — you don't." The woman smiled lightly, took a sip, and a familiar music rang in Liz's ears.

She remembered the feeling. Craving, elation, revelry. The beat of the music from downstairs thumped in her chest and she imagined swaying to it. She suddenly felt a driving thirst and stared at the glass in Sameedha's hand. She remembered the bottle that the serving woman had thrown away, nearly full. The man had to use both hands to restrain her.

"Elizabeth, you don't really want to leave before all the

fun, do you? You would rather go downstairs, find something to drink, and dance with Matt. That's what you want
to do, isn't it?"

Drinks downstairs. Yes. Just have fun. Enjoy. "Yes."

Beautiful Sameedha laughed like tinkling glass. "Bring
her down to Anthony, he'll entertain her while we wait. Oh,
and tell everyone to prepare for our guest."

CHAPTER 31

HADDIE CRIED AS SHE DROVE.

Each corner she turned, she expected the police to pull in behind her. A man jogging along the sidewalk could be a demon racing toward her. Portland seemed dark and dangerous. The RAV4 stunk from the thin film of slime that covered her. The crack in the windshield had grown, webbing toward the middle. She ached from every joint, and her fingers tingled painfully on the wheel. The nail holes in her shoulder had barely bled, but they stung.

Somehow, the man she'd pushed into traffic felt more like murder than Dmitry or the guard shooting at them when she escaped with Liz. It had been self-defense — she'd told herself more than once. Still, he lay in that gutter, face deformed from the car. She'd pushed him. It had all happened so fast.

Wilkins had found her in Portland, and the agent had nearly died because of it. The FBI would never understand demons or powers like her own. She tried to formulate lies to tell them. Nothing would hide what had happened outside the hotel. Wilkins had seen it all. All because the agent thought Haddie still searched for Harold Holmes. What could Haddie possibly explain? She barely understood any of it herself.

The people who ran the raves had found her at the hotel. They had to know about Liz. *Is that how they found me?* Had they tortured Liz? Haddie's jaw tightened. She shouldn't blame Liz for going back for Matt, but she did. *I should have made the call to the police.* Liz would still have gone.

The car's screen displayed a text from Terry. She hit read. "I'm worried. Are you okay?"

She didn't have time to worry about Terry. Still, she'd shoot him a quick text when she stopped. According to the map on her phone, her destination lay up the street on the right. She drove through an industrial area that had more trees than expected. Passing under a streetlight, she could see a black Chevy Tahoe parked near the entrance right where she would be turning in.

A light glowed in the window of the SUV. A yellow haze.

Haddie drove by steadily, careful not to glance at the two men who sat there. Her pulse rose. She sucked a breath into her tight chest. They didn't follow.

She didn't pull into the next parking lot on the right; only a short hedge and some sparse trees blocked the two lots. Instead, she drove past a long building to her left painted dark green on the first floor and white on the upper. Haddie watched her rearview mirror. She pulled into an empty lot to the left. The back had a closed gate and a handful of parking spots on the right. Glass windows covered this side of the building. They were dark, so perhaps they were offices.

She pulled to the gate and then backed into a parking

spot out of sight from the men guarding the entrance. Her pulse pounded in her ears. *Are they waiting for me?* They might expect Haddie to come back for Liz again. A trap. No, they had been looking for her at the hotel.

She turned off the RAV4 and she picked up her phone to respond to Terry. Tell him what? *I'm fine - just running in to steal Liz from some demons?* She opened her messages and saw new ones from Dad and Terry. She'd missed calls as well.

Terry's were not short.

"So. It seems that billionaire Anthony Prizer isn't a billionaire anymore. Made some flimsy property deals in South America and India. His net worth is plummeting. All connected to Indian companies. There's a bunch of theories."

"Boards have lit up about hellish creatures racing around. A pic too, could be faked. Just happens to be near that address of the rave you were investigating. Did you see anything? All good?"

"?"

"Worried. Haven't heard from you in a couple hours. The boards are nuts about this demon thing. You were in the same area . . . Just let me know."

"Half the day without hearing back from you. Assuming something wrong. Checking police and hospitals. Don't make me find your dad."

"Just got a DM from a Dr. Aaron. Says he knows you and wants your number. About the demons."

Haddie raised her eyebrows. The scientist from the ski lift? He'd known about the demons before her. Of course he'd follow any discussions about them. How had he connected with Terry? She quickly skimmed the last two messages; the last had come in while she drove.

"I left a voicemail. Seriously trying to find your dad's number."

"I'm worried. Are you okay?"

Haddie peered into the darkness, making sure no yellow hazes or orange eyes had followed her to the parking lot. Then, she dialed Terry. She could imagine what his voicemail sounded like.

"Haddie." He'd answered immediately. "Where are you?"

"Portland. I'm okay." She stopped, just short of touching her hair. Tilting, she could see in the mirror that it had turned pinkish brown.

"What's going on?" he asked. The question held an admonishment as well as curiosity.

Haddie sucked in a breath. She'd left Terry out of the Harold Holmes situation, though he'd asked some odd questions. He believed she'd had a skiing accident last winter with Liz. She hadn't wanted to drag him into her problems. Ever. Not to mention, she doubted he could resist comments on the forums. She'd have to work around telling him, but she needed help. She sighed. "What have you found out about these — this demon?"

"More than I believe. Some believe they're government super soldiers gone wrong. The usual Apocalypse prophecy. The Portland pic that got posted has disappeared; they always do. But it could easily be a photoshop. I've got a copy. It —" he paused. She could hear him taking a sip through a straw. "It's just that it happened near the address I gave you. I was freaking. Thought I killed you."

Haddie nodded, still watching the guarded building. She had a view of the side. When would the ravers show up? None of the usual conspiracies helped her. Somehow, the demons were involved with or worked for the people who put on the raves. Demons for hire?

"Oh," Terry sounded excited. "We've got someone who went down and looked for the demon. I didn't say anything, but the warehouse, the address I gave you, the police have it locked down tonight. Cordoned off. The pictures are too dark — from cell phones. When I heard that, well I freaked. I got your dogwalker's number, Sam."

Haddie waited as Terry paused.

He spoke a little slower, almost meekly. "I might have just texted her that I couldn't get hold of you, and that I was worried. She might have freaked, a little. Sorry."

Haddie swore. No wonder Dad had been calling. "Tell her I'm fine. Just looking for Liz."

"And Dr. Aaron?" Terry sounded relieved that she didn't go off on him.

"How do you know him?"

He swallowed audibly. "Well, I mean, he's been a constant in these demon groups. A bit of a fanatic. But I got worried, and asked if anyone had seen a friend of mine around this sighting. He messaged me immediately and started demanding that I put him in touch with you. Said he knew you from last winter. That was the ski trip, right?"

Terry had posted a description of her in the forums. It didn't matter. The fight outside the hotel had to have attracted some attention, though she'd had pink hair part of the time. She opened her mouth, about to ask Terry if he'd heard anything about the fight outside the hotel, and stopped.

Wilkins would be after her shortly. The FBI wouldn't just let something like this go. She'd killed someone, no matter the circumstances.

"Haddie?"

"Huh?" She stared at the building where the rave would be happening. She needed to find Liz. Get past those guards.

"What about Dr. Aaron? Do you want me to give him your number?"

She did want to know about the demons. He'd been suspicious of her and her powers, and had disappeared right after the fight. "Yes."

He paused and she could hear him typing. "So what's going on? Still haven't found Liz? I mean, this could be serious. The more I look, the worse it gets. Missing people, on top of the suicides. One mom swears her son is in a mental hospital because of these raves."

That sounded about right. Whatever the song did, she could imagine it driving her crazy. "I'm about to go into the rave now. I'm hoping to get Liz out. I'll let you know."

"You're alone?"

"Yes." She'd rather have Dad with her.

She peered at the building where the rave would be. If the guards were looking for her, likely considering the attack at the hotel, then she'd have to scout for a back way in. Before, she'd planned on walking in as if going to the rave, then scoop up Liz — and Matt.

"Maybe you should just call the police."

She thought of a swat team facing down demons or the fanatical yellow-hazed men, with Liz in the middle. "Not yet." This needed to be quiet. She looked into the mirror at the spray of pinkish brown covering the right side of her hair and leaving a shock of white down the left side of her face. *Not very stealthy, Haddie.* Maybe she had a hoodie in the back from last winter.

"When?"

Call the police? Haddie raised her eyebrows. It couldn't

hurt to have a backup plan. Though, if it came to that, she'd probably end up in jail herself. She looked at the time: 9:22 p.m.

"If you don't hear from me, can you make an anonymous report around 11:30?"

"Anonymous is just my style." Some of Terry's usual cheery tone rebounded. He dropped back to a serious note. "How much about this are you going to tell me after?"

Haddie swallowed. He'd known how little she'd said about Harold Holmes. They avoided the topic now. She didn't want to lie to him, but some of it he wouldn't believe. She couldn't accept half of it herself. "We'll see."

"Fair enough, Buckaroo. Good luck."

Haddie hung up, feeling her emotions sag to nearly tears. Terry was a good friend. Like Liz. They'd taken all the unusual mystery, the lies, and still been there for her. She felt dirty for hiding everything from them. What else could she do? Most of it she couldn't explain even to herself. She'd thought Dad insane when he tried.

Liz needed her. Haddie couldn't imagine what had been going on inside the building, but Liz had come here looking for Matt. She couldn't know the danger she put herself in. At least Haddie understood the risk. A little more rest, and she might have been in better shape for it.

She groaned opening the door, and her hips threatened to fail as she got out of the RAV4. Hopefully there'd be a dark hoodie in the back.

PART 6

Our nine, the Noveilm, lost our youngest, Makabetza, before we founded our kingdoms.

CHAPTER 32

THOMAS WALKED out the office of his garage. Clouds hid any stars, but the air didn't smell of rain, just of grease and petroleum. Still, he could make out the dark silhouettes of the mountains sleeping on the horizon. Here, in Goshen, they didn't have the immediate majesty of some that he had lived beside, but they were a comfort. For the mountains alone, he'd moved to Lom, Norway across multiple identities and considered moving back.

Biff waited for him in the cab of the idling truck. He preened his hair in the rearview mirror and checked his teeth.

Haddie had found and lost Liz. All over a boyfriend. Not surprising. Whatever Haddie's friend had gotten herself involved with didn't seem like the usual mishaps that young people got into.

His former self, his first identity, would probably be in Boone, North Carolina right about now. The exact dates were a bit fuzzy after so many centuries. No, maybe the rally is next month. Either way, he'd made plenty of trouble for himself at that age.

He grunted, sliding into the cab, and shoved his thermos into the console. "Let's do this."

Biff shifted into gear and they lurched across the parking lot. "Where is she?"

Thomas absently grabbed the charger line as he pulled out his phone and plugged it in. He opened the app and connected to the equipment hidden under Haddie's car. She wouldn't have appreciated him tracking her, but after Harold Holmes, he'd taken precautions. The map loaded. "She's driving. No, it looks like she's parked. Still in Portland." He minimized it and texted her again, "Call me."

"They're probably having a good time. No reason to go crashing down the bedroom door." Biff smirked. He knew better, and hadn't hesitated to head over for what might end up an all-night mission. Likely, he still remembered the night he'd picked them up from Harold Holmes.

"Liz. That's the cute professor, right?"

Thomas rubbed back his hair and sighed. "She's got a boyfriend." Maybe not after this adventure. Some people you didn't know until they got a few drinks in them.

Biff turned, likely leering. "Not the job I'd be applying for."

Thomas watched the traffic ahead. They had a couple of hours to drive, and Biff would do most of the talking. One of the reasons he liked a bike was less talk. It would help keep his mind off Haddie, though. She usually responded to texts unless she'd gotten pissed over something. Hell. He didn't like this. He hadn't liked leaving her in Portland to come back for Meg.

At least Meg seemed settled. He'd need to watch Sam, to make sure the woman didn't get too curious. They both seemed focused on the pup for now. It had been a good idea. Meg had nearly smiled.

He insisted that they bring the pup to Meg's room at the garage. They'd been fine with it, and Sam had been there to get the dog settled in. It had worked out when he decided to return to Portland. Sam offered to spend the night with Meg, as long as she could get dropped back to her apartment in the morning. He hoped it wouldn't take that long to help Haddie.

The entire situation left a bad taste in his mouth. He'd been to some pretty wild parties and festivals, some of which had turned violent. This one just felt wrong.

"You got the kid a puppy. Garage trained?"

Thomas grunted. Biff hadn't been there but a couple months before Haddie and Rock moved to college. Most dogs did well in a garage, with a little training.

It had taken Biff longer to acclimate than Rock. Thomas had seen Biff around a couple times before he got clean. For some reason, Thomas had taken him under his wing and cleared up some of the misunderstandings with the authorities and a bike club in Nevada. Biff had been called Slo Jack back then. Now, he had a fresh identity and a new start. Thomas could understand that. And Biff didn't ask questions. Not serious ones, at least.

CHAPTER 33

Haddie found a patch of dirt and began rubbing the brown and white Peruvian chullo into the dirt, darkening the whites. Wearing a bright, patterned hat to cover her white and pink hair wouldn't help.

She stuffed her hair inside and tied the dangling tassels under her chin. "This is insane, Haddie." As she stood up, the ball in the back bounced annoyingly.

Across the street, on the same side as the rave, stood another warehouse with plenty of greenery. The bordering parking lot extended deep into the back. Hopefully, it would give her enough cover to slip down the side and come into the rave from the rear door. Gratefully, she'd worn dark clothes this morning. It seemed days since she'd had coffee with her dad while Meg, Sam, and Rock played.

Behind the rave where the men guarded, a fenced-in lot would be one of her only obstacles. She'd grabbed a towel in case there was barbed wire, but she imagined her aching joints were her biggest problem. The idea of climbing a fence in her condition exhausted her. Taking a deep breath, she bundled the tan towel under her arm and started across the lot.

The windowless warehouse on the other side of the street had a garden of bushes at the corner exposed to the guards. It looked as though she could make it behind those and never be visible. Crossing the street, even this lot, would expose her directly to the guards. Hopefully, they were watching the other direction where traffic would arrive.

Her heart pounding, she walked straight across the street, not too fast, not too slow, and not looking in their direction. A streetlamp lit the area, and she kept to the dimmest edge, farthest from the guards.

Her phone vibrated and she twitched, swearing. Don't look. What if Liz hadn't come here? Went out for tacos? Without a purse. Still, Haddie hit the yellow wall of the warehouse where the bushes blocked the guard's car and dug for her phone; an unknown number texted. She didn't recognize the area code.

"Haddie. This is Aaron. We've met over the snow," the text read.

Dr. Aaron Knox. She stared for a moment. Aaron was the scientist, who she remembered as tall and handsome, if a bit sheepish. His statement sounded like a code.

Haddie imagined he couldn't be sure he'd been given the right number, or that she had her phone. She raised her eyebrows; she didn't really have time for this, but he also might have information she needed. There could be more demons inside the rave.

"High above," she texted. Hopefully, that would be enough.

It seemed to work. "Your friend mentioned you are in the vicinity of a sighting? What can you tell me?"

"I don't have time. Another friend, who you met in the snow, might be in trouble. She's in a building where I'm afraid there might be," she paused, not wanting to worry through codes, "demons."

Aaron texted, "Just call the police. The FBI if you want. Don't go in there alone."

Haddie imagined a swat team firing at a demon bearing down on them. Their last concern would be over a mob of drugged out losers on the dance floor.

"Why do you call them demons?" she typed. She'd gotten the term from him. It certainly fit.

"The first sighting, in DC, got reported to the boards by someone with a religious bias. It stuck. After my first encounter, and subsequent research, I simply adopted their terminology. I have no better frame of reference to use. Perhaps, you might?"

Haddie nodded to herself. Had she expected a divine implication? She ached to know more, just not right now. Liz needed her help.

"What are they?" she texted.

"I don't know," he replied.

He had to know something. Her lips tightened, frustrated. "I've got to go. I'll call you after. I have a lot of questions."

"I have questions about you as well. If you survive, text me."

His last sentence didn't help calm the tightening in her chest as she prepared to sneak into another lair where a yellow-hazed man guarded out front. It was unlikely to be any easier inside than the last, but she couldn't imagine a better option.

Down the front of the windowless building, bushes had been planted out from a decorative awning and wrapped around the corner, leaving plenty of room to sneak behind. She would be able to catch a glimpse of their car at points, but only if she tried.

No other cars had shown up; the front lot remained empty except for the guards. She worked her way to the side, along the windows and the heavily planted entrance to the building. She felt sure that no one saw her as she made her way to a back corner.

Leaning over, hands on her knees, she stood beside a pungent green shrub with small leaves and stiff branches. Mosquitoes found her. Her hands had turned nearly black with all the purpura; she tried to ignore both as she waved the bugs away.

Ahead of her, a barren lot led to the fence behind the rave. Of course, it had barbed wire. The gate, facing the front and more exposed to the guards, stood half the height, even with the wire. She frowned and crouched, scurrying toward the higher fence. A small hedge between the lots protected her. Hopefully. She'd used her powers three times already, and her body felt like she'd been run over. She ached so badly it didn't feel like she stooped low enough. Being nearly six foot tall made it more difficult.

Four truck containers were parked on the far side of the back lot. Three sedans and a silver SUV sat in the parking spots at the back of the building. There was no glimpse of a yellow haze in any of them, but that didn't mean there weren't people sitting there, watching. Haddie veered left toward the back of the fence.

She set the towel over her shoulder and climbed. Her knuckles complained the worst, threatening to stay locked around the stiff wire. She felt exposed as she twisted the towel around the barbed wire at the top. Sweating and cursing all insect life, she stepped onto the wire, holding onto the towel-wrapped section with both hands. Hips and knees complained, but she climbed to the top.

Her dismount failed. She swung a leg over, but the same fingers that had refused to disengage slipped off the cloth. She dropped sideways and hit a bush that looked far fluffier than it actually was. Branches dug into her thigh, and her hip twisted as she rolled into the mulch. She lay there for a moment, snuffing in bugs, and stared at the freight containers. Three were colored in various stages of rust red, and one was white.

I am horrible at sneaking. Even in D&D, she'd rather charge into the melee with an axe than sneak around with a bow. A bow would be nice, right about now. Nope. An axe. She could feel blood where the branch had stabbed her.

She groaned. *I forgot to text David.* She wouldn't be texting any time soon.

Haddie shifted, the ball of her hat under her cheek. No one ran out of the cars parked in the back. No guns blazed. No demons. She groaned as she pushed herself up from the ground. She crawled to her feet, trying to use an underfed bush for support.

The back of the building had a door directly in front of the parked cars. The freight containers took up the spaces near the dumpster and would give her cover. A canopy covered the area, and recycling bins lined the wall. A section of the warehouse jutted out on the corner farthest from her. The dumpster sat behind a privacy fence, and a dim shape gave her a hint of a door in the wall beyond.

Haddie worked her way along the back fence, her eyes locked on the parked cars. At the corner she walked through bushes, hugging the fence. The lack of trees made it seem more exposed, but no light made it through the blanket of clouds above. The dumpster reeked that particular smell that each one seems to have.

She leaned around the privacy fence to watch the cars. The back of a dark blue Lancer blocked the other sedans, and the silver SUV stuck out enough that she could see the driver's window. Dashing, she hit the wall of the building and pressed against it.

Her heart beat faster than she realized until she tried to listen; her breaths came too loud. She swallowed, waiting for the sound of a car door to close or footsteps.

A white plastic gate, unlocked, stood beside her at the corner of the building. If she'd come in from the other side, she could have walked in.

She could still call the police and wait from her hiding place by the dumpster. No, it put Liz in too much risk. Haddie had reverted to not caring what happened to Matt, except Liz might. She didn't wish ill of the man. Maybe a little.

Sidling along the wall, she came to the door. A chill flushed over her. Closing her eyes, she grabbed the handle and took a breath. *Please.*

It opened.

Haddie smiled, almost wanting to laugh.

A boot kicked the door out of her hand, whipping her tortured wrist out to her side. The man that followed wore black clothing. He punched at her face as soon as his right shoulder cleared.

Haddie shifted too slowly. The momentum of her arm had put her off balance.

His face wore a snarl, emphasizing a long thin nose. His fist grazed her opposite cheek. The one that hadn't swelled yet.

She jerked at his blow, a glancing impact that turned

her. She could smell him. He stunk of aftershave and sweat. Her left arm moved in defense, almost in a dance, but too late to stop his punch; it slammed inside his elbow.

The strike shifted him to the door frame. His eyes furrowed, as if angered.

Haddie spun with her turn, and his hips flared at the sudden movement. Driving her right elbow into his throat, she felt his head crack against the wall. Her knee followed a moment later, ramming everything he owned against the building.

She danced back. Behind her, she felt the branches of the vegetation loosely planted around the dumpster's fence. She'd used a move Dad had taught her, without a thought, instead of the taekwondo she'd been trained in.

The man slumped at the knees, sliding down the wall. Then his body sagged forward, and he landed face first in front of her.

Haddie sucked in ragged breaths. Eyes wide, she stared down into a dark hall, waiting for someone to come to his rescue. Exposed to the cars, she stood, breathing in and out.

No one came. No footsteps. Her cheekbone ached from the punch, and joints vied for what hurt worst.

They had guards out front; why wouldn't they have guards at the entrances? How many guards, though? What chance did she have of getting inside, grabbing Liz, maybe grabbing Matt, and getting back out? *I have to try*. She couldn't leave Liz until the police came shooting their way in. Haddie didn't even know if Liz hadn't been tortured. They'd figured out what hotel they stayed at. What did they have, a list of guests?

The man had a holster — with a gun. He could have just shot her in the face. She must have surprised him. He lay on the ground, face down with his back legs splayed like a frog.

Did I kill him? He's breathing. The back of his head shone wet with blood.

Haddie leaned down for his gun. She flinched when the ball of her hat swung around and tapped her cheek. Some model of a SIG. No safety. Full magazine. Dad had always said he found guns unreliable. Considering the power he had, she understood the statement better. Still, she didn't think she had enough left in her to attempt to use her power again. *I might need a gun.*

Stepping over the man, she held the gun and eased around the door frame. The dark hall only stretched a few paces before a door let in hazy light from the other side. A low beat thrummed in rhythmic dance music.

Haddie stepped into the hall and her phone vibrated. Her lips tightened, but it could be Liz. Her only real hope, if she had one.

Terry sent a photo at 9:51. It only took a second for her to recognize the scene. A mottled reddish demon wrestled with agent Wilkins against the wall in the center of the grainy picture where someone had zoomed in, likely with a cell phone. In the left corner, Haddie, a blob of pink hair, leaned against a blue sedan. They hadn't caught her face. Not in this picture.

CHAPTER 34

HADDIE FELT NAUSEOUS. She couldn't escape the consequences of the murder outside the hotel. Why Wilkins hadn't called baffled her. Would the agent call, demanding that Haddie turn herself in, or were they busy getting warrants? What would they do with her? Terry would imagine them dissecting her to figure out her powers.

None of it mattered at the moment. *Just get Liz out of here.*

The music thrummed inside.

At the end of the hall, colored light undulated from the crack under the door. Haddie took a step in, holding the gun down at her right side. She'd never been a good shot, even when she'd gone to the range every week during a freshman thing in college.

The rave, and Liz, were on the other side of the door ahead of her. Or, they had Liz locked in some closet like the madman at the first rave.

Haddie took another step. The light from the back door, albeit faint, would highlight her silhouette when she entered the rave. She returned, pushed the man's boot out of the way, and closed the door. Taking a deep breath, she started back down the hall, tracing the left wall with her hand and gun to the side. The weapon seemed to grow in weight; her wrist joints complained, and her fingers around the grip seemed stiff and weak.

Her left hand crossed a door frame, and she swept across the door until she found the knob. Inside, the darker room buzzed with electricity, and she could smell equipment. A trio of red lights flickered in the back, above her head height. She imagined it to be a utility room of some sort. A flashlight would be useful. Along with her lock-picking kit. She didn't plan on making this a habit.

The music volume suddenly escalated, causing her to jump and spin to her right. A pair of orange dots, so small they had to be distant, shone — through the wall. A demon. How could she see their eyes through walls? She hadn't seen them before, possibly because she had been focused on the slit of light under the door. The dots moved, giving her the sense of a head turning, until they joined as one as if she viewed its profile.

She swallowed. The darkness, terrifying in its own way, also felt comfortable and cloaking. Opening the door to the rave petrified her. *Liz. Focus.*

Haddie closed the utility room door and rested her left hand on the knob that would open to the rave. Music thudded through her chest, and the bass seemed to shake the walls.

They'd left it unlocked. Security seemed contradictory, with open doors and armed guards. *Maybe that's their plan.*

Haddie leaned her face against the door jamb and winced. The guard outside had managed a good bruise. Maybe she could just scare her way in, considering how her face looked. The thought made her smile. Instead, she remained where she was and held the door open a crack, just enough for one eye to see.

Light strobed against the bay wall to her right and the pair of doors in it. The room rose to the top of the building. Flashing colors danced across ceiling, walls, and floors, distracting her. Close to the right, a stairway led above Haddie's head.

The orange dots had disappeared in the light. A white-robed woman stood in the right front corner at an entrance. She stood at a podium talking with a couple who had dressed for the rave in short skirts and neon tube tops. The two ravers took back what looked like their IDs and skipped toward the dance floor, out of Haddie's sight.

She could see a man dressed like the guard she'd left outside. A large wolfhound sat behind him — with tiny orange dots for eyes.

Haddie sucked in a breath and pulled back. She stopped just short of closing the door. *Demon dogs. Of course.*

She leaned against the utility room door, heart thumping and right hand shaking with the weight of the gun.

The guard, and the demon, had a clear view of the door. She couldn't just stroll in, gun or not, and rescue Liz. If she tried to use her power on them, she'd have trouble walking anytime soon, let alone grab Liz and start running.

Haddie could still give up. She could head out the back door, get back to her car, and wait for the police. Risk Liz. Or she could go into the rave and hope that Liz danced there. Hope that no one noticed a tall, bruised woman wearing a dirty chullo with a bouncing tassel ball. Hope that Liz came quietly and they could sneak out the back.

She closed the door quietly.

The utility room seemed to stretch to the far wall; maybe it had a second entrance. She sighed and slipped into the darkness and burnt ozone of the side room, stuffing the gun into the back of her jeans behind her waistband. She shook her right hand, trying to get the joints to loosen. The orange eyes of the demon remained distant through the wall to her right.

The flickering red lights began to give her some sense of the room. Empty.

Walking along the wall bordering the rave, she swept her right hand up and down it. Stepping back, she checked the other side of the door and found the light switch. Did she dare?

Teeth clamped, she flicked the switch.

The light, two stories up, had one bulb missing. The dim light it shone on the room was sufficient, if not anti-climactic.

Electrical panels lined the back wall. Equipment, possibly alarm systems, was affixed above them. Ahead, a large air conditioner attached to aluminum vents that climbed the wall flanking the rave. Winding loops of black, blue, and white cable lay discarded in the corner opposite her.

No door.

She stopped with her hand poised over the light switch. The air handling vents had an access panel — two, one on top of the other. The aluminum shaft ran straight up the wall, then split at the ceiling. She could climb up and use a vent to get into the rave. The bay stood three stories tall, so there wouldn't be any air vents on the ground level; they'd be at the ceiling, forcing cold air down against the rising warmer air.

Haddie snorted. She hadn't been able to get down an

eight foot fence. Three stories. She'd break her own head; the demons wouldn't have to go through any effort.

Her choices consisted of popping in through the back door and strolling onto the dance floor, or dropping onto them from the ceiling. Neither seemed particularly promising, and Liz might not even be there.

Haddie leaned against the wall and then slid down, exhausted. The gun pressed painfully against her spine. She didn't want to give up.

During the past few months since Harold Holmes, she'd tried to learn how to let go. Not obsess. Talk things over with Dad, Liz, or even Terry before jumping into a new cause. Listen to their feedback. They would all say the same thing right now: Wait for the police. Let it go.

Haddie picked at the wet hole in her jeans. She'd stopped bleeding. Liz had been so beaten up by these raves. *I can't let her go through this alone.*

"Three stories, it is," Haddie murmured.

She frowned at the spools of cable. *With some rope.* She smiled, then winced trying to get up. Wincing hurt. She'd look like a purple Halloween pumpkin if her face kept swelling.

A thin blue cable seemed the longest, not three stories by any stretch, but she wound it around her middle and twisted a knot into it. She wouldn't have to worry about making too much sound in the aluminum shaft; they likely vibrated from the pounding music. The worst part of the plan came from imagining herself climbing up a shaft pressed shoulder to foot. She'd seen it done in movies, but those characters didn't ache in every joint like she did.

She readjusted her gun and opened the lower panel; it resisted until she had it cracked and air sucked in.

Light splashed in from a grate. DJ equipment was piled

on the other side, and someone danced lightly in white pants among it. She shut the panel and it slammed out of her fingers at the end.

Haddie blinked and raised her eyebrows. She'd found an opening on the ground floor — with someone right next to it. The upper panel, high enough that she'd have to climb into it, led to a shaft that went up quickly; cool air flowed out across her body. She shut it and stepped back.

Making her decision, she crossed the room, shut off the light, and then opened the bottom panel. She didn't trust herself three stories up.

Air sucked around her as she climbed in. The trunks and containers blocked much of her view, but also hid her. Some neon diamond hung from the ceiling. The air vents dropped down half the height of the room, but she doubted she would have fit. If she had, she probably would have fallen straight down.

She assumed the white pants belonged to the DJ. Their equipment and table blocked the top of their body, leaving white sandals and dirty feet that tapped and scraped across concrete.

Haddie pressed her face against the left side of the duct, trying to get a view. The stairs climbed toward a spot above her. Focusing, she could make out the orange pinpricks of the demon's eyes as they swiveled back and forth watching the incoming ravers.

She tested the grate, a yard square, in each corner. The bottom left was missing a screw, gave completely, and began to bend halfway up. The edges dug into her hands. Purpura covered much of them and hurt where the metal stabbed. The rave already smelled like alcohol.

The middle screw didn't budge. The metal bent out easily, but a triangle the size of her head wouldn't work.

Haddie pressed against the grate, viewing her surroundings. *This might get loud.* Working her body around, she placed her left boot heel near the stubborn screw and bounced her shoulders with the music. Pulling her foot back she gave it three more beats before she kicked.

The grate flared out in a tall triangle. Not bad. Except for the burns in her hip, knee, and every bone in her foot.

She waited, hoping that the noise had been caught up in the rave. It didn't seem possible that she'd be able to climb back out of the duct and get across the utility room in time to escape, if they'd heard. Not in her shape.

No one peered in. Head first? *At least, I'll see them coming.* She pulled the gun out and began.

Along the wall next to the grate, someone had provided refreshments. Bottles and red cups lined the table and floor. Cardboard cases of alcohol were piled against the wall between the tables and the opening Haddie climbed out of.

A woman wearing a plastic skirt poured gin or vodka into her mouth, holding the bottle a good six inches from her lips. Half a dozen others used cups. No one gave Haddie a second look.

Haddie pushed out faster.

The DJ, a dark brown woman with dreads, wore only pants. White painted handprints covered her chest, stomach, and sides. Her eyes stared up at the glowing neon above while her hands worked across the equipment.

Don't look down. Squirming, Haddie found a piece of glass on the concrete as it dug into her left shoulder. She swore and had to lay the gun on her chest to reach over and pluck it out. Wonderful. She remembered the floors of the other raves; some places had sparkled with broken bottles.

The woman in the sci-fi plastic skirt paused for a moment and watched with a lecherous smile.

Haddie shuffled out, freeing her legs and hoping she'd only found a random piece of glass.

The woman walked over and offered the bottle over Haddie's head. "Open up," she said, possibly. The music swept away most of the sound.

Haddie rolled to her side as the vodka hit. Most of it soaked into her hat, but a good portion found the wound the demon's nails had left, and the new hole the glass had made. *Damn.* Anger flushed up her face. She kicked out, finding a shin to push the woman away.

As she crawled to her hands and knees, the DJ still ignored her, but Haddie could feel the tone reaching out to her, coaxing her.

The woman had returned to pouring the vodka into her own mouth.

A guard with a holstered gun and black shirt stood in front of the DJ. He had a baton hanging from his hip and watched the pile of ravers dancing just a few steps from him.

Liz.

She danced in the same black shirt Haddie had put her to bed in. The man in the white suit stood in the center again, his eyes closed and hands upraised.

Her exit hadn't gained her much. Haddie would have to slip past the guard, but the crowd had grown enough that she might blend in. Without the gun. She reached back to tuck it into her belt and had to work past the loops of cable.

Behind the DJ, against the wall, some ravers sat, or knelt, still urged to dance, but too broken or weary to stand. She might have a chance coming in from that side, and she'd be less exposed to the demon.

Sliding along the wall, she made it past the corner behind the DJ.

There in solely a black concert shirt, and hopefully a pair of tighty-whities, Matt sprawled on the floor.

Haddie's jaw clenched. If it hadn't been for him, Liz would be home safe, Haddie wouldn't have thrown a guy into traffic, and she wouldn't be wearing a vodka-scented chullo. *I should just leave him.*

She sighed. *I can't do that to Liz, or Matt for that matter.*

CHAPTER 35

HADDIE KNELT beside the group of exhausted or unconscious ravers, the stench of sweat and urine overpowering the vodka in her hair.

"Matt?" She tapped his face.

He didn't move; a nasty scrape along his neck led to a torn collar on his new T-shirt. His legs had dark stains running down them that she didn't want to think about.

The tone had gotten into her head, but she fought the urges. The music pounded in her chest. *I don't have time for this.* Haddie slapped his cheek, hard enough that her own knuckles screamed at her.

He mumbled and shifted his head.

Liz drifted into a pocket of ravers, barely visible. The tone tugged at Haddie, compelling her. The vodka smelled good. She swore at Matt, steeling herself for the pain, and slapped his already pink cheek.

His eyes opened, glazed and unfocused, but immediately he started to rise.

Finally. Haddie dismissed him for the moment.

Crouched, she glanced around the room. *Could I have*

just walked in the back door? The guard in front of the DJ seemed unemotional, hardly glancing at some of the nudity. They would go out the back. The table with food and drink ran right up to it. Ravers bounced there and back without a second look.

She could see the demon's eyes shine through the crowd, now that she knew what to look for. What are they, really? Surely not an evil spirit, or a creature from an underworld.

A woman danced toward her, shaking enough to arouse Haddie. *That tone is getting to me.* She had to get Liz, maybe even Matt, and sneak them out of here.

Matt had started to stumble in a semblance of a rhythm against one of the women and she obliged, rubbing against him.

The sight made it more difficult to control herself. Haddie pushed back against it.

Grabbing Matt's arm, she tugged him. She made a motion of drinking and he shuffled along. *They are nearly mindless.* The tone urged her to focus only on the most pleasurable desires, forgoing any other thoughts. It wouldn't have been hard to forget all her worries and succumb. *Focus. You probably have less than an hour before Terry makes that call.*

Liz danced alone, close to the man in white. He looked asleep with haggard features and fluttering eyelids, but he posed in a fresh white suit with only one brown stain near the cuff of his left leg. He wore the same white sandals that the DJ did.

He emanated that echo of a tone — that driving compulsion. Haddie pushed against the urges, constantly snapping her mind back to focus, her hand clenched around Matt's sweaty, grimy arm.

She tapped Liz on the shoulder and made the same drinking motion. Haddie stood so close to the man in white. *Just one drink.* It sounded so good. The music had such a deep, inviting beat. Simply enjoy. *No.* Haddie grabbed Liz's shoulder with her left hand.

The tone had become too much. Haddie growled, flaring out against the tone, beating it back. Her own song, different, pressed out. The driving compulsion melted away.

The man in white gasped, opening his eyes.

Time to go. The dancing ravers had grown thick around them; many were newer guests with more energy. Haddie pushed Liz toward the back where a crowd worked the food and drinks and her exit waited.

A voice somehow cut through the music, not necessarily louder, but vibrant and timed. "Stop her." An old lady in a villain cosplay with her face made up for the rave stood at the top of the stairs. The tone, the original and not the echo, flooded from her, nearly overwhelming. She spoke with confident authority, without any alarming emotion.

Haddie staggered at the strength of the tone. It seemed focused on her. She fought against it and felt her own song tremble. Dull pain rose in the joints of her fingers; her grip on Matt and Liz stiffened and threatened to lose them. She scrambled to keep hold of Liz who pushed past a raver, seemingly intent on getting the promised drink.

A gunshot cut through the music, close and deafening.

Haddie felt a searing burn across the top of her arm. Her black shirt tore, and red flesh welled dark blood. She'd been shot. Or at least nicked by the bullet. *It doesn't look that bad.*

A hand reached out from behind, limply waving toward her arm. She spun to find the man in white, his shoulder and chest speckled with blood. The side of his neck had a gaping hole that gushed blood. The ravers dancing close to him had been sprayed, but they seemed not to notice, or care.

They fired at me. They killed their own man.

Matt pushed into her as a second shot rang out. Blinking and numb, she stumbled. She'd lost hold of Liz. *Focus.*

Someone to her right, closer to the shooter, grunted. The guard. The one in front of the DJ had to be the one firing.

She glanced for Liz, hoping she'd moved away toward the back tables before she got caught in a crossfire. *Exactly what I didn't want.*

Haddie fell to one knee and reached back for her gun. The feet had started to stumble and stomp around her. She'd blocked the tone, but guessed that the man in white's death had released the others.

A young shirtless man fell on her with a dead weight. Haddie sprawled to the floor.

Another gunshot sounded, echoed by one from the other side of the room. A sharp twang and a ricochet sounded on the concrete beside her.

Somehow, she'd lost the gun.

Barely cutting through the ringing and music, the woman's voice from above yelled, "Stop!"

Two more shots rang out, and someone screamed.

Haddie crawled up to her knees. She didn't need her gun. She needed to find Liz and get to the exit. Her ears rang so loudly that only the highest notes of the music made it through; the bass she felt in her chest. Her heart raced faster.

Some of the dancers had fallen to the floor, while others ran for the front door. Gunshots continued.

Through their legs, she saw the demon.

Fur and skin sloughed off with a shake. Orange eyes gleamed. A large beak formed its true face. A thin, pink-skinned neck wound up like a bird. A small gold medallion hung tight on its neck, reflecting a faint yellow light. The hairless, skinless legs could have been that of a dog's, thick and sturdy.

Haddie plowed through someone's legs as she made for Liz. Her friend huddled with a group by the tables. One man, dressed in what looked like an iridescent leotard, had climbed underneath with the discarded bottles and cups.

The room had broken into pandemonium. Most tried to flee; others dropped to the floor beside unmoving bodies. Some just stood, too drunk or shocked to react.

This had been exactly what Haddie didn't want the police doing, starting a gunfight. No, she'd started a massacre. *I did this.*

The woman on the stairs, directly above the tables, had been joined by another small demon. Fleshy and pudgy, it slobbered at her legs. The woman shouted angrily, leaning on the railing of the stairs, but Haddie couldn't hear her — couldn't hear anything but the ringing in her ears.

Except the gunshots; those resonated through the ringing.

Haddie broke from the frantic crowd and made straight for the back tables. She cringed, scrambling across the concrete. The bulk of the ravers moved toward the front door, leaving an open area by the back. She knew the guard in front of the DJ stood to her right. *He's got a clean shot.* She could only hope he'd emptied his magazine.

Matt hid behind a group of a dozen other ravers. Not one had thought to go to the door.

Liz crouched with her hands over her head. Gratefully, she stood at the edge of the group, close to the door.

Haddie barely slowed, grabbing Liz's arm and yanking her toward the door.

A finger-sized bullet hole silently formed in the door. The metal just sucked inside itself. She'd heard the continuing gunshots, but not the bullet as it tore through metal. *Just go.*

Bottles shattered at the table, and glass sprinkled across her side. She caught a faint hint of the garbage outside as she jerked open the door. The hall waited, dark, safe, and slightly more humid. Haddie could only hope that the guard outside hadn't recovered. How long had she been inside?

"Come on," she said. Her own voice barely registered except as vibration.

Liz stumbled along as Haddie pulled.

They'd almost made it. Just get outside and to the open gate. Hopefully, they could run along the side of the building and disappear into some other property. Haddie didn't dare go down to the street even if her car did wait a short distance away. The guards parked outside might still be there. Haddie would be on the wrong side of the building, but they couldn't risk the fence around the back lot.

She was lucky not to have been shot already. How many people had died? The guards had shot into the crowd trying to get to her.

Why had the woman wanted her alive? She'd seemed angry over the shooting. Who was she?

Haddie never let go of Liz as they moved through the back hallway. There'd been no resistance, but she couldn't take a chance that Liz wouldn't go back for Matt. *I'm not losing her now.* Not after all this.

The guard still lay prone on the ground. Haddie might have caused his death as well.

The air stunk of the dumpster, a welcome smell at this moment. As she jerked right, she could see a crowd of people following down the hall. Ravers, and Matt among them. Good. She could tell Liz he made it out.

They poured into the parking lot as she pulled Liz to the white gate. A thin hysterical woman with pasties moved to follow her. Matt stumbled with others into the back lot.

Haddie didn't pause as she pulled Liz behind her through the open gate.

CHAPTER 36

HADDIE SUCKED in a deep breath as she tried to calm herself.

Liz stared wide-eyed, still hunched over, cowering.

A row of head-high cedars stretched along the building leading all the way to the front. Haddie couldn't risk that the two guards weren't still parked there. They might not even know about the mayhem inside. Surely some of the ravers had made it out the front door, but she couldn't chance it.

She pushed through the cedars to her left. Their fragrant branches were a pleasant break between her own stench and the dumpster. Her arm stung from the gunshot, but her joints ached worse.

A huge warehouse sat across the parking lot. Semi containers and trailers parked randomly in spaces or in front of bay doors. Lights and canopies marked a few entrances, but she didn't even want to try getting inside. The building stretched so far back that it surely intersected with another street.

They'd have a better chance hiding on some property

back there, until the police came and cleaned everything up.

A hysterical woman raced along the side of the building behind them, heading for the front. Another crashed through the gate.

Haddie pulled Liz to the parking lot. The sky hung dark above with no stars or moon. The clouds had to be blanketing overhead.

Liz couldn't move fast. She stumbled and shuffled no matter how much Haddie pulled on her.

They were exposed. The back lot of the rave sat to their left behind the fence and containers. Figures ran and moved there. If she could see them, they could see her. Their movement, so close, disturbed her more in their silence — unheard over the ringing in Haddie's ears. She glanced back, nervous they were being followed.

Docks, containers, and trucks created tempting hiding places along the massive building, but she wanted to be far away. She wouldn't feel safe until they couldn't see the building or anyone from it. Then, Liz might be safe, but Haddie would have to deal with Special Agent Wilkins and the death in front of the hotel. Imagining the man's blood in the gutter reminded her of the nightmares that flashed in front of her each time she used her ability.

She doubted she'd ever be free of the image and memory, let alone the consequences. How could she even explain what had happened on that street? The man's death by car would be clear. But the demon? Technically self-defense, she'd used abilities that no one could comprehend and she couldn't clarify.

The parking lot ended at a road ahead, parallel to the one she'd driven in on. Another business lined the opposite side with more trailers and trucks. A light seemed to be on in an open bay; maybe they had a late delivery, and Haddie could find a place to hide inside.

To their left, a business backed up to the rave. She didn't see fences, except along this property line. She might be able to circle around into the same lot and get back to her car. She drew in a breath, feeling some hope and excitement over the options.

Slightly behind them, she caught a motion as the demon leaped to the top of the barbed wire fence. Like a bloody flamingo, it perched for a second atop the wire.

"Run!" Haddie yelled, almost hearing her own words through the ringing.

Liz couldn't. Haddie pulled, but she would end up yanking Liz to the ground before her friend could take any quicker steps.

The creature ran with dog-like speed, its head flopping back and forth on its spindly curved neck.

Other shadows scurried across the parking lot. They could have been ravers escaping behind Haddie and Liz or guards bent on killing them. She didn't intend to pause to find out. She might make it to the end of the building before the creature caught up with her. If she hadn't lost the gun, she'd at least have something to defend herself with other than fists and boots. Taekwondo hadn't really trained her for fighting demonic flamingos.

They wouldn't make it. Liz moved too slowly, stumbling in steps that seemed too painful. She had looked back and seen the danger, but didn't seem able to handle even the slow footsteps she took.

Haddie had to turn before they reached the street.

As the demon leaped, she swept it aside with an inside block. Her right forearm caught it in its flexible neck, and its body folded around it. Its momentum carried its bulk forward, but she'd stepped to the side.

It still managed to drag the tip of its beak across her shirt, tearing the cloth and scratching her skin.

Haddie danced back, exhausted. Her joints protested every position.

Liz had dropped to the ground and was sitting with her legs to the side on the asphalt, waiting for death. She should be running.

The demon scurried to its legs and leaped a good ten feet, sailing directly toward Haddie.

Jumping, Haddie tilted back and aimed a side kick to the creature's face. it was the wrong kick for this demon's shape.

The face and neck folded back from the impact, which did little to affect the creature. The body continued bending backward and landed at Haddie's feet. Before she could get away, the beak swung around and jabbed behind her left knee.

The fresh pain nearly crumpled her leg. It felt wet instantly. How was she supposed to fight this thing?

She scrambled to the side and crouched with both hands open. Maybe she could catch its neck and snap it.

It gave her the chance. Lunging, it pecked at her face. She caught the neck with her right hand and pulled back from the beak. Her left hand grabbed on as its hind claws raked down both of her thighs. Her pants slit open, and her and skin shredded.

Haddie screamed in pain. She stumbled back. Her hands wrung a loose but muscular neck. How was she supposed to kill it?

Its legs scraped a new set of tracks on her legs, and the

beak poked into her arm as neatly as if a stiletto had been driven in.

Her boot slipped on the asphalt. She fell trying to hold the demon away from her face.

Squirming, it dug into her arm with a back leg.

Muscles on her left arm felt torn. It would be only moments before she wouldn't be able to hold it back.

Haddie closed her eyes and growled. Even through the ringing in her ears, the air sang with her tone.

Pain convulsed through empty hands. The demon disappeared and the nightmares began. Surely her dad's experience, she watched south Asian soldiers fade at his hands from a long-failed war. The horror took seconds, but she felt every moment of it. His feelings. His remorse. His fear. She'd always considered Dad fearless.

Gasping, she couldn't react when two pairs of rough hands grabbed her under the armpits. Lifting her torso and legs off the ground, they dragged her backward, toward the rave.

A third collected Liz, causing a flicker of anger in Haddie, but she didn't have any energy left to do anything. She could barely breathe. Her lungs fought the movement.

Liz didn't resist, hobbling behind with a guard gripping her arm.

Haddie's head flopped back, staring up at her captors and the gray blanket of clouds above. One of the men had the yellow haze. Dancing yellow sparks, like fireflies, raced in circles in and out of his skin. Looping through his head, they surfaced and spun about his face and eyes before diving back in again. There were hundreds, like a swarm of tiny bees of light.

She doubted she could use her power again. Her heels

ground and vibrated on the asphalt. Pulling her head up nearly caused her to lose consciousness.

Liz and her guard had fallen back.

Haddie might be able to use the last of her strength to make Liz's captor disappear. There might be others nearby. Wouldn't her captors just split and retrieve Liz, who wouldn't, or couldn't run?

Haddie couldn't bring herself to do it. *How much pain can I endure?* Worse, she felt that too much more, and her body wouldn't survive.

We're likely both dead anyway. Whatever purpose the woman had for them, they'd soon find out.

The police would be out to the rave soon. What had she told Terry? 11:30 p.m.

CHAPTER 37

HADDIE MANAGED to strain her head up as they passed back inside the white gate.

Through the fading ringing in her ears, she could hear sharp words from the guard leading Liz; they'd trailed farther behind.

Mosquitoes had found Haddie's ears and neck, mercilessly poking around for a free meal. The sky felt dead and gray. She'd failed in every way tonight. People had died because of her, and they had Liz again. *This is my fault.* If she'd answered Liz's call, they could have ended it that first day. It seemed a lifetime ago.

The dumpster welcomed her back to the rave with its familiar, sharp taint. Her captors raised her up higher to get around corners, their grip digging into her armpits. She might have been able to walk. What were they going to do with her? If they'd just wanted her dead, they could have finished her in the parking lot. Perhaps they didn't want to leave a mess.

They dragged her heels over the guard she'd first encountered, pausing as they opened the door. Three bodies lay in the back parking lot, none with Matt's black T-shirt. Maybe he had escaped. They didn't seem worried about leaving corpses lying around, at least for the moment. Why not just kill her out here?

The dark hall felt like a death sentence. She could possibly work up enough strength to take out one of her captors. However, once she did that, she'd likely go unconscious. She'd been near that after she took out that last demon. The thought of more nightmares emblazoned forever in her memory sounded worse than dying, at the moment.

Her legs hurt from the demon's claws. They spiked into sharp pain as her captors jostled her over a body on the floor. She almost lost consciousness. Even the dim rectangle of the door to the back faded close to the black of the hall.

They dragged Haddie halfway into the silent rave, over the body of a dead woman, before they dropped her against a door along the wall. The woman had worn a pink and black outfit, and her bare arm lay on the first step of the stairs, as if she intended to crawl up.

The two men took positions on each side of Haddie, their guns drawn but held at their waists. Empty hands clasped over their gun hands.

Bodies littered the floor. The room smelled like alcohol and it pooled, thinning the blood on the floor around those who had died near fallen tables and broken bottles. The DJ packed up quietly into her containers, as if there hadn't been a massacre.

I caused this. Haddie fought nausea looking from one raver to the next.

They hadn't turned on the lights. The only source of light was the elongated diamond above, continuing to cycle through neon colors, flashing at odd moments. Another guard stood at the front of the bay with a white-robed woman kneeling beside a podium. Blood splattered her clothes. Two pairs of bloody bare feet lay in the hallway beyond. The door stood ajar against bodies. At the far end, beyond any hope, the dim gray light from outside shone through windows by the front door.

Haddie couldn't count the dead. Dozens. A pile started under the light and trailed toward the exit. There was a small pile by the tables. Why kill them all?

The front door opened, and she sucked in her breath. For one brief moment she thought the police had arrived. Instead, a silhouette with a yellow-hazed head walked down the hall toward them. Despite already having three guards, her pulse rose.

Liz crumpled down beside her, and Haddie jumped.

"You okay?" Haddie asked.

"Silence," said the man who had escorted Liz. He wore a tight crew cut, nearly shaved. He walked past and headed toward the front.

Liz stared wide-eyed, trembling. She barely made eye contact with Haddie before looking at her lap.

A door opened, far above to Haddie's left.

Carrying a champagne glass in a white glove, the tall woman began descending. The monstrous pudgy demon, wearing a glowing gold medallion, followed her trailing purple gown, its nails clicking on each metal step. She'd painted her face white and decorated it with sparkling rainbows, appropriate for a rave.

This was the woman with the power. Haddie steeled herself. Did she have enough strength left to resist?

Four women in white robes followed. No, they were gowns, long-sleeved satin with a sash at the waist. The bottoms were dirty, as if they had been kneeling. Three carried silver laptops, and the fourth an unopened bottle of champagne and an empty glass.

The woman paused dramatically near the foot of the stairs, inspecting Haddie with a growing smile. She waited for a moment, sipping her champagne.

Haddie waited, tense. Her body ached, her face and fingers as well, but she might have enough strength to use her power.

The woman smiled, then continued, striding directly among the corpses, stopping when she could go no farther without stepping on them. Blood soaked into the hem of her gown, darkening it.

Her entourage followed. Blood soaked into their hems, climbing pink into the cloth.

The woman studied the faces of the dead. "I've lost some very important and rich opportunities because of you." She paused at one of the bodies, shaking her head. "This man is worth millions."

Is that what this was all about? Money? The billionaire who lost all his money? Matt's credit card declined at the hotel? Haddie found her jaw tightening despite her aching joints.

The woman turned, her face wrinkled from frowning. It eased as she looked at Haddie. "At least, he'll have you. Otherwise, this loss would be a disaster." She smiled a secret smile. "You're priceless."

What did that mean? Who was this "he" that would have her? "Who —?"

The guard to her right slammed the back of his fist into Haddie's forehead. As her head smacked against the door, Haddie sucked in a breath, reeling with sparks winking against the neon light. The alcohol in the air had become so thick that she tasted it.

The woman resumed her inspection of the massacre. "Anthony had come to the end of his usefulness, I suppose."

Haddie flushed with anger. Whatever game this woman played, it would end soon when the police arrived. She ached to dig out her phone and check the time. It had to be close to 11:30. How long would it take them to respond after Terry's call?

The woman's entourage followed dutifully. The pudgy demon trotted slowly, sitting at her right side as she stopped. It glared more at the purple gown than anything else in the room, seeming to resent the woman as much as Haddie. What held it back?

Haddie took a deep breath, her face composed and attentive. *I'm listening to your rant. I'm giving you an audience until the police get here.*

What if this woman worked her powers on the officers? Had them dancing and lapping up the alcohol pooled on the floor? Liz still had a chance to survive, if the police came in and she stayed still on the floor. The guards had lined up from the front door to the back. Surely the police would see the bodies in the parking lot and come in expecting guns.

The woman whirled. Her gown would have twirled, but for the blood. She stalked over to them. "I will need a replacement for Anthony; perhaps your little friend will do."

The demon sat near its master, with its look of resentment and hatred. Something held it back.

Haddie's teeth clenched. She imagined Liz standing there, half dead, in a circle of dancing police officers.

She growled and the tone squelched in the air.

The impact felt like a wave of air pressing back. No visions came, and her joints ached no more than they did before. No prickling pain seared across her skin as blood shattered. Her power had failed.

The woman laughed and drained her glass. "My mentor has trained me well, as you see. I can even resist her."

The girl with the champagne popped the cork, a celebration to Haddie's failure.

She hadn't expected that. A hollow desperation opened up in her chest. She'd been ready to sacrifice herself, all in the hopes that the police would arrive in time to save Liz.

The woman spoke to the guard beside Liz while her serving girl poured her another glass. "Get the men to clear the equipment out of here. I want to be underway immediately. There's been too much gunfire; we might have gathered some unwanted attention."

He bustled off toward the men at the front, and the woman took a fresh sip from her newly poured drink.

The emptiness in Haddie's chest grew. They might not even be here when the police arrived, and there was nothing she could do. She might be able to take down one of the guards and survive, albeit unlikely in her condition, but there were four more in the building, and possibly others outside.

The woman gloated over Haddie. "You will be an exquisite gift for my mentor. She will enjoy the opportunity, I'm sure. You've managed to rebuke my power, as I have yours. We will see if you can resist Lady Erica. Your time with her will be limited before our Lord will seek to bring you back to the original ambition." She cracked her face paint with a smile. "We'll keep you a secret for just another day or two."

The attendants stood emotionless behind the woman. The demon waited beside her, its orange eyes focused on the purple gown. The little medallion on its chest glowed with the same yellow haze as some of the guards.

Nothing Haddie could do would stop this. The police were her only chance, and she might miss them. The guard who had hit her stood close. Liz might end up as another of the woman's lackeys, replacing the man in the white suit. Or worse, killed and left among the dead. Haddie had been responsible for the deaths of dozens, and still no closer to saving Liz.

I have failed.

CHAPTER 38

HADDIE LOOKED at the man's legs who stood beside her. If she didn't feel so weak, she'd try and wrestle him to the ground and take his gun. Shoot the woman square in the forehead. *Dust off some of that glitter.*

An ache swelled in her chest. The anger and frustration had risen to hate. *I don't want to be like this.* Haddie just needed a distraction so that Liz could run. All of this would be worth it if Liz survived. No one else needed to die. The mound in the room belonged to Haddie already.

Two guards, one with the yellow haze, stepped over the bodies to help the DJ pack up her equipment. From the front, the guard who'd been watching Liz dragged a thick collapsible aluminum ladder down the hall. Bright lights turned on above, and the neon winked off.

No one guarded the back door. If Haddie did tackle her guard, would Liz take the opportunity to escape out the back?

The woman turned to watch them pack. Her four servants knelt in alcohol and blood. The demon seemed to snarl, whipping about, coerced.

Liz tucked her knees to her chin, her arms holding them tight. She seemed to watch the blood, thinned by alcohol, spreading closer to them. Did she blame Haddie for that? Did she know Matt escaped?

Haddie leaned her head down, risking another blow from the guard. She whispered, "Matt made it out."

"Silence," the guard beside Haddie hissed. He didn't strike her.

Liz lifted her head up slowly and looked at Haddie as if she were a stranger. It hurt. Then, she nodded before turning her chin back to its resting place.

Haddie's throat closed, and tears threatened. She couldn't blame Liz. Learning your friend had horrible powers and lied about them would be difficult, if not impossible, to accept. That the woman who ran the raves had a similar power made it worse. Like they were related.

Liz would remember the ski trip, and how Haddie had let her believe she'd hallucinated the demon. The lies. Would there be a difference, in Liz's mind, between the woman in the purple gown, Haddie, and the demons? Were they all just monsters — mutants? Liz had to see the difference.

Haddie couldn't put her dad in that category; he'd always been a good man. She felt like a murderer, just seconds ago willing to kill more people.

The ladder opened and extended to rest against the opposite wall. One guard held it while a second climbed up with a socket wrench. The DJ's bench had been broken down, and parts were stored in black plastic containers. They worked around the dead as if they were discarded litter from the rave. Would they leave the bodies? Likely, since Terry's suicide raves would have had some proof — corpses left behind.

Haddie and Liz they would take.

The woman moved to get a closer view of the dismantling, bumping into the demon and angering it. She gave it no thought as it snarled.

Its medallion glowed slightly. The yellow haze enlarged in a pulse. Was there some connection in controlling the demon?

I have no intention of being someone's gift. Liz would not become the next zombie in a white suit echoing the woman's song. If a distraction enabled Liz to leave, it would be enough.

Haddie growled. Her tone rang out, causing the woman to turn.

The medallion winked away. Haddie had hoped that affecting such a small object wouldn't hurt as badly, but it felt worse. Pain sparkled across her skin, and she couldn't breathe. Her joints flared. Her hands trembled.

The nightmares came. Dark grisly memories played out in her eyes: one man being dismembered by two others, her dad's shout, and two people faded, leaving only a dying man hung from a limb. A young child, the bomb it carried, and an explosion that never happened.

Haddie trembled against the door.

The demon snarled and flesh sloughed free. Its teeth clamped around the woman's leg, tearing her gown. Muscles bulged around the creature's jaws where flabby jowls had rested. Though small, it brought her down with one shake of its head.

The woman screeched as she fell. A bone snapped, audible even to Haddie's dulled ears.

Haddie felt nearly unconscious, her dry mouth trying to speak. Liz needed to use the distraction and run. However, she just watched, aware, but motionless.

Four white-robed servants descended upon on the demon, trying to pull it off the screaming woman in purple. It released its grip and caught one of their faces in a too-wide jaw. The woman's cheeks distorted as bones crushed.

The guard beside Haddie stepped forward, gun raised, but they made a pile that included the woman in the purple gown.

"Run," Haddie said. Her voice, hoarse and barely a whisper, seemed lost in the pandemonium.

Liz shifted back, but didn't try to rise. Haddie pushed her left hand limply against Liz's leg, trying to push her toward the back door. With her right hand, Haddie pushed her hand up the door she leaned against, searching for the knob above her head. There could be another way out. There had been a second door in the back, in front of the parked cars.

The scribe raced across the room and tackled the demon, who had moved back to the woman in the purple gown after killing two of the servants. She stabbed at it with a pen, and the demon oozed dark red blood.

Haddie found the knob of the door behind her. If she could just crawl in there. Her legs were cold, and each breath took effort.

Liz still sat, watching as if entranced.

"Run," Haddie said. Her croak, no louder than before, seemed to go unheard.

The guard from the front stepped closer, his gun drawn, focused on the demon but unwilling to fire at the woman in the purple gown.

Haddie cringed, trying to turn the knob with her knuckles burning and her fingers too weak. She'd caused the distraction; now she needed to get Liz out. Why couldn't she just run for the back?

The demon lunged at the scribe, and the guards opened fire. The woman's white gown blossomed red blood, and the demon shifted to the side with a hit on its hind quarters.

The guard on the ladder fired. A thin column of flame appeared beside him. Haddie paused, entranced. It hung there, swaying and growing before it climbed over his head. He had barely turned toward it when the top half of the building concussed with flame.

Heat cracked against Haddie's body. Her head and back slammed into the door, her arm pinned above her.

Liz grunted beside her and finally moved, raising hands.

Bulbs burst in the lamps above, but the light blinded Haddie.

Then the floor in front of them roared. The entire quarter where the DJ had been packing was suddenly engulfed in flames. The woman in purple sat up and screamed as fire roared through her alcohol-soaked cloth. Her remaining two servants disappeared in the blaze, still wrestling the demon. The guards behind, the DJ, and the man on the ladder disappeared behind the inferno.

Run, Liz. Run. Haddie didn't have the strength. Her legs had gone numb, searing in pain if she tried to shift them. She barely held onto the knob above.

Liz just needed to escape.

They couldn't both burn up in Haddie's firestorm. Her body count kept growing. No wonder Liz couldn't stand to look at her.

The demon skittered away, its flesh smoking. It leaped on the guard standing directly in front of Haddie, the one who'd slammed her in the forehead.

Bones crunched in the man's arm. Gunshots rang in the bay, echoing. They sounded distant.

Liz climbed over Haddie, brushed her hand off the

knob, and opened the door. She moved with determination, no longer stunned.

Haddie's head slammed to the floor, and the ceiling above exploded into stars. Even the flames at her feet dimmed. The red glow on the ceiling looked dark and ominous. Hellish. Liz had escaped the burning room.

Bullets tore through the guard's back, and he dropped. The pudgy, round demon rolled off the fallen man and moved erratically, loping with short legs toward the final guard.

Smoke choked the air. The roar in her ears might have been the flames. It might have been the echo from the gunshots, or the explosion from the alcohol fumes. The muffled screams came from the last guard. The people in the fire had become silent.

The demon did appear indestructible, as Aaron had warned. Fire and bullet holes slowed it, but she doubted the last guard would hold it off for long. Haddie would be next. She'd try her powers. Her lungs barely seemed to work. She might not survive another use of her abilities, but if it gave Liz more time to escape, then she'd try it.

Haddie felt Liz grabbing her under the armpits.

No. "Run," she said. Pleading, her eyes clouded with tears.

CHAPTER 39

LIZ STUCK the heels of her sneakers to the floor and yanked. Her bruised, blistered, and bloody feet screamed in pain. Noxious smoke clogged the room.

Haddie, her face swollen purple and eyebrows nearly gone from the heat, moaned. "Run." Her voice sounded scratchy and faint.

Liz blinked against the smoke and daze. Her head swam. She didn't know where that fleshy horror had bounced off to, but if Haddie didn't get up they'd die by fire or that red Slimer. "Kick with your damn feet, you weigh a ton."

Liz coughed. The air smelled of burning corpses and melting plastic. She couldn't imagine what filled her lungs. If they'd asked, she might have told them not to fire their guns inside an alcohol-fumed room. Didn't they smell it? She'd been breathing it the entire time she listened to Sameedha. Not that she could blame getting drunk on that. The vague memory of chugging schnapps returned to her.

Inside the bay, glass shattered and the fire roared, like it had found a new source of fuel. Fresh heat poured through the open door.

"Haddie, kick."

Haddie's hips had just crossed the threshold. Blood slicked her pants, glistening in the firelight.

Fire spread like liquid, no longer satisfied with the bodies and plastic containers. It would be at Haddie's feet soon.

Liz backed up a step and leaned into her load. Blistered and bruised heels screamed at the torture. *Either Haddie weighs more than she says, or I need to up my workout.* Being half-drunk didn't help.

She hadn't forgotten about Slimer. So, when the gunshots stopped, she dropped her voice to a whisper and swore. "Pull your legs up, or we're both dead."

Haddie managed it. She was groaning and whining, but she rolled and her legs moved out of the doorway.

Liz dropped her friend and leaped behind the door. *Last chance.*

Years in classrooms doing drills taught her a good door when she felt one. Steel. She slammed it closed with her shoulder. That last second before it latched, she felt the creature slam against it, sliding toward the opening.

A single red digit, looking disturbingly human except for the pointed black nail, caught on her side of the door jamb. The latch had clicked, though. She held her breath as she backed away from the door. The nail wiggled, and she could hear vicious scratching and snarling from the other side. The door stayed, and so did the nail.

The heat had been stopped, but smoke filled the room.

A single double-paned window looked over a dull gray parking lot and a hedge. It had no hinge or way to open it.

The room had been piled with office furniture, including two stacking chairs with black padding.

The creature stopped scraping at the door. Hopefully it had died from smoke or fire.

Haddie lay face down, mumbling for Liz to run. *That's not happening.*

Each step a wet, painful moment, Liz grabbed both chairs in a stack, surprised by how heavy they were. First, she held the legs and smacked the backs into the glass. They nearly slapped her forehead on the rebound. Her second attempt did as little damage when she tried to jab the legs into the window.

I need something dense and heavy, like a fire extinguisher. She snorted, thinking of the conflagration on the other side of the door.

She coughed and stepped gingerly through the clutter of office chairs and desks. *I didn't escape that room just to die in here instead.*

She tried a swivel chair, failed, and dropped it to the floor.

Haddie rolled over at the noise, her eyes bleary and her face bloated. Liz grimaced. Blood stained the floor where Haddie had lain face down. The gouges down her legs looked deep. They had to get her to a hospital.

Could Haddie's magic or superpower, whatever it was, make glass disappear? *I didn't hallucinate during the ski trip; it actually happened.* The scientist had shot something, which survived to become a skinless mutant that tried to kill them several hundred feet above the earth. Haddie had made it vanish. Another that looked like a lobster had attacked them when they got off the ski lift. Haddie had made something it threw disappear. Then, there was the creature that had broken the windshield earlier today. And just now in the parking lot, the one with the beak had vanished.

No wonder Haddie always seemed tired and barely got her schoolwork done. *Surely a little glass wouldn't be a problem.*

"Haddie?" Liz leaned down over her friend's brutalized face.

She should have left when Matt went weird. Haddie lay there, who knew how close to death, only because she'd saved Liz. Tears welled in Liz's eyes. She wanted to hold her, but there didn't seem to be anywhere on her that didn't have a bruise. How could Haddie have put herself through so much over Liz's stupidity? She'd never had a better friend. It was her turn to save them.

Haddie's eyes closed, and her head rolled to the side.

Liz knelt, coughing. "Haddie?" Her friend breathed in and out slowly, but didn't respond. Usually, she would slap someone's face to wake them. Liz couldn't bring herself to do it. Haddie looked like a purple volleyball with eyes.

Liz stood up, wiped away her tears, and carefully looked around the room. If she could pick up a desk, then that should break the window. It wasn't really an option, but she did size up both desks. One lay against the outer wall near the window, stacked with swivel office chairs. The other, smaller, stood on its end near the door. Liz jumped to it.

Its legs pointed toward her and the window, and the two sections of drawers attached to each end. She grabbed the edge of the drawer cabinet at the top and managed to drag the desk, wincing with each step. Measuring the distance between the legs and window, she shuffled backward, then squeezed from behind it and ran to the other side.

The building groaned above her. *Just give me a minute.*

She coughed and pushed the top edge, throwing a pair

of legs down and against the window. It shattered the safety glass into a dull hole. Not completely satisfying, but a cool waft of fresh air rewarded her.

As Haddie slept, Liz pulled the desk back up, pushed it about six inches to the side, and let it fall again to create another break in the glass. Then she moved it out of the way and used one of the stacked chairs to open a decent hole in the window. She was careful to break off the shards of glass that were sticking up from the lower edge of the frame.

She leaned against the side of the window, breathing in and out. She wouldn't be able to drag Haddie through that opening before the building collapsed. Who knew where the little bundle of joy had hopped off to — hopefully not outside for a walk? Getting out of this parking lot would be a good idea; she doubted she wanted to explain any of this to the police. She looked out the window. Maybe Matt would be nearby to lend a hand? *Nope. Didn't think so.*

Liz left the window and stood over her sleeping friend.

By the fifth slap, Haddie opened her eyes; Liz felt as guilty as if she'd been torturing the sensitive skin of newborn puppies. However, she needed her friend alive and well, no matter how horrible everything was at the moment. They would get through this, then Liz could figure it out.

CHAPTER 40

HADDIE COULDN'T BREATHE. She could hear the fire outside their room. Acrid smoke burned the inside of her nose.

Liz looked down on her with a pained look. Disgusted perhaps. *How can she even look at me?*

Haddie had left a trail of death behind her. Fragments flashed through her memory, interspersed with the nightmares that came from using her powers. "Run." Her throat dry, she spoke with a crackling voice.

Liz shook her head. "No, you've got to crawl over here. I've got the window open."

Haddie couldn't imagine raising her head. Her legs felt numb. Her left arm ached everywhere, and her joints burned. Her face stung.

"I can't." It hurt to speak. "Run."

Liz frowned and donned a determined expression. "Nope. We'll both die in here together. The roof is going to collapse soon, I believe. It should be fairly quick. We've been sucking in burning plastic, and whatever else you can imagine."

Liz couldn't risk her life now, not after everything Haddie had done. The woman who ran these raves, she'd died in the fire, along with everyone who served her, though they likely didn't deserve it. Where had the pudgy demon gone? Burned in the fire? Would that work as well as a bullet to their brain?

Haddie coughed and felt the burn in her lungs. The room looked like half office, half storage. A desk stood on its end. She could see the dim shape of the window behind her and to her right. Groaning, she pushed up and swiveled her head for a better look past Liz.

"Can you stand?" Liz put a hand behind Haddie's neck.

Shredded pants and blood covered her thighs. She winced, remembering the pain of the demon's claws. Moving her foot, she sucked in a breath at the searing stab that ran through her leg. She shook her head. Her left arm ached — everywhere. "Move, let me try to crawl there."

Liz shifted behind her.

Haddie rolled to her side, pain flushing through her legs and hips. *Had her friend forgiven her? Accepted what she was?* Pressing her elbow and forearm on the concrete, she dragged her body toward the window. Her head pounded with the effort, and the room dimmed. Smoke bit her nostrils and throat. Pain throbbed through her left arm as she touched the concrete, stabilizing her torso as she placed her elbow out again.

Two more drags across the floor and she could rest against the desk by the outer wall. Deep ragged breath brought in noxious smoke, and whiffs of fresh air from the broken window teased her. Crumbled safety glass rimmed the top and the upper sides of the hole. The edge of the window looked impossibly high above Haddie's head.

The building groaned above them. Haddie pulled

herself up to the wall under the window, where dull glass bit into her forearm. "Why don't you go outside and pull me up?" she asked.

Liz snorted. "Good try. I'll stay right in here with you until we can get you up to the window. I've got most of the glass out of the frame and a floor mat to throw over it."

She produced a black mat and draped it halfway down the wall. Grabbing Haddie under the arms, she managed to get them closer.

Haddie got a firm grip with her right hand and dragged her butt over to the wall. She'd have to go out head first, which meant dragging her shredded thighs over the sill. Shivers ran down her spine, and she swallowed a hint of bile. *You can do this, Haddie.*

They'd managed to survive the firetrap that Haddie had caused and escape the woman in the purple gown and her four demons, all at the cost of a few dozen innocent lives. Calling the police would have been the safer plan, though Liz might not have survived.

Haddie pulled herself up, trying not to black out as her knees bent.

CHAPTER 41

THOMAS JUMPED out of Biff's tow truck and gave Haddie's RAV4 a quick glance. The windshield had been shattered on the passenger side. Had she hit someone?

Biff walked down the parking lot toward the road. "I don't think it was on fire when we passed it."

Thomas smoothed his hair and walked up to look. Flames shot from a small spot on the roof of the warehouse with all the cars. There'd been a couple of oddly dressed people walking the streets when they'd first approached. Then they saw one warehouse with a half-full parking lot. He'd assumed Haddie would be in that building, but had wanted to check her SUV first.

"Hell," Thomas broke into a run, grunting as he forced stiff joints.

Biff kept up easily.

All the upper windows in the front showed signs of flames. A single gray sedan screeched out of the parking lot, turning the opposite way on the road. A hedge stood between them and the other cars. Thomas aimed toward the back of the hedge where the plants looked sparse enough to run through. The single torrent of flames shot from the roof near the back, like the fire had found a skylight.

A small animal, engulfed in flames, bounced against one of the upper windows. Haddie would likely be inside trying to save it.

"Hell, Haddie." Thomas dove through the hedge, eying a glass door ahead of them.

To the left, a dark shape hung out a first floor window, and smoke trailed through its broken glass. They weren't trying very hard to get out. Sirens sounded in the distance. Police or firefighters were on their way. He needed to find Haddie and not be here when they started digging through all this.

He paused when he saw the first body, lying near one of the parked cars in the front. More lay in the back parking lot behind a gate rolled closed. It didn't look good. He pushed back his doubts and fears. He'd find Haddie, safe.

Thomas sprinted toward the figure lightly struggling to wriggle out. They had on one of those Peruvian ski hats with the little tassels. The ball dangled down along with their arms. The smoke smelled acrid. Biff ran at his side and they reached the window at the same time.

A familiar face looked out from the dark room, bending down to speak through the broken glass. "Hey, you're Haddie's dad. Sure am happy to see you." Liz coughed. "Could you help pull her out?"

Haddie hung, barely moving, half out the window. Thomas motioned Biff to the other side. She stiffened and cried out as they dragged her through the opening.

Liz exited quickly, looking scuffed up. Soot smudged her face, her hair looked matted, and her eyebrows had dwindled to faint lines. She stepped back and looked toward the roof.

They laid Haddie on the grass and rolled her over.

"Dad." Her voice sounded like gravel.

The dirty hat framed her purple face, swollen, scratched, and with as little eyebrows as her friend. Her legs had been sliced open, deep enough to need stitches. Her left arm didn't look much better. She'd heal, quicker than most people. Better, if they got her some fluids and stopped the bleeding.

Biff put his hands on his hips. "Hell, Haddie, you look like shit."

Thomas threw Biff a look.

Biff spread his hands out. "Nice hat."

"Jerk." Haddie spoke in a dry squelch.

Thomas leaned down, gesturing to Biff. "Help me get her on my shoulder. I've got a vet I know in Rosewood. We'll head there."

They juggled Haddie up and over his shoulder. Her pants were still wet with blood, and Thomas could feel it through his own clothes.

Liz hobbled, barely able to walk. "We should hurry. There's a little critter out here we probably shouldn't let find us."

Thomas looked up at the windows of the third floor. Nothing seemed to move there. "Biff, can you carry Liz? I'd like to hurry, and she seems in pain."

Liz nodded as Biff leaned in, and she held on as he tossed her onto his shoulder.

Lightning crackled in the west, backlighting the clouds. The building groaned as he walked away.

They'd gotten as far as the hedge when Biff opened his mouth. "You're not wearing a bra, are you?"

Liz swore. "I hate men."

Thomas glared at Biff. "He tends to bring that out in women. Keep it shut, Biff."

When they got to the RAV4, Biff placed Liz on the front seat. He then opened the back and folded down the seats so they could lay Haddie flat. There were enough miscellaneous pieces of clothing, towels, and blankets that Thomas could try and make her comfortable.

They got them water and he had Biff get ready to follow in the tow truck. Thomas leaned in the back door, wanting to stroke her hair and try and sooth her. However, he could only imagine how much she hurt. Much of the bruising came from purpura. She would have had to use her powers a lot to get that bad. She'd survive. Then, she could tell him what the hell happened.

"I'm going to get you to a vet I know. He'll get you stitched up."

"You know every EMT and vet on the west coast?" she asked, trying to smile but managing a wince.

"Pretty much." He smiled. "Rest."

Liz sat quietly in the passenger seat, clutching her second bottle of water. Biff followed in the truck as Thomas drove to the edge of the parking lot.

The fire had burst through the top of the building. Firetrucks lit the trees with flashing lights and blocked the street. Thomas looked left and pulled up the map on his phone.

"Police?" asked Haddie. She still lay down, but light lit the windows.

He checked. "Nope, just fire."

She sounded weary. "What time is it?"

"12:11."

"They should be here." Haddie sounded surprised.

So, she had called the police. That might get complicated, especially if they could place her at the scene.

Thomas took the street to the left; it wound around and would bring them back out the way they'd come in. A short bit to I-5. He dialed the vet, a biker who worked mainly on horses and the occasional gunshot wound when you didn't want to go to the hospital.

They'd just turned the wide corner, the lights from the fire to their right, when Liz stiffened. "Matt."

A man with a black shirt and bare legs sat in the grass on Thomas's side of the road. He had his face in his hands and didn't react when they stopped.

"This your boyfriend?" He hoped they weren't in for drama; he didn't have time.

"Was." Liz looked at the man in a way that told Thomas they weren't quite done yet.

"I'll have Biff take him in the truck."

Liz nodded, relieved.

Thomas waved to Biff and gestured to the man, who still hadn't reacted to them.

Biff jumped out, tucking hair over his ear. "What's up boss?"

"That's Liz's boyfriend, Matt. Give him a lift. Don't be a jerk." It looked like Matt might just sleep most of the way. Hopefully, for his sake.

Biff shrugged and walked over, calling out to Matt. He stopped short, a pace away. "Aw, Boss, he reeks."

Thomas smiled.

CHAPTER 42

HADDIE STARED up at the white light above her, drowsy and thirsty despite all the liquids she'd had. The vet's husband had made her some tea, and she'd drunk enough water that she might need to pee again soon, a task she didn't relish with the fresh stitches.

The vet had let Haddie sleep, even given her a mild sedative, but the stiff gurney and the nagging pain kept waking her. She didn't know the time, and Dad had taken her phone on the car ride here.

The room smelled like antiseptic, but the stink of burning plastic remained in her nose. Her gurney sat by a wood-framed window overlooking a gray landscape, lit by the occasional lightning and blurred by rain. A long white counter spanned two walls and the corner, and wood cabinets were affixed above and below, larger than most doctors' examination rooms she'd been in. The vet had left some clothes of her husband's and Haddie's water on the metal table in the center, just out of reach. The door to the next room was closed, but she knew she could call out and Dad would be just on the other side.

Her thighs were stitched and wrapped from crotch to knee in white bandages, and her left arm had stripes of them.

Lightning flashed outside in the storm. It could be morning already; she couldn't tell through the clouds and rain.

The door cracked open silently, and Dad peeked in. "You're up." He walked in waving her phone. "Just turned your phone back on. Terry's been messaging you." He set the phone on her stomach.

She pulled her right hand from under the sheet and picked it up: 7:42 a.m. It looked like night outside. David had evidently given up on her, or was just giving her space. She'd never texted him after the hotel. Could she really expect him to put up with a relationship like this? *I'll call when we're on the road.* What could she even tell him?

There were two messages from Terry, but he'd be asleep at this hour. He tended to stay up until two or three. The time on the last message marked it at 4:29 a.m. She should let him know she made it — she imagined it wouldn't wake him.

Dad slipped behind and raised the back on the gurney, leaning her up. "How much does he know?"

Haddie showed him the picture of her in the background of the demon fighting Wilkins. "Only what he's seen."

"We need to be careful. Watch what you tell him." His lips tightened, and he rubbed his hair back. He had bloodshot eyes and looked tired.

"Does it matter now? An FBI agent saw me vaporize a demon and throw a man into oncoming traffic."

"That's why I turned on the phone. Wanted to see if they tried to reach you." He searched her eyes. "Are you sure she made it? You were a little vague when we got you here."

"I think so."

She remembered Wilkins, her gun, the wound in her shoulder, and she mouthed something to Haddie. *Could there have been a third attacker?* One that the agent saw and wanted her to run from? Had Wilkins survived? The idea that the woman might have died saving Haddie worried her. Is that what she wanted? Just to keep her secret safe?

"Liz knows," she said.

"You mentioned that earlier." Unasked, he offered her water.

She had been fuzzy right after they reached his friend's clinic. Finishing the water, she started texting Terry. "All good. Sorry, I've been sleeping. Liz safe. Heading back."

The response came too quickly. Terry hadn't been asleep. "You're sure?"

"Yes. Why?"

His typing lasted a while before a large block showed. "You've got a black hole up there in Portland. Nothing from the police about the raves.

"Any pictures of demons drop off the internet in seconds. We've got some bots going, grabbing them as they come up, only way we have anything. We know this is a cover-up. Even Dr. Aaron is keeping out of it."

He followed with a quick text, "Was that you? Near the Chinese restaurant?"

Haddie remembered a large red sign from the parking lot. What could she tell him?

Terry didn't wait. "News says two crazed locals. One in custody."

That made no sense. No one could be in custody, unless

there had been a third. She ached and her stomach rebelled against the water. Hunger and nausea mixed.

"Let me work through this." She couldn't think of anything to say. Terry wanted answers that she wouldn't give. *Not now.*

"Ok."

Her chest tightened, and her eyes watered. He'd been a friend and helped her every step of the way. Who knew where Liz would be without Terry? Haddie wouldn't have found her. He'd been up all night worrying about her, and she couldn't tell him anything. It didn't seem fair. She glanced over to Dad who watched her, silent and grim.

"The police never came." It didn't really matter, at this point. It did bother her. She couldn't imagine Terry had forgotten, but it gave her something to move past an awkward impasse.

"Really. So they were covering up, even then. Glad I didn't give them any information."

She typed out, "The fire department did." Stopping before she sent it, she showed it to her dad. It was like throwing Terry a bone. *Am I thinking it through?*

Dad frowned, but shrugged. She sent it.

"What?" he texted.

When she didn't respond, he continued. "I'll dig into it. Everybody likes to report fires."

She texted slowly, "Thank you. Someday I'll have more to say."

"Understand, Buckaroo. Come home."

She flipped the phone onto her stomach and wiped her eyes. "I hate keeping him in the dark, after all he's gone through."

"Might be for his own good. Whoever they — we — are, bodies pile up." He shook his head. "It's beginning to feel like a war." He rested his hand on the gurney. "Are you up for seeing Liz? Heard her squeaking around the kitchen."

Haddie nodded. She stared at the open door as he left. They'd be heading back to Eugene soon. Dad had said morning, despite the vet's concern over the stitches. He likely didn't want to put his friends at risk. That's part of what she'd become. A risk to those around her. Wilkins might have saved her tonight.

Liz rolled in on her wheelchair. For a vet's office, they oddly had a gurney and wheelchair. She imagined they'd taken out a few bullets over the years.

Liz wore a fresh dark blue T-shirt, and her hair looked damp. Scratches still covered her face and arms. Her eyebrows were nearly gone. Absently, Haddie searched for her own.

Pulling up to face Haddie, Liz tucked between the steel table and the gurney. "I remember you saying you didn't know what you are. Is that true?"

Haddie could feel her pulse rise, not wanting to have this conversation. She nodded.

"What is it that you do know? How do you make things — disappear? When did it start?" Liz rattled off each question, beginning to frown as if frustrated.

"I've learned to control it, but initially it just happened. There's a tone, like ringing a bell, then whatever I'm focused on disappears. I believe I push it back in time."

Liz jumped on the answer and shot out a question. "Why do you say that?"

"I don't know."

Liz scowled.

"The first time, I saw like — a misty ghost of the person I would later do this to. In the same position as when I made him disappear."

Liz pulled hair away from her face. "Have you tested, to see if you really do push things back in time, like with an object, not a person?" She almost sounded excited.

Haddie shivered. "No. It hurts to use it. And there's memories, other people's memories, of using the power. I get the purpura, the little bruises. My joints ache."

"Oh." Liz looked a little disappointed.

Dad walked in and shut the door behind him. "Unless you'd like Haddie to end up a government lab rat, we need to be careful about when and where we discuss this."

Liz pursed her lips and nodded, glancing at Haddie. She likely wanted to know more. They would have time, at home.

He reached over to Haddie's glass, grabbed it, and headed for the sink. "How's Matt? What does he remember?"

"Not talking, like he's barely connecting to anything." Liz shrugged.

Dad ran the sink, snorting. "He connected with food pretty well last night. Biff said Matt ate a chicken leg while he hosed him off. Wouldn't put the food down."

Liz squirmed. "I'd gone to sleep by then, I guess."

Dad handed Haddie a fresh glass and nodded for her to drink it. "Sent Biff to go pick up Matt's car. He'll let us know if it's still there." He waited for the glass. "We're leaving soon. Okay with Matt in Haddie's car with us?"

"Sure." Shifting her wheelchair around, she didn't look at them.

Would Liz and Matt's relationship survive this? Haddie couldn't tell if she wanted that. *I'm angry at Matt.* Not his fault. *I should worry about David.* How much more will he put up with? She stared as Dad opened the door for Liz.

Aaron would be waiting for a message. Had she

mentioned him to Dad? They needed to get home. Sam and Meg were alone at the garage. Dad needed to check in on them. Haddie needed to worry about Wilkins. The FBI or police could be waiting at her apartment.

"Dad, we need to talk about Wilkins. What should I do?"

"I'd disappear. Are you ready for the consequences if you don't?" He rested his hand on the gurney, about as close as he got to her, like she'd break.

Leave Liz, David, Sam, Terry, school, and Andrea? *Not ready to do that.*

He kept speaking when she didn't continue. "Sounds like you could end up in jail. Worse. The internet, they'll have pictures of these things. The attack."

"Terry says it's all being covered up."

"You're going to rely on it being covered up?" He tilted his head. "What if you're a witness they need to get rid of?"

Haddie hadn't thought of that. *Thanks, Dad.* She took in a deep breath, steeling herself. "I'm not going to disappear. I killed a man. I'll talk with Wilkins. If it goes bad, just get Liz home safe. I won't involve anyone else, obviously."

"Your choice." It didn't seem as if he agreed with her decision. However, he was used to making up a new identity. Would she have to — someday?

Haddie looked through her recent calls, dialed the number, and held her breath. A man answered, not Wilkins.

"Um, is Special Agent Wilkins there?"

"Unavailable at the moment. Who's this?"

She almost hung up, but they had her number. "Had-hira Dawson." Pausing, she expected a tirade insisting she report somewhere immediately. Finally, she continued, "I missed an appointment, so I wanted to apologize and reschedule."

The voiced sounded cold, bored. "We'll let her know." They disconnected

Odd. She'd expected some reaction to her name. Staring at the phone, she waited. Perhaps he'd look up the name and call her back, demanding that she go somewhere.

Dad's phone dinged. "Biff has Matt's car, dropping it at garage." He pocketed the phone. "I'll get Liz and Matt in the car. I pulled up under the carport. Come back for the gurney."

She still stared at the phone.

He took it out of her hands and turned it off. "We'll get you settled in. Liz agreed to help you get back on your feet. I need to check on Meg and Sam."

Outside the window, lightning struck close in the back yard. Earth exploded into the air, frozen in blue light.

THOMAS RETURNED from walking Rock after giving Liz enough time to get Haddie settled in her bed. Sam had texted twice to remind him, and Rock insisted after he had greeted Haddie upon their return.

Rock followed him as he filled a glass with water for Haddie, then bounded ahead over the clutter of spent clothes as Thomas kicked them aside to make a path across Haddie's bedroom.

Liz took the glass as she sat on the bed. "Matt outside?"

Thomas grunted. "Waiting on the taxi. He seemed to understand."

Haddie looked ready to drop back into sleep. She'd slept through most of the ride. They'd only had a few private moments to go over the details; hopefully she'd be up for a longer conversation at another time. He'd have to return later to change some bandages.

"I'll be back tonight. How you feeling?"

She shrugged and winced. The swelling in her face would go down soon, and the purpura would fade over the next week. "Sore." Her face contorted, almost ready to cry.

"How do you deal with it? All the death? I can't get the images — " She shook her head.

Thomas nodded. "Best I've learned to do is focus on what is saved." He glanced at Liz pointedly.

Haddie let out short breaths, still fighting not to cry. She nodded. "I'll be okay. I've got Sam and David. Get back to Meg. Sam's going to be crazy to get back to her animals."

"She is." He leaned down and gave her a kiss at the hairline. "Love you."

"Love you, too, Dad."

He walked out knowing the load that rested on his daughter's shoulders. The second-guessing. The regrets.

Thomas met Biff by the truck. Inside it still stunk from Matt like a concert port-o-potty. He cracked the window to get fresh air. Once Thomas had shut down his questions during their first mile of the ride, Biff had gotten quiet. He wasn't angry or resentful; they'd gone through a similar situation last fall. They drove back to Goshen in silence.

I need to set someone up to watch the apartment. This issue with the FBI wouldn't go away, not without some repercussions. Worse, she'd been in a fight with someone else with powers, again. The first two were gone, but the last had made it sound like there were others. For centuries, he'd considered himself some anomaly. Some genetic defect or touched by the gods. *Alone.*

Was this going to be the end of it, or the beginning? Had this woman who ran the raves told others about Haddie? It sounded like they'd gone to the hotel looking for her.

I want to take Haddie and Meg away. Disappear.

They pulled into the drive of the garage, and he noticed the boyfriend's car parked in the back of the lot. Thomas had packed Matt into a taxi before he'd left Liz with Haddie. The man still hadn't spoken. Eaten, yes.

Sam knew he'd be home soon. He'd received six photos of the puppy, and Meg, since he let her know that he was bringing Haddie home. Biff would have to get Sam back to her apartment. It sounded like she had a zoo there from the list. He'd have to tell the lie about Haddie being in an accident.

When Thomas walked into the office, the door buzzer went off. The small sitting area and desk smelled like something had been fried for breakfast, instead of the usual garage grease.

Sam bounced out of Haddie's – Meg's — bedroom in the back hall. "Hey T." She swayed with her hands behind her back, wearing a spare mechanic's shirt.

Under her feet, Louis fell out of the bedroom and scrambled across tile to jump on his knee. Thomas knelt down with a wince and ruffled soft puppy fur. "Hey, Boy. They treating you good?"

Sam huffed. "Good? He's pampered."

Thomas looked up. "He's been behaving? No mistakes?"

She offered a knowing smile. "None that you'll find."

He'd finally identified the woman's accent as southeastern, likely from a city. Maybe Georgia? It was very faint, as if she'd been away for a long time or worked hard to discard it. He understood wanting to leave old lives behind.

Biff walked in the office door and the puppy shot to him for a couple laps.

Thomas approached Sam, nodding toward the bedroom and speaking quietly. "How's she doing?"

"She likes to draw. No cap, she's good."

Not exactly what he asked, but it would do. "I'll see if Biff will pick up some supplies." Drawing would be a good hobby, something to connect the girl here. He'd expected video games for some reason. He nodded to Sam and walked past her toward the door.

Meg sat on the bed, leaning against the wall wearing a pout and one of his T-shirts, and her auburn hair reminded him of so many of his descendants. She glanced up and her face lightened, a little. *That's hopeful.* Louis wriggled through his ankles and leaped for the bed. Scrambling up with his awkward puppy hind legs, he bounced on top of Meg and licked at her face. Her smiling face.

CHAPTER 44

HADDIE SWALLOWED and pushed herself higher on the pillows Sam had stacked behind her. Rock grumbled, trotting out of the bedroom toward the front door.

Haddie's sheet covered the worst of the bandages on her legs. Sam had tied her hair back, but that only made the black eyes and purpura stand out worse.

The room looked neater than usual, thanks to Sam. She'd even changed Jisoo's litter box for the occasion. The apartment smelled like spicy black beans from lunch.

Haddie hadn't wanted David to see her like this, but he'd been more insistent than usual after she'd lied about being in a car accident. It was rather endearing. Yesterday when she'd called during the ride back from Portland, he'd tried to leave work and meet her at the apartment. She'd convinced him to wait until Friday after work to come over.

Even now, as she heard him greet Sam at the door, her throat swelled and she blinked away tears. He hadn't been angry about her not texting after the hotel. There had been some reservation and perhaps sadness in his voice, but he hadn't dumped her. Instead, he'd been understanding and grateful that she'd found Liz. Right up until Haddie started lying about a car crash, then he'd become worried and insisted on seeing her.

She took in a deep breath as his footsteps crossed the apartment. Haddie turned toward the door of her bedroom.

David looked paler than usual, but his eyes were bright and dark. His eyebrows drew together and his head tilted. Freshly shaved, he looked handsome despite the expression. He carried a florist's vase with sweet pink roses.

Haddie touched her lips and tried not to cry. She already looked frightful. "They're beautiful."

David nodded and motioned toward her dresser. "You're okay? Nothing broken?"

"No, I've told you three times. Scratched up, a couple stitches. I'll be running around soon." Haddie ached to have him just hold her.

He came back to the edge of the bed, tentatively. "So you'll be ready for that hike we missed. Tomorrow?" His lips turned into a gentle smirk.

Haddie chuckled. "Okay. Not broken, but bruised. You'll have to give me a week before I'm ready for that." She patted the edge of the bed, hoping he just waited for permission.

David sat as if she were fragile. "So what happened? You haven't really gotten into any details."

Because I don't want to lie any more than I have to. "It was all so stupid, I don't want to sound like an idiot." She reached out for his hand. "They gave me next week off work — more than I need — so I'll have plenty of time to hang out. If you're not busy."

He frowned slightly, perhaps at her avoidance. "Of course." Holding her hand gently, he leaned in for a light kiss. "Any chance I get."

She'd hidden so much from him that he had to notice. *He hadn't run away though.* Haddie just had to make sure she didn't end up in any more situations that caused her to lie. It didn't feel right keeping secrets from him.

She reached around and pulled him to her.

Gingerly, he slid his hands under her shoulders and held her. "I love you."

"I love you," she said, holding back tears.

CHAPTER 45

A WEEK after they'd returned to Eugene, Haddie had healed somewhat, physically, and been walking enough to go to work. Her legs hurt, but partially due to her new abilities, she healed much quicker than she could imagine.

In the summer heat, Toby walked beside her on their way to lunch. Haddie needed to get out of the office; Josh had been singing opera all morning, despite Grace's calm promise of stapling his lips. Andrea had been cold, accepting Haddie's lame excuse with a stern warning against further absences. Haddie's new metabolism demolished calories, a nice side effect she imagined partly due to the intense healing. She could have eaten two hours ago.

The memory, the images, and the horror of the killing at the raves lingered. The guards, soldiers as Dad called them, less so than the innocent ravers. She'd played a large part in their deaths. Some nights she lay awake thinking how she might have saved them too.

Walking on this city street in the sun, it all felt like a nightmare, not reality. The people bustled around with their busy lives, never knowing about demons or people like her. They had their lives, TV shows, relationships, and drama.

A cold chill ran up Haddie's shoulders. Special Agent Wilkins leaned casually against a car in the parking lot across the street from the restaurant. If this was a stakeout, the agent hadn't been very discreet.

Catching her eye, the woman made the slightest nod of her head and walked alongside the building toward the back. A handful of scruffy unkempt trees sprouted at the corner. The lot looked empty.

Was this some trick? The FBI wouldn't play like that. They'd just pull up and take her. Wilkins wanted something, perhaps just to talk about that night. Had she understood what happened?

"Hey, Toby. Order me some chow fun, I'll be right there." Haddie jogged into the street without a discussion. She'd think of something later. If she didn't get arrested.

The parking lot stretched from two nearly identical buildings about one and half stories tall. White paint peeled off the concrete blocks, and more sand than grass bordered the wall and asphalt. The thin oaks, young enough that their branches came to her chest, grew at the corner of the building where a gap formed between the larger building behind. Wilkins had gone around that corner and was hidden from her view.

Brushing leaves away carefully, Haddie found the agent waiting between the buildings. There was enough room to clear the trees and join her.

"Special Agent Wilkins?"

"Ms. Dawson." She watched behind Haddie, glancing as if nervous. "I won't take much time. Who was it that attacked you — us, that night?"

Haddie swallowed. She had no intention of giving the

agent any information that she didn't already know. Certainly not about the raves. Terry suggested that it had been buried by the government. It hadn't made the news. "I don't know who they were."

Wilkins frowned, then nodded. "Of course. I ask, because I never got to make my report. They didn't want to hear about that creature." She paused, studying Haddie. "A statement was provided for me. They wanted the incident silenced. A naked, burned man attacked me, drug induced, evidently. One man died trying to shoot the other. A car accident."

Haddie waited, absorbing what the woman said. Good news? She didn't have to worry about getting arrested. Her nightmares would have to be her punishment. Bad news — someone powerful didn't want this story out there. *Terry was right.*

Rubbing her earlobe, Wilkins looked hopeful, as if something she'd said would prompt Haddie to speak. When Haddie didn't, the agent sighed. "Something is wrong inside the FBI. I'm assuming you were the victim here. I also believe that you've dealt with these — things before. In your own way."

Wilkins emphasized the last sentence carefully, leaving no doubt that she'd witnessed Haddie's power. *She knows.* Haddie didn't trust herself to speak. She stood silently in an alley that smelled of kitchen grease listening to an FBI agent who knew about her powers.

When Haddie didn't reply, Wilkins took a long blink before she continued speaking, her voice low and bitter. "Later, they asked about the woman in pink hair. I told them I didn't know anything about that woman." She tilted her head, an expression of regret twitching across lips and eyebrows. "We will need to discuss this, at some point, Ms. Dawson. I can't be seen with you, but I will see you soon."

Wilkins walked toward her, brushing past as she moved.

Haddie stood there with the open alley ahead of her. Terry had been right.

CHAPTER 46

HADDIE DROVE Terry in her RAV4 down Hilyard, preparing to take the right onto East 30th for the third time.

Terry drank nervously from his giant cup of soda, the red straw dented from all his worrying at it. "I mean, you're a girl, right? What does it mean?" A strand of straight, black hair dangled over his brown forehead, threatening to poke into his eye.

Haddie stared at the traffic light. "That she suggested you bring one of your nerdy sci-fi posters to decorate her new apartment? First, that she has no sense of taste."

He closed his eyes and pressed his fingers to his lips. "Haddie."

"I'm sorry. You're worrying over nothing. If she mentions how nice someone's ring is, then start thinking."

"Ring?" His eyes went wide. "You don't think —?"

"Relax, let her use the poster. She'll regret it on her own." She turned behind a black Tacoma and started down the block toward her next turn into the residential neighborhood behind Albertsons.

Sun hit her rearview mirror and she blinked. Dr. Aaron

Knox had been specific about the time and the route they were supposed to take. The man seemed obsessed — paranoid. They were supposed to find him walking the sidewalk in front of Albertsons. Maybe he'd bailed.

The lawns looked dry from the summer heat, despite plenty of rain. A 1959 blue and white Ford F100 was parked to the left as she passed the grocery store again. It sat under a tree with leaves in the bed. The spots of rust bubbling under the paint hinted that it had been restored years ago.

Dirty-blond and sharp-nosed, Aaron walked on the sidewalk on the passenger side. Not where he'd said to pick him up. Perhaps his mistrust included her and Terry. He turned as she approached and strode briskly toward her back door. He wore a white, short-sleeve button down shirt and jeans and had a small, gray backpack over his shoulder.

Hot air and the smell of fresh cut grass poured into the car when he slid inside.

"Keep on the route. Pull into Albertsons' parking lot. I'll find a place to park there." He spoke in quick clipped sentences and slouched down into his seat.

Haddie raised her eyebrows. "Nice to see you again."

Terry turned in his seat, peeking around the headrest. "Nice to meetcha, Doc."

"Eyes forward. Don't look back here like there's someone in the back."

Terry turned and worked on his straw.

Haddie kept to an even speed. "What brings you to Eugene?" She had a slew of questions. They all boiled down to what the demons were. He'd already answered that he didn't know. Still, it had been exciting when Terry had mentioned Dr. Knox wanted to meet with her. Any information might help ease some of the obsession. She'd been trying hard not to, but all she could think about were the demons, the men with yellow haze, and people like herself and Dad. What had her world become?

"You. You brought me to Eugene." His eyes tightened when she looked into the rearview at him. "And the sighting of the two demons."

Haddie pulled up to the corner, waiting for traffic. "Terry says there have been other sightings." She carefully avoided the topic of when they'd met at the ski lift.

"These demons have been showing up for the past six years. Random sightings that governments are covering up."

She drove for a bit before asking him the same question she had before. "What are they?"

"As I said, I don't know." His tone implied annoyance with the question. It took a moment before he continued, "Whatever you're involved with is very dangerous."

Haddie turned the next corner, bringing them back on Hilyard, without saying anything else. She'd explained to Terry that she'd want to talk with Dr. Knox alone. He'd whined a bit, but understood. Though itching to know, he'd accepted her need to keep this from him, not that it stopped the occasional snide remark or puppy dog eyes.

Dr. Knox motioned them to an empty spot in the back of the lot, facing some young oaks.

Haddie looked at Terry, and when he didn't move, she said, "Give us a moment."

He rolled his eyes and opened his door. "You'll regret it though. I've got an awesome brain that you'll really miss."

Aaron waited until the door closed before speaking. "How many demons were there?"

Haddie locked eyes in the mirror. "Two more. Smaller, inside the bodies of large dogs. I spotted one, an Irish

Wolfhound that acted fairly normal — until it ended up with a beak."

Aaron tilted his head. "You can see them — their eyes?"

"Yes." *He sees the orange as well.* Liz hadn't. Could it be the use of an ability? Her chest tightened. Another one of her – of them – someone with ability. "Do you hear a tone when you do something? Something that shouldn't be possible?"

Aaron's eyes widened and his body pulled back into the seat. "That's the connection?"

"Then you do?" she asked, pushing. Her pulse raced at meeting someone like herself — who wasn't trying to kill her. *Yet.*

"Did. Once." He looked away, his eyebrows furrowed.

Haddie waited, hoping he'd continue. Finally, she broke the silence. "What happened?"

His voice started with broken statements, as if distracted or thinking. "College. Frat party. I'd tried to protect a friend; she'd been drugged. I think. They threatened me. I yelled. After I did, they all did what I told them to, immediately." His voice sharpened as he said, "It never happened again."

"Little bruises?" she asked.

Aaron took in a deep breath and looked back to the mirror. "Yes. Purpura. I went into human medical research after that." He touched the bridge of his nose, as though pushing up glasses that weren't there. "Thought the first demons were a form of human mutation. Still do."

Haddie didn't quite understand. Could he control people? She sucked in a breath. Would she even know if he controlled her? If he did, she would see purpura on him after he used his power. Could he make her ignore that, though? *I'm being paranoid.*

Hurriedly, she offered, "The demons wore little medal-lions with the yellow haze. The same — I see the same yellow fog on some of their guards."

"Yellow haze?" He seemed surprised. "Like a cloud on their face?"

"Yes." What did he know?

"I saw that once, on the people who I — on the men who I yelled at. They always had it after that." Aaron seemed to shudder.

So, the yellow-haze meant they were being controlled by someone with that power — another like herself and Dad. *No, more like Aaron.* Aaron might not even know he'd become immortal or had someone in his family with the same power. He looked to be in his mid-thirties; college would have been mid-twenties. Maybe immortality had only hit her dad. *Am I relieved?*

"Do you think anyone in your family has found this power?" she asked.

"Genetic?" He frowned. "No. What makes you think it is?"

She wasn't about to give up Dad. Haddie shrugged. "Nothing. I'm no scientist."

CHAPTER 47

HADDIE DROVE over to Liz's with Terry sulking in the front seat. Dr. Knox had left from the Albertons' parking lot before Terry'd returned from the store. He'd picked up some more snacks for Livia's party, and the bag lay at his feet, smelling of some flavor of opened chips.

Her mouth felt dry and tasted chalky. The talk with Dr. Aaron had left her with more questions than answers. Healthy fears, as well. She looked forward to discussing it with Dad, the only one she could be completely open with about all this. Liz had broached the topic once more, as if it could be considered a science experiment.

Haddie pulled into the dead end. Liz's house stood on the corner, angular and awkward with just one peak to the roof. It looked as if someone had split a house in half to convert one end for a duplex.

"Here," she texted.

Liz's Avenger was parked in the driveway, and she ran past it on her way to the RAV4, wearing a long blouse with black shoulders that faded to turquoise at the waist. As usual, she wore sunglasses even though the sun had begun to set.

Tossing her bag into the back seat, she climbed in behind Haddie. "Hey, Terry. I figured you'd be at the party, setting up."

"We — I had something to pick up for the party." He rustled the bag at his feet. "How's Matt?"

Liz's tone quieted. "Okay. He's on sabbatical." Matt had checked into a rehab for depression; they probably took one look at his bloodwork and welcomed him in.

"Nice." Terry emphasized the word as if Liz had just said, "vacation in Hawaii." He turned in his seat, facing the back. "Livia's apartment still smells like paint. I did up her bedroom in purple. She loved it."

Most of the drive, they kept the topic on Livia's new apartment, a safe enough discussion. Haddie would eventually mention some of Dr. Knox's conversation to Liz; she had a more logical view of things. Liz called it empirical.

Red colored the clouds layered against a dark blue sky when they pulled up to the apartment. David wouldn't make it back from the coast in time to join them, but Haddie had a light hike planned with him for Sunday. Terry collected his poster and three boxes of games from the back.

Liz gave Haddie a hug. "How are you feeling?"

"Stiff." Haddie motioned across her thighs.

"I'm nervous." Liz nodded toward the building. "I haven't been around drinking since."

"I don't expect that kind of party. Terry's a nerd."

"You're right. I'll be fine." Liz let out a long breath and squeezed Haddie's right arm. "Thanks."

"For what?" Haddie closed her door.

"Being my friend."

Haddie gave Liz another hug. "Ditto."

Terry closed the back, trying to juggle his oversized drink with his load. Haddie reached out and he handed her the poster.

Livia opened the door before they reached it. Her dark brown hair had red highlights dyed into it. Her dark eyes and bright red lipstick were a contrast to her light skin. "Oh, I heard the car door. Still waiting on pizza."

Terry gave her a kiss, then looked back at Haddie, raising his eyebrows. "Beautiful, isn't she?"

Haddie laughed. "Yes, what does she see in you?" She leaned around Terry and offered her hand. "Haddie, it's good to officially meet you."

"You don't look near as dangerous as Terry makes you sound," Livia said.

Terry blushed.

Wait until you get to know me, Haddie thought.

<<<*The End*>>>

Continue the AngelSong series at
www.KevinArthurDavis.com

ALSO BY KEVIN A. DAVIS

If you haven't read the Origin story, *Shattered Blood*, then download a free ebook or purchase paperback on Amazon.

AngelSong Series

Penumbra - Book One

Red Tempest - Book Two

Coerced - Book Three

Demons' Lair - Book Four

Infrared - Book Five. (End of the AngelSong Series)

All books in the series have been written and at the time of this printing are waiting on edits.

Please join my mailing list if you'd like to be kept up to date on this series and the upcoming Khimmer Chronicles series.

ACKNOWLEDGMENTS

My wife April continues to support me emotionally at every turn of my writing career. She listens to my ideas and reads the very first, and very worst drafts. Some of the pieces you may have enjoyed in Penumbra you may have to thank her for.

Robyn Huss, my editor, has once again transformed my writing to levels I could not achieve without her. Her insight goes far beyond pure grammar and she shows her skill in every paragraph you have read in this book.

I will dearly miss a beloved and irreplaceable mentor, David Farland; our loss is felt around the world. Please pick up one of his books and enjoy the magic he evoked. If you are are a writer, study his teachings at Apex Writers.

My writing groups from JordanCon, DragonCon, and Apex are instrumental in making sure I keep on track.

Thank you.

CPSIA information can be obtained
at www.ICGtesting.com
Printed in the USA
LVHW091353130322
713344LV00018B/83